MASS EFFECT

ASCENSION

By Drew Karpyshyn

BALDUR'S GATE II: THRONE OF BHAAL

TEMPLE HILL

STAR WARS: DARTH BANE: PATH OF
    DESTRUCTION
STAR WARS: DARTH BANE: RULE OF TWO

MASS EFFECT: REVELATION
MASS EFFECT: ASCENSION

MASS EFFECT™
ASCENSION

DREW KARPYSHYN

BALLANTINE BOOKS • NEW YORK

A Del Rey Books Mass Market Original

Published in the United States by Del Rey Books, an imprint of The Random House Publishing Group, a division of Random House, Inc., New York.

ISBN 978-0-345-49852-6

Printed in the United States of America

www.delreybooks.com
www.bioware.com

OPM 9 8 7 6 5 4 3

To my wife, Jennifer.
I couldn't do this without your
never-ending love and support.

ACKNOWLEDGMENTS

This is the second Mass Effect novel, and once again I want to thank the entire BioWare Mass Effect team for helping to make all this possible. I consider it an honor and a privilege to work with such incredibly talented men and women. Without their creativity, hard work, brilliance, and passion, Mass Effect would not exist.

PROLOGUE

The news report on the vid screen flickered with a constant stream of images capturing the death and destruction Saren's attack had wrought upon the Citadel. Bodies of geth and C-Sec officers were strewn haphazardly about the Council Chambers in the aftermath of the battle. Entire sections of the Presidium had been reduced to scorched, twisted metal. Melted, blackened chunks of debris that had once been ships of the Citadel fleet floated aimlessly through the clouds of the Serpent Nebula—an asteroid belt born from the bloodshed and carnage.

The Illusive Man watched it all with a cool, clinical detachment. Work had already begun to rebuild and repair the great space station, but the repercussions of the battle went far beyond the widespread physical damage. In the weeks since the devastating geth assault, every major media outlet across the galaxy had been dominated with the graphic—and previously unthinkable—images.

The attack had shaken the galactic powers that be to their alien cores, stripping away their naïve sense of invincibility. The Citadel, seat of the Council and the symbol of their unassailable power and position, had very nearly fallen to an enemy fleet. Tens of thousands of lives had been lost; all of Council space was in mourning.

Yet where others saw tragedy, he saw opportunity. He knew, perhaps better than anyone, that the galaxy's sudden awareness of its own vulnerability could benefit humanity. That was what made him special: he was a man of vision.

Once he had been just like everybody else. He had marveled with the rest of the people on Earth when the Prothean ruins were discovered on Mars. He had watched the vids in amazement when they reported on humanity's first, violent contact with an intelligent alien species. Back then he had been an average man, with an average job and an average life. He had friends and family. He even had a name.

All those things were gone now. Stripped away by the necessity of his cause. He had become the Illusive Man, abandoning and transcending his ordinary existence in pursuit of a far greater goal. Humanity had slipped the surly bonds of Earth, but they had not found the face of God. Instead, they had discovered a thriving galactic community: a dozen species spread across hundreds of solar systems and thousands of worlds. Newcomers thrust into the interstellar political arena, the human race needed to adapt and evolve if they wanted to survive.

They couldn't put their faith in the Alliance. A bloated coalition of government officials and disparate military branches, the Alliance was a clumsy, blunt instrument weighed down by laws, convention, and the crushing weight of public opinion. Too interested in appeasement and kowtowing to the various alien species, they were unable—or unwilling—to make the hard decisions necessary to thrust humanity toward its destiny.

The people of Earth needed someone to champion their cause. They needed patriots and heroes willing to make the necessary sacrifices to elevate the human race above its interstellar rivals. They needed Cerberus, and Cerberus couldn't exist without the Illusive Man.

As a man of vision, he understood this. Without Cerberus, humanity was doomed to an existence of groveling subservience at the feet of alien masters. Still, there were those who would call what he did criminal. Unethical. Amoral. History would vindicate him, but until it did he and his followers were forced to exist in hiding, working toward their goals in secret.

The images on the vid changed, now showing the face of Commander Shepard. The first human Spectre, Shepard had been instrumental in defeating Saren and his geth . . . or so the official reports claimed.

The Illusive Man couldn't help but wonder how much those official reports left out. He knew there was more to the attack than a rogue turian Spectre leading an army of geth against the Council. There was *Sovereign,* for one, Saren's magnificent flagship. The vids maintained it was a geth creation, but only the blind or the foolish would accept that explanation. Any vessel able to withstand the combined power of the Alliance and Council fleets was too advanced, too far beyond the capabilities of any other ship in the galaxy, to have been created by any of the known species.

It was clear there were certain things those in charge didn't want the general public to know. They were afraid of causing a panic; they were spinning the facts and distorting the truth while they began the long, slow process of hunting down and exterminating the last pockets of geth resistance scattered across Council space. But Cerberus had people in the Alliance. High-ranking people. In time, every classified detail of the attack would filter down to the Illusive Man. It might take weeks, maybe even months, before he knew the whole truth. But he could wait. He was a patient man.

Yet he couldn't deny these were interesting times. For the past decade, the three species seated on the Council—salarians, turians, and asari—had fought to keep humanity at bay, slamming door after door in its face. Now those doors had been blown off their hinges. The Citadel forces had been decimated by the geth, leaving the Alliance fleet unchallenged as the galaxy's single most dominant power. Even the Council, fundamentally unchanged for nearly a thousand years, had been radically restructured.

Some believed this marked an end to the tyranny of the alien triumvirate, and the beginning of humanity's unstoppable rise. The Illusive Man, however, understood that holding on to power was far more difficult than seizing it. Whatever political advantage the Alliance might gain in the short term would be temporary at best. Little by little, the impact of Shepard's actions and the heroics of the Alliance fleet would fade in the galaxy's collective consciousness. The admiration and gratitude of alien governments would slowly wane, replaced by suspicion and resentment.

Over time they would rebuild their fleets. And inevitably, the other species would once again vie for power, seeking to elevate themselves at humanity's expense.

Humanity had taken a bold step forward but the journey was far from complete. There were many more battles still to be fought in the struggle for galactic dominance, on many different fronts. The attacks on the Citadel were just one small piece of the greater puzzle, and he would deal with them in their proper time.

Right now there were more immediate concerns; his attention needed to be focused elsewhere. As a man of vision, he understood the necessity of having more than one plan. He knew when to wait, and when to push forward. And the time had come to push forward with their asset inside the Ascension Project.

ONE

Paul Grayson never used to dream. As a young man he had slept untroubled through the night. But those days of innocence were many years gone.

They were two hours into the flight; another four until they reached their destination. Grayson checked the status of the ship's engines and mass drive, then confirmed their route on the navigation screens for the fourth time in the past hour. There wasn't much else a pilot needed to do en route; everything was fully automated while a ship was in FTL flight.

He didn't dream every night, but almost every other night. It might have been a sign of advancing age, or a by-product of the red sand he dosed himself with on occasion. Or maybe it was just a guilty conscience. The salarians had a saying: the mind with many secrets can never rest.

He was stalling; checking and rechecking the instruments and readouts to hold what was to come at bay. Recognizing his own fear and reluctance allowed him—forced him—to confront the situation. Deal with it. He took a deep breath to collect himself, his heart pounding in his chest as he rose slowly from his seat. No sense putting it off any longer. It was time.

On some level he always knew when he was dreaming. There was a strange haze over everything, a bleary film that left the false reality feeling washed out and muted. Yet through this obscuring filter, certain elements would register with exacting precision, minor details indelibly etched into his subconscious mind. The juxtaposition added to the surreal nature of his dreams, yet also made them somehow more vivid, more intense, than his waking world.

His feet padded softly over the carpeted aisle as he made his way aft from the cockpit toward the passenger cabin. There, Pel and Keo occupied two of the four seats, sitting kitty-corner across from each other. Pel was a big man with broad shoulders and olive skin. His hair was cropped in a tight afro, and he had a thin black beard extending along the length of his jaw. Seated in the chair facing Grayson as he came into the cabin, Pel was swaying gently back and forth in time to the song coming over his headphones. His fingers tapped lightly against his thigh, his perfectly manicured nails rustling softly against the dark material of his suit pants. His tie was still tight around his neck, but his jacket was unbuttoned and his mirrored sunglasses were tucked away inside the right breast pocket. His eyes were nearly closed; he'd lost himself in the rhythms of the music—a peaceful, easy image at odds with his reputation as one of Terra Firma's top personal protection agents.

Keo wore the same suit as her partner minus the tie, but she lacked the imposing physical size one typically expected in a bodyguard. She was a full foot shorter than Pel and maybe half his weight, though there was a tautness to her wiry muscles that hinted at the violence she was capable of inflicting.

Her exact age was difficult to pin down, though Grayson knew she had to be at least forty. With advances in nutrition and gene therapy to reduce the effects of aging, it was common for people to look as young and healthy at fifty as they did at thirty, and Keo's unusual appearance made it even harder to estimate how old or young she might be. Her pale skin was the color of chalk, giving her a ghostly appearance, and her silver hair was shaved short enough to glimpse the pasty-white flesh of her scalp beneath.

Intermarriage between the various ethnicities of Earth over the past two centuries had made alabaster skin a rarity, and Grayson suspected Keo's stark complexion was the result of a minor pigment deficiency she had never bothered to reverse . . . although it was entirely possible she had undergone elective skin-lightening for cosmetic purposes. After all, visibility was a key aspect of her job: let people know you're on duty, and they'll think twice before doing anything stupid. Keo's odd appearance definitely made her stand out in a crowd despite her stature.

She was facing away from Grayson, but she twisted around in her seat to watch him as he entered the cabin. She looked tense and coiled, ready for anything—a complete contrast to Pel's easy calm. Unlike her partner, she seemed incapable of relaxing, even under the most mundane circumstances.

"What's wrong?" she demanded at his approach, eyeing the pilot suspiciously.

Grayson froze and raised his hands in the air so

they were level with his shoulders. "Just getting a drink," he assured her.

His body was charged with nervous anticipation, the tips of his fingers were actually tingling. But he was careful to betray no hint of this in his voice.

This particular dream was all too familiar. Over the past ten years he had relived his first kill hundreds, if not thousands, of times. There had been other assignments, of course; other deaths. In the service of the greater cause he had taken many, many lives. If humanity was to survive—to triumph over all the other species—sacrifices had to be made. But of all the sacrifices, of all the lives he had taken, of all the missions he had completed, this was the one he dreamed of more than any other.

Satisfied the pilot posed no immediate threat, Keo turned away from him and settled back down in her seat, though she still seemed ready to lash out at the slightest provocation. Grayson made his way behind her toward the small fridge in the corner of the passenger cabin. He swallowed hard, his throat so dry and tight it actually hurt. He half-imagined he saw her ears twitch at the sound.

From the corner of his eye he saw Pel remove his headphones, dropping them casually into the seat beside him as he stood up to stretch. "How long till we land?" he asked, his words partially stifled by a yawn.

"Four hours," Grayson replied as he opened the fridge and ducked down to inspect the contents, struggling to keep his breathing calm and even.

"No complications?" Pel asked as the pilot rummaged around in the chilled contents of the fridge.

"Everything's right on schedule," Grayson replied,

wrapping his left hand around a bottled water while his right grasped the handle of the long, thin serrated blade he had stashed inside the icebox before the journey began.

Even though he knew this was a dream, Grayson was powerless to change anything that was about to happen. The episode would continue without variance or alteration. He was trapped in the role of passive observer; a witness forced to watch through his own eyes as events unfolded along their original course, his subconscious refusing to allow him to alter his own personal history.

"Guess I'll go check on sleeping beauty," Pel said *nonchalantly, giving Grayson the code phrase for the final go. There was no turning back now.*

There was only one other passenger on board: Claude Menneau, one of the highest ranking members of the pro-human Terra Firma political party. A man of vast wealth and power, he was a charismatic, though not necessarily likable, public figure; the kind of man who could afford a private interstellar vessel, complete with his own pilot and a pair of full-time bodyguards to accompany him on his frequent trips.

In what had become a familiar routine, Menneau had locked himself away in the VIP room in the aft of the vessel just after takeoff. There he would rest and prepare for his upcoming public appearance. In a few hours they were scheduled to touch down at the civilian spaceport on Shanxi, where Menneau would address a fevered crowd of Terra Firma supporters.

In the wake of the Nashan Stellar Dynamics kickback scandal, Inez Simmons had been forced to step down from her role as party leader. It was clear either

Menneau or a man named Charles Saracino would succeed her at the Terra Firma helm, and both were making frequent trips to the various human colonies to drum up support.

Menneau was currently ahead in the polls by a full three points. But things were about to change. The Illusive Man wanted Saracino to win, and the Illusive Man always got what he wanted.

Grayson stood up from the fridge, shielding the knife from view with the bottled water in case Keo happened to be looking his way. To his relief, she was still seated facing away from him, her attention focused on Pel's back as he made his way with long, easy strides toward the VIP room in the tail of the vessel.

The chilled condensation on the water bottle made his left palm cold and damp. The right was damp, too—hot and sweaty from being clenched too tightly around the handle of his weapon. He took a silent step forward so that he was standing only inches behind Keo, her bare neck exposed and vulnerable.

Pel would never have been able to get this close to her; not without raising suspicion and putting her on guard. Despite nearly six months working together as bodyguards for Menneau, she still didn't completely trust her partner. Pel was a former mercenary, a professional killer with a murky past. Keo always kept half an eye on him. That was why it had to be Grayson. She might not trust him—Keo didn't trust anybody—but she didn't watch his every move like she did with Pel.

He held the weapon poised to strike, took a deep breath, then stabbed forward with the blade, slashing at an upward angle toward the soft spot in the skull just behind Keo's ear. It should have been a quick, clean kill. But his momentary hesitation cost him; it gave Keo a chance to sense the attack before it came. Reacting with a survival instinct honed over countless missions, she leaped from her seat, spinning to face her attacker even as the blade plunged home. Her incredible reflexes saved her from instantaneous death; instead of sliding smoothly up into her brain the knife buried itself deep in the flesh of her neck, where it stuck fast.

Grayson felt the handle slide free from his sweaty palm as he stumbled backward, away from his would-be victim. He stopped when his back struck the wall near the small fridge; there was nowhere to go. Keo was on her feet now, staring at him from across the seat. He saw the cold certainty of his own imminent death in her eyes. Without the advantage of surprise, he was no match for her years of combat training. He didn't even have a weapon anymore: his knife still jutted awkwardly out from the side of Keo's neck, the handle quivering slightly.

Ignoring the pistol on her hip—she wasn't about to risk firing her weapon inside a passenger vessel during flight—she yanked a short, savage-looking knife from her belt and leaped over the seat separating her and Grayson.

It was a critical mistake. Grayson had botched what should have been a quick kill, showing his inexperience. That had led Keo to underestimate him; she came at him too aggressively, trying to end the fight quickly instead of holding her ground or coming cautiously around the seats. Her tactical error gave her opponent the split second he needed to take back the advantage.

The instant she left her feet Grayson lunged forward. Flying through the air Keo couldn't stop her momentum or change her direction, and their bodies crashed together in a tangled heap. Grayson felt her knife slicing across his left bicep, but in the close quarters the small woman couldn't get enough leverage, and the wound was superficial.

She kicked at him and tried to roll away, looking to disengage so she could take advantage of her speed and quickness. Grayson didn't try to stop her. Instead, he reached out and seized the handle of the knife still lodged in her neck. He yanked it out in one long, smooth pull as she scrambled back up to her feet.

As the blade slid free, a crimson geyser came gushing out of the wound. The serrated edge had torn open her carotid artery. Keo had just enough time to register a look of surprised disbelief before the sudden drop in blood pressure to her brain caused her to black out and collapse, her limp body falling to the floor beside Grayson.

A gout of warm, sticky fluid splashed across his face and hands, and he scampered to his feet with a grunt of disgust, backing quickly away from the body until he struck up against the wall by the fridge once again. The blood continued to pour from the hole in her throat, the intensity of the stream increasing and decreasing with each beat of her still pumping heart. When the muscle gave out a few seconds later, the pulsating flow was reduced to a slow but steady trickle.

Pel returned from the back room less than a minute

later. He raised one eyebrow at the blood covering Grayson, but didn't speak. Moving calmly, he approached Keo's body on the floor and bent down to check for a pulse, stepping carefully over the expanding pool of blood so as not to stain his shoes. Satisfied, he stood up and settled back into the seat he'd been relaxing in earlier.

"Nice work, Killer," he said with a soft chuckle.

Grayson was still standing against the wall beside the fridge. He had watched Keo's life rapidly bleeding away without moving, transfixed by the gruesome scene.

"Menneau's dead?" he asked. A stupid question, but as the adrenaline rush of his first kill faded his mind felt dull and slow.

Pel nodded. "Not nearly as messy as this, though. I like to keep my bodies neat." He reached for the headphones still sitting on the seat beside him.

"Should we clean up the blood?"

"No point," Pel informed him, sliding the headphones over his ears. "Soon as we rendezvous with the pickup team, they're just going to dump this whole ship into the nearest sun.

"Don't forget to claim your trophy," the big man added as he closed his eyes, his body beginning to rock in time to the music's rhythm once again.

Grayson swallowed hard, then forced himself into motion. He pushed himself away from the wall and made his way over to Keo's body. She lay half on her side, the pistol on her hip easily within reach. He stretched out a trembling hand toward the weapon . . .

The dream always ended in exactly the same place. And each time it did, Grayson woke with his heart pounding, his muscles tensed, and his palms sweating, as if his body had been reliving the experience along with his subconscious mind.

He didn't know then—and he didn't know now—why Menneau had to die. He only knew that it served the greater good in some way. Yet that was enough. He was dedicated to the cause, completely loyal to Cerberus and its leader. The Illusive Man had given him an order, and he had followed it without question.

Apart from the mistake of allowing Keo to briefly survive his initial attack, Grayson's first mission had been an unqualified success. The pickup team had met with them at the designated rendezvous, and the ship, along with the bodies of Keo and Menneau, had been disposed of. There were suspicions and theories surrounding the disappearance of Menneau and his crew, but with no evidence to back them up they had amounted to nothing. And with his chief rival removed from the race, Charles Saracino had claimed the leadership of the Terra Firma party . . . though how that played into the long-term plans of the Illusive Man was anyone's guess.

Grayson's performance had impressed his superiors within the Cerberus organization, leading to dozens of assignments over the next decade. But that all ended once Gillian was accepted into the Ascension Project.

He didn't like to think about Gillian. Not like this, alone in his apartment with the darkness pressing in. He pushed her face from his mind and rolled over, hoping to fall back asleep. He froze when he heard a noise coming from beyond the bedroom door. His ears pricked up intently, and he could just make out voices coming from the living room of his small apartment. It was possible he had simply left the vid screen on when he'd staggered into bed, too sand-blasted to shut it off. Possible, but not likely.

Moving silently he rolled out of the bed, leaving a tangled mess of covers behind. Wearing only a pair of boxers, his thin body shivered in the chill air of the room as he carefully opened the drawer of the night-stand and pulled out his pistol. *Keo's pistol,* his mind corrected, dredging up her memory once again.

Suitably armed, he crept barefoot across the bed-room and through the half-open door into the hall beyond. The apartment was dark, though he could see the soft glow of the vid screen spilling out from the living room. He moved forward in a low crouch, presenting less of a target should the intruder attempt to take a shot at him.

"Put the gun away, Killer," Pel's voice called out as he approached. "It's just me."

Cursing under his breath, Grayson stood up straight and made his way into the living room to meet his uninvited guest.

Pel was lounging on the overstuffed couch in front of the vid screen, watching one of the news channels. He was still a big, powerful figure but he had gained weight over the past ten years. He looked somewhat soft now, a man who was clearly enjoying a life of luxury and indulgence.

"Jesus, you look like hell," Pel noted when Grayson came into view. "Stop spending all your money on red sand and buy yourself a goddamned meal once in a while."

As he spoke he reached out with a foot and kicked at the small coffee table in the center of the room. Grayson had been too high to bother cleaning up before going to bed—a mirror, a razorblade, and a small bag of red sand sat in plain view atop the table.

"Helps me sleep," Grayson mumbled.

"Still having nightmares?" Pel asked. There was something mocking in his tone.

"Dreams," Grayson replied. "About Keo."

"I used to dream about her, too," Pel admitted with a lopsided grin. "Always wondered what she'd be like in the sack."

Grayson tossed the pistol down on the table with the drug paraphernalia and slouched into the chair opposite the couch. He wasn't sure if Pel was joking with him or not. With Pel he was never sure.

He glanced over at the vid screen. They were showing images of the newly repaired Citadel. Two months ago the attack had dominated the media, along with the thoughts and awareness of every being in Council space. Now, however, the shock and horror were beginning to fade. Normalcy was returning, creeping in slowly but surely from all sides. Aliens and humans alike were falling back into their everyday routines: work, school, friends, family. Ordinary people moving on.

The story still had life in the media, but now it was left to the pundits and politicians to analyze and dissect. A panel of political experts—an asari ambassador, a volus diplomat, and a retired salarian intelligence operative—appeared on the vid screen, debating the political stances of the various candidates humanity was considering for the Council.

"You think the Man has any pull in who we pick?" Grayson asked, nodding toward the screen.

"Maybe," Pel answered, noncommittal. "Wouldn't be the first time he got involved in politics."

"You ever wonder why he wanted Menneau dead?" The question was out of Grayson's mouth before he even realized he was asking it.

Pel shrugged indifferently, though there was a wary look in his eye. "Could be any of a hundred reasons. I don't ask questions like that. And neither should you."

"You think we owe him blind obedience?"

"I just figure it's done and there's nothing you can do to change it. People like us can't afford to live in the past. Makes a man sloppy."

"I've got everything under control," Grayson assured him.

"Clearly," Pel snorted, nodding at the red sand on the table.

"Just tell me why you're here," Grayson said wearily.

"The Man wants to hit the girl with another batch of meds."

"She has a name," Grayson muttered. "It's Gillian."

Pel sat up and leaned forward, his hands on his thighs as he shook his head in exasperation. "I don't want to know her name. Names make things personal. You get messy when things get personal. She's not a person; she's just an asset on the inside. Makes it easier when the Illusive Man decides she's expendable."

"He doesn't want that," Grayson countered. "She's too valuable."

"For now," Pel grunted. "But down the line someone might figure they can learn more if they cut her skull open and poke around inside her brain. Then what happens, Killer?"

An image of Gillian's butchered body lying on a medical gurney sprang to Grayson's mind, but he wasn't about to rise to Pel's bait.

Besides, that's not going to happen. They need Gillian.

"I'm loyal to the cause," he said out loud, not wanting to argue the point with Pel. "I'll do what's necessary."

"Glad to hear it," Pel answered. "Hate to think you've gone soft."

"Is that why you're really here?" Grayson wanted to know. "Did he bring you all the way back from the Terminus Systems so you could check up on me?"

"You don't answer to me anymore, Killer," Pel assured him. "I'm just passing through. Had to come in to clean up some business on Earth, so I volunteered to stop by on my way back out to drop off the supplies."

The big man pulled a small vial of clear liquid from his coat pocket and tossed it to Grayson, who caught it cleanly with one hand. There was no label on the vial; nothing to mark what it was or what it might do; no indications of where it came from.

His work done, Pel rose from the couch and turned to go.

"You going to report the red sand?" Grayson called out after him just as he reached the door.

"Nothing to do with me," he said without turning around. "You can get dusted every night for all I care.

I'm off to meet a contact on Omega. This time tomorrow I'll be up to my ass in aliens."

"It's part of my cover," Grayson added defensively. "Fits my character. Troubled father."

Pel passed his hand in front of the door panel and it swooshed open.

"Whatever you say, man. This is your assignment."

He stepped out into the apartment hallway, then turned back to deliver a parting warning.

"Don't get sloppy, Killer. I hate cleaning up someone else's mess."

The door swooshed shut, perfectly timed with the end of his words and cutting off any chance for Grayson to reply.

"Son-of-a-bitch always has to get the last word," he muttered.

With a groan he pulled himself out of his chair and set the vial on the small table beside the bag of red sand, then wandered reluctantly back to bed. Mercifully, the only dreams he had for the rest of the night were of his daughter.

TWO

Kahlee Sanders moved with quick, confident steps down the halls of the Jon Grissom Academy. A space station constructed seven years ago in orbit around the human colony of Elysium, it had been named after Rear Admiral Jon Grissom, the first man to travel through a Mass Relay and one of humanity's most revered and respected living heroes.

Grissom also happened to be Kahlee's father.

Her shoes, sensible, half-inch wedge heels, clacked softly as she made her way down the dormitory corridor, and her lab coat swished faintly with every step. It was almost an hour after supper, and the students were in their rooms, studying in preparation for tomorrow's classes. Most kept their doors closed, though the few who preferred to leave them open looked up from their e-books and computer screens as she passed, their attention drawn by the sound of her footsteps. Some smiled or nodded to her; a few of the younger ones even gave her an enthusiastic wave. To each she replied in kind.

Only a handful of people actually knew Jon Grissom was her father, and their relationship, if it could be called that, had nothing to do with her position here at the Academy. She didn't see her father often; the last time she had spoken to him was over a year ago. And that had ended, as every visit seemed to, in an argument. Her father was a difficult man to love.

Grissom was approaching seventy, and unlike most people in this era of modern medicine, he actually looked his age. Kahlee was in her early forties, but her appearance was that of a woman at least a decade younger. Average in both height and build, she was fit enough to still move with the spryness of youth. Her skin was still smooth, apart from a few tiny wrinkles around the creases of her eyes when she laughed or smiled. And her shoulder-length hair was still blond with darker, sandy streaks; she wouldn't have to worry about gray hairs for another thirty years at least.

In contrast, her father looked *old*. His mind—and tongue—were still as sharp as ever, but his body seemed dry and withered. His skin was leathery and hard, his features sunken and drawn, his face lined from decades of dealing with the pressure and stress that came with being a living icon. Grissom's thinning hair was mostly white, and he moved with the slow, deliberate actions of the elderly, even walking with the hint of a stoop.

Picturing him in her mind, it was hard to imagine the great hero the media and history books portrayed. Kahlee couldn't help but wonder how much of that was intentional, a facade Grissom maintained in order to keep others at bay. Her father had turned his back on his fame, unwilling to allow himself to be held up as a symbol for Earth or the Alliance. He'd refused to attend the consecration of the Jon Grissom

Academy, and over the past seven years he'd declined dozens of invitations from the board of directors to visit the facility, despite the fact it was orbiting the planet where he made his home.

Probably for the best, Kahlee thought to herself. Let the public cling to his memory; it served as a better symbol of nobility and courage than the misanthropic old bastard he had become. Besides, she had plenty to keep her busy here at the Academy without having to deal with her father.

She pushed the thoughts of Grissom aside as she reached her destination. She rapped once on the closed door.

"Come in," a young boy's voice grudgingly called out, and a second later the door *whoosh*ed open.

Nick lay on his back in his bed, scowling up at the ceiling. He was twelve, though somewhat small for his age. Despite this, there was something about him—an almost unconscious air of arrogance and cruelty—that marked him as a bully rather than a victim.

Kahlee stepped in and closed the door behind her. Nick stubbornly refused to look over and acknowledge her presence. His school computer sat, closed and ignored, on the small desk in the corner of the room. It was obvious he was pouting.

"What's the matter, Nick?" she asked, coming over to sit on the edge of his bed.

"Hendel put me in lockdown for three weeks!" he exclaimed, sitting up suddenly. His expression was one of outrage and utter indignation. "He won't even let me play on the 'net!"

Students at the Grissom Academy were well taken

care of, but when they misbehaved certain privileges—access to games on the Extranet, watching favorite shows on the vid screens in their rooms, or listening to popular music—could be taken away. Nick, in particular, was very familiar with this form of punishment.

"Three weeks is forever!" he protested. "That's totally not fair!"

"Three weeks is a long time," Kahlee agreed with a somber nod, struggling to keep the hint of a smile from playing across her lips. "What did you do?"

"Nothing!" There was a pregnant pause before he continued. "I just . . . I kind of . . . *pushed* Seshaun."

Kahlee shook her head disapprovingly, her urge to smile completely gone. "You know that's not allowed, Nick," she said sternly.

All the students at the Grissom Academy were remarkable in some way: mathematical geniuses, technical savants, brilliant artists, world-class musicians and composers. But Kahlee only ever dealt with those students involved in the Ascension Project—a program designed to help children with biotic aptitude maximize their potential. Once fitted with microscopic amplifiers wired throughout their nervous system, it was possible for biotic individuals to use electromagnetic impulses generated in the brain to create mass effect fields. With years of training in mental focus and biofeedback techniques, these fields could become strong enough to alter their physical surroundings. A powerful biotic could lift and throw objects, freeze them in place, or even shred them apart with nothing but the power of the mind. Given such dangerous potential, it was no surprise that there were strict rules against the students using their abilities outside of properly supervised settings.

"Did you hurt him?"

"A little," Nick admitted, grudgingly. "He banged his knee when I knocked him down. It's no big deal."

"It *is* a big deal," Kahlee insisted. "You can't use biotics on the other kids, Nick. You know that!"

Like all the Ascension Project students in his age group, Nick had undergone his implantation surgery a little over a year ago. Most of the children were still struggling to access their newfound abilities, practicing the drills and lessons that would allow them to coordinate their new biotic amps with their own biological systems. In the first two years, the majority could barely lift a pen a few inches off the surface of a desk.

Nick, however, was a quick learner. Based on initial testing, most of his classmates would almost certainly catch up to him over the coming years; several might even surpass him. But right now he was far more powerful than any of his peers . . . strong enough to knock another twelve-year-old down.

"He started it," Nick protested in his own defense. "He was making fun of my shoes. So I just *pushed* him. I can't help it if I'm good at biotics!"

Kahlee sighed. Nick's attitude was completely normal, and completely unacceptable. The Ascension Project had two primary objectives: to work with biotic individuals in an attempt to maximize human potential in the field, and, more important in her eyes, to help biotics integrate themselves into so-called normal human society. The students were not just trained in biotic techniques, they were also exposed to a curriculum of philosophical and moral instruction that would help them understand the responsibilities and obligations that came with their remarkable talent.

It was important the children didn't grow up with a sense of entitlement, or the belief they were somehow better than others because of their abilities. Of course, this was often the hardest lesson to teach.

"Seshaun's bigger than you, isn't he?" Kahlee noted after a moment of thought.

"All the boys are bigger than me," Nick mumbled, crossing his legs. He hunched forward to rest his elbows on the bedspread, then balanced his chin on his hands in an amazing display of the flexibility that all young children possess.

"Before you got your implants, did he pick on you? Did he push you around just because he was bigger than you?"

"No," Nick answered, rolling his eyes as he sensed a lecture coming. "That would be wrong," he dutifully added, knowing it was what she wanted to hear.

"Just because you're bigger or stronger or better at biotics doesn't mean you can do whatever you want," Kahlee told him, knowing he was only half-listening. Still, she hoped enough repetitions might get the message through someday. "You have a special gift, but that doesn't make it okay to hurt other people."

"I know," the boy admitted. "But it was mostly an accident. And I said I was sorry."

"Saying sorry isn't always enough," Kahlee answered. "That's why Hendel put you in lockdown."

"But three weeks is *sooo* long!"

Kahlee shrugged. "Hendel used to be a soldier. He believes in discipline. Now let's check your readings."

The boy, still resting his chin in his hands, tilted his head further downward to expose the nape of his neck. Kahlee reached out and touched him gingerly just above his collar, bracing against the tiny spark that jolted the tip of her finger. Nick jumped slightly, though he was more used to it than she was. Biotics often gave off small, sharp discharges of electricity; their bodies naturally generated static, as if they had just walked across a carpet in wool socks.

She pinched the skin on his neck between the thumb and forefinger of her left hand, while her right drew out a small needle from the pocket of her lab coat. There was a tiny, ball-shaped transmitter on the needle's head.

"Ready?" she asked.

"Ready," Nick said through tightly gritted teeth, and she pushed the needle into the gap between two of his vertebrae with a firm, steady pressure.

The boy's body tensed up and he let out a soft grunt as it entered, then relaxed. Kahlee pulled an omnitool from one of her other pockets and glanced at the readout to make sure Nick's data was transmitting properly.

"Did you used to be a soldier, too?" Nick asked, head still bent forward.

Kahlee blinked in surprise. The Grissom Academy was a joint Alliance-civilian facility. Much of the funding came from the Alliance, but for the most part it was modeled after a boarding school rather than a military academy. Parents were free to visit their children at any time, or to withdraw them from the curriculum for any reason. Security, custodial, and support services were provided by fully uniformed

military personnel, but the majority of the instructors, researchers, and academic staff were civilian.
This was particularly important for the Ascension
Project, as it helped allay fears the Alliance was trying
to transform children into biotic supersoldiers.

"I used to be in the Alliance," Kahlee admitted.
"I'm retired now."

A brilliant programmer with a knack for synthetic
and artificial intelligences, Kahlee had enlisted at the
age of twenty-two, shortly after her mother died. She
had spent fourteen years working on various top-
security-clearance projects for the Alliance before returning to civilian life. The next few years she had
served as a freelance corporate consultant, cementing
her reputation as one of the foremost experts in her
field. Then, five years ago, she had been offered a lu-
crative position on the Ascension Project by the Grissom Academy board of directors.

"I figured you were a soldier," Nick said a little
smugly. "You look all tough, like you're ready for a
fight all the time. Just like Hendel."

Kahlee was momentarily taken aback. She had
basic combat training; it was mandatory for all Alliance personnel. But she didn't imagine herself bearing any resemblance to a battle-hardened veteran like
Hendel. The majority of her service had been spent in
research labs surrounded by computers and other scientists, not out on the battlefield.

*Except for that time you helped Anderson kill a
krogan Battlemaster,* a small part of her mind chimed
in. She tried to push the memory away. She didn't like
to think about Sidon and everything that came after
it: too many friends lost there. But with Saren's face

constantly appearing on the news vids over the past few months, it was hard not to dredge the memories up. And every time she saw images of *Sovereign* attacking the Citadel, she couldn't help but wonder if there had been some connection between Dr. Shu Qian's illegal research at Sidon and the massive alien starship Saren had used to lead the geth assault.

"Miss Sanders? I think I'm done."

Nick's voice snapped her thoughts back to the present. The transmitter in his neck was beeping faintly.

"Sorry, Nick," she muttered, withdrawing the needle. Nick sat up straight, rubbing the back of his neck.

She pocketed the needle, then checked the readout on her omnitool again, verifying she had the data she needed. This was the core of her work on the Ascension Project. The newest biotic implants, collectively called the L4 configuration, were equipped with a network of virtual intelligence chips. The VI chips monitored the brain wave activity of a biotic, learning the complex thought patterns of their host and adapting their own performance to maximize biotic potential.

By analyzing the data collected in the chips, Kahlee and her team could also make subtle, customized adjustments to the VI program coordinating an individual's amps, resulting in even greater gains. So far tests showed a 10 to 15 percent increase in biotic ability over the older L3 configurations in 90 percent of the subjects, with no apparent side effects. But, like most research into the field of biotics, they were only beginning to scratch the surface of what was possible.

Nick lay back on his bed again, drained by the ordeal of having his spine tapped. "I'm getting stronger, right?" he said softly, smiling ever so slightly.

"I can't tell just by looking at the readout," Kahlee replied, evading the question. "I need to get back to the lab and run the numbers."

"I think I'm getting stronger," the boy said confidently, closing his eyes.

A little alarmed, she patted him gently on the leg and stood up from the bed. "Get some rest, Nick," she said, leaving him alone in his room.

THREE

As the door to Nick's room closed behind her, Kahlee noticed Hendel coming down the hall, wearing his customary attire of tan pants and a black, snug fitting, long-sleeved shirt. He was a tall man, a few inches over six feet, and thick through the neck, chest, and arms, with a closely cropped beard and mustache that covered his chin and upper lip but left his cheeks bare. His rusty-brown hair and first name were clear evidence of his Scandinavian ancestry. However, the darker tone of his skin and his last name, Mitra, hinted at his mixed heritage, and he had actually been born in the suburbs just outside of New Calcutta, one of Earth's wealthiest regions.

Kahlee assumed his parents still lived there, though they were no longer a part of his life. Her dysfunctional relationship with Grissom was nothing compared to Hendel and his family. He hadn't spoken to them in over twenty years; not since they'd abandoned him to the Biotic Acclimation and Training program when he was a teenager. The BAaT program, in contrast to the openness the Ascension Project enjoyed at the Grissom Academy, had taken place in a top-secret military facility before it was shut down as a dismal failure. The minds behind the program had wanted the BAaT instructors to act without interference from the families, so they had made every effort to convince the parents that biotics were dangerous. They tried to make them feel ashamed and even afraid of their own children, hoping to drive a wedge between the students and their families. In Hendel's case they had done a wonderful job.

He was approaching with both speed and purpose, propelled by his long, quick strides. He ignored the children peering curiously out at him from their rooms as he went by, a frown etched on his face as he stared intently at the floor.

Now there's someone who walks like a soldier, she thought.

"Hey!" Kahlee called out in surprise as he blew past her, seemingly oblivious to her presence. "Watch where you're going!"

"Huh?" he said, pulling up short and glancing back over his shoulder. Only then did he seem to notice her. "Sorry. In a hurry."

"I'll walk with you," she offered.

Hendel resumed his pace, and Kahlee fell into stride beside him. Every few steps she had to break into a quick jog to keep up.

"You were just with Nick?" he asked.

"He's sulking," Kahlee replied. "Thinks you're being unfair."

"He's lucky," Hendel grumbled. "Back in my day he would've gotten a smack upside the head hard enough to make his ears bleed. Now all we have are lockdowns and lectures. No wonder half these kids leave here as arrogant, snot-nosed punks."

"I think that has more to do with being a teenager than being a biotic," Kahlee noted with a small smile. Hendel talked tough, but she knew he'd never allow any harm to come to the children he worked with.

"Somebody needs to straighten that kid out," Hendel warned. "Or he'll end up as one of those guys who goes into a bar, hits on another man's date . . . then uses biotics to knock the other guy on his ass when he takes a swing.

"He'll think it's all just a big joke . . . until someone in the bar freaks out and bashes him over the head with a bottle when he's not looking."

Kahlee liked Hendel, but this was an example of his pessimistic, often bleak view of life. Of course there was some truth to what he said—there were biotics who acted as if they were indestructible, blessed with super powers. But there were limits to their talents. It took time to generate a mass effect field, as well as intense mental concentration and focus. Fatigue set in quickly. After one or two impressive displays a biotic was drained, leaving them as vulnerable as anyone else.

There were several documented cases of biotics flaunting their power: cheating at dice or roulette in a casino; altering the trajectory of the ball in the middle of a basketball game; even playing practical jokes on people by yanking their chairs out from under them. And the consequences for these actions were often severe. Enraged mobs had been known to assault or even kill biotics in retaliation for such minor offenses; driven to extreme overreaction by their ignorance and fear.

"That's not going to happen to Nick," she assured

him. "He'll learn. We'll get through to him eventually."

"Maybe one of the teachers needs to hit him with a stunner," he deadpanned.

"Don't look at me," Kahlee objected with a laugh, taking two quick hop-steps to keep from falling behind. "I never carry mine."

The stunners—small electroshock weapons manufactured by Aldrin Labs and capable of rendering a student unconscious—were standard issue to all personnel on the Ascension Project; a precaution in case any of the students ever unleashed a serious biotic attack against a staff member or classmate. For legal reasons, all nonbiotic personnel were supposed to carry a stunner while on duty, but Kahlee openly defied the rule. She hated the stunners. They seemed to hearken back to the mistrust and fear prevalent during the days of the BAaT program. Besides, in all the years of the Ascension Project, no staff member had ever needed to use one.

God willing no one ever will, she thought. Out loud she asked, "So where are we headed in such a hurry?"

"To see Gillian."

"Can it wait?" Kahlee asked. "Jiro's taking her readings."

Hendel raised a curious eye. "You're not supervising?"

"He knows what he's doing."

For some reason, Hendel had never warmed to Jiro. It could have been the age difference—Jiro was one of the youngest members on the staff. Or it could have simply been a clash of personalities—Jiro was cheerful, extroverted, and talkative, whereas Hendel was, in a word, stoic.

"I've got nothing against Jiro," he assured her, though she knew that wasn't completely true. "But Gillian's not like the other students."

"You worry about her too much."

"That's funny," he replied, "coming from you."

Kahlee let the comment slide. She and Hendel both spent a lot of extra time and attention on Gillian. It wasn't really fair to the other students, but Gillian was special. She needed more help than the others.

"She likes Jiro," Kahlee explained. "He'll do fine without you hovering around like an overprotective parent."

"This has nothing to do with getting her readings," Hendel grunted. "Grayson wants to come for another visit."

Kahlee stopped and grabbed her companion by the elbow, knocking the bigger man off stride and spinning him halfway around to face her.

"No," she said firmly. "I don't want her hearing that from you."

"I'm in charge of security for this wing," Hendel replied defensively. "All visitation requests go through me for approval."

"You're not seriously thinking of denying his request?" Kahlee asked, horrified. "He's her *father*! He has rights!"

"If I think the visit poses a danger to the child I can deny a parent's request," Hendel replied coolly.

"Danger? What kind of danger?"

"He's a drug addict, for Christ's sakes!"

"You can't prove that," Kahlee warned. "And you

can't deny his request based on suspicions. Not without getting fired."

"He wants to come the day after tomorrow!" Hendel objected. "I just need to see if Gillian's up to it. It might be better if he waits a few weeks so she can get used to the idea."

"Yeah, right," Kahlee replied sarcastically. "It's all about what's best for her. Your personal feelings about Grayson have nothing to do with it."

"Gillian needs routines and consistency," Hendel insisted. "You know how upset she gets if her schedule's disrupted. If he wants to be part of her life, he can come see her every month like the other parents, instead of once or twice a year whenever it's convenient for him. These unexpected visits are too hard on her."

"She'll cope," Kahlee said, eyes narrowing. "I'll tell Gillian her father's coming. You just go back to your office and approve Grayson's request."

Hendel opened his mouth to say something else, then wisely closed it.

"I'll get right on that," he muttered, then walked off in the opposite direction, heading back toward the administrative wing of the building.

Kahlee watched him go, then took a deep breath to try and calm herself. Gillian was surprisingly perceptive; she tended to read and react to other people's emotions. And the girl looked up to Hendel. If he'd delivered the news of her father's trip, she almost certainly would have picked up on his disapproval, and had a sympathetic negative reaction. That wasn't fair to Grayson, or his daughter.

Gillian's room was at the far end of the dormitory, where there was less noise to disturb her. By the time Kahlee reached the door, she had plastered an expression of cheerful expectation on her face. She raised her fist and rapped lightly. Her knock was answered not by the girl, but by Jiro.

"Come in."

The door slid open to reveal Gillian sitting at her desk. She was thin and angular, the tallest child in her age group by several inches. She had fine black hair that hung down almost to her waist, and eyes that seemed too wide and too far apart for her long face. Kahlee suspected she took after her mother, as apart from her slender build she didn't bear any real resemblance to Grayson.

Gillian was twelve, the same age as Nick. In fact, almost half the children in the Ascension Project came from the same approximate age group. Thirteen years ago three major industrial accidents, each at a different human colony, had occurred over a four-month span. The circumstances were suspicious, but investigations had uncovered no connection between the incidents. Of course, this had done little to quell the conspiracy theorists on the Extranet who refused to believe it was all just a tragic string of negligence and coincidence.

The third accident was by far the most devastating; some reports had initially called it the worst toxic disaster in human history. A fully loaded Eldfell-Ashland transport ship had exploded in atmosphere, killing the crew and spewing a deadly cloud of element zero over the entire Yandoa colony, exposing thousands of children in utero.

While the majority suffered no long-lasting harmful effects, several hundred of the unborn children developed significant symptoms ranging from cancer to organ damage, birth defects, and even spontaneous abortion. However, some good did come from the otherwise tragic statistics: thirty-seven of the exposed children had been diagnosed as not only healthy, but also with significant biotic potential of varying degree. All of them were now here at the Grissom Academy.

Gillian was staring with a disturbing intensity at the assignment on her computer screen. Sometimes she would sit like this for hours, motionless. Then, as if some undetectable switch went off in her mind, she would explode into a flurry of action, typing out answers so quickly her fingers were nothing but a blur. Her answers were, without variation, 100 percent correct.

"All done here?" Kahlee asked, directing the question at her assistant gathering up his equipment in the corner of the room.

"Just finished," Jiro replied with a smile.

He was only twenty-five, handsome, and well put together. His features were a pleasing mix of both his American and Asian ancestry, and he wore his hair, dyed a dark red, in a spiky, tousled style that made it look as if he'd just rolled out of bed. An easy, confident charm and impish smile made Jiro appear even younger than he actually was.

Cradle robber, a small corner of her conscience chided. She pointedly ignored it.

"Gillian did very well today," Jiro added, turning his smile toward the girl. "Didn't you, Gillian?"

"I guess," the girl muttered softly, though she didn't turn her head from the screen.

Gillian had good days and bad days, and the fact that she was speaking hinted to Kahlee that this might be one of the good ones.

"I have some exciting news," she said, coming over to stand beside Jiro.

With any other child Kahlee would have sat on the edge of the desk, or rested a comforting hand on their shoulder. But for Gillian even the softest brush of a fingertip against her skin could sometimes cause her to react as if she'd been touched with a burning ember. Other times she seemed oblivious to all sensation, as if her nerve endings were completely dead. This made it difficult to get the daily readings Kahlee needed for her research. Fortunately, Gillian seemed to react well to Jiro, and he was usually able to get the data without causing her significant discomfort.

"Your father's coming to visit. He'll be here in two days."

She waited for a reaction, and was relieved to see the faint hint of a smile touch the girl's lips. Jiro picked up on the subtle change in Gillian's mood and reacted to it quickly.

"I bet he can't wait to see you again," he said, his tone overflowing with exuberance.

The girl turned her head to them, her face now sporting a full-blown grin. "I can wear the dress he gave me," she said, her voice distant and dreamy.

Grayson had given his daughter the dress on his last visit, almost nine months ago. Kahlee doubted it would still fit, but she didn't want to bring it up and spoil the moment.

"I bet he'd rather see you in your school uniform," Jiro chimed in without missing a beat. "Let's show him how hard you're working on your classes."

Gillian furrowed her brow and scowled, processing the information. Then her brow relaxed and the smile returned. "He likes to talk about school."

"That's because he's so proud of how smart you are," Jiro added.

"I need to finish my assignment," Gillian said abruptly, the mention of her studies bringing the concept of academics to the forefront of her thoughts. Her mind latched on to the idea, fixating on it to the exclusion of everything else. She turned back to the computer screen, staring at it once more with unwavering focus.

Kahlee and Jiro, familiar with her unusual behaviors, didn't bother to disturb her by saying good-bye as they left.

"What say we get a little alone time?" Jiro whispered as they walked down the hall, sliding his arm around Kahlee's waist.

"Not where the kids can see," she chided, elbowing him playfully in the ribs. He flinched, but didn't let go.

"We could go back to Gillian's room," he suggested, pulling her closer. "She won't even notice we're there."

"Not funny!" Kahlee gasped, giving him another, much sharper, shot with her elbow.

His hand fell away as he gave an exaggerated grunt and doubled over, pretending to gasp for air. Kahlee rolled her eyes and kept walking.

"Careful soldier," he said, standing up straight and

trotting to catch up with her. "You can't go around beating up innocent civilians like that."

"You hardly qualify as innocent," she told him. "Besides, I'm a civilian now, too."

"You can take the girl out of the army, but you can't take the army out of the girl," he countered with a grin.

It was a harmless joke; Jiro was always teasing her about her military background. But it made her think back to Nick's comment comparing her and Hendel.

"Gillian seemed to be doing well today," she said, eager to change the subject.

Jiro shrugged, his expression becoming more serious.

"She still doesn't interact with the other kids at all. And she's way behind the rest of the class."

Kahlee knew he was referring to biotics, rather than academics. Even among the remarkable children of the Ascension Project, Gillian was special. At age three she had been diagnosed with a mild form of high-functioning autism; it had almost caused the board to reject her application to the Academy. Ultimately they had relented, partly because of a large donation Grayson had generously provided and partly because Gillian had shown far greater potential than any of the other students . . . or any other individual in the short history of recorded human biotics.

Accepted science held that biotic potential was established in early childhood as a fixed and unalterable rating. The purpose of a program like the Ascension Project was to teach biotics how to fully utilize their talent so they could get the most from their inherent abilities. With Gillian, however, regular testing at the Academy charted a rating that was continuing to rise in erratic, but undeniable, fits and starts—a previously unheard-of phenomenon.

The gap between Gillian's biotic ability and the rest of her classmates had been large to begin with; now it was enormous. Despite this advantage, however, Gillian had difficulty translating her potential into observable results. Because of her unique cognitive processes, she struggled to grasp the mental focusing techniques necessary to coordinate her amps with the electrical impulses of her brain. In short, she didn't know how to tap into her power, and none of the instructors seemed to know how to teach her.

"Maybe the board was right in the first place," Kahlee said with a sigh. "This might be too much for her."

"Seeing her father might help," Jiro suggested, without much hope. After a moment he added, "How did Hendel react when he found out Grayson was coming?"

"Like you'd expect," she answered. "He was trying to figure out some way to deny his request."

"Let me guess," Jiro chimed in with another smile. "You pulled rank on him."

"Enough with the army talk," she said wearily.

"Sorry," he apologized, his smile disappearing. A second later it was back in full force. "Hey, why don't you knock off early tonight?" he offered. "I can run your numbers for you. You go back to my room, make yourself comfortable, and relax, and I'll meet you there when I'm done."

"Now that's the best idea I've heard all day," she

said with a suggestive smile, handing over her omni-tool.

She glanced around to make sure they were alone in the corridor, then gave him a quick kiss on the lips. "Don't keep me waiting all night."

FOUR

"Watch where you're going, human."

The krogan Pel had inadvertently bumped into glared down at him, clearly looking for any excuse to start a fight. Pel didn't normally back down from anyone, especially an alien, but he was smart enough to make an exception for an angry, eight-foot-tall mountain of scaled muscle.

"Sorry," he mumbled, avoiding eye contact until the oversized reptile thumped away to satisfy his bloodlust somewhere else.

Normally Pel wouldn't have been careless enough to bump into a talking lizard the size of a small tank, even on the crowded streets of Omega. But he had other things on his mind at the moment. Cerberus had sent him to meet a new Terminus Systems contact, but the contact had never showed. That alone was enough to make Pel nervous. Then, as he was making his way back to his rented apartment in a neighboring district, he had the feeling he was being watched.

He hadn't noticed anyone suspicious following him, but Cerberus taught its agents that ignoring their instincts was a good way to end up dead. Unfortunately, Omega wasn't the kind of place to walk around while constantly looking back over your shoulder. You had to pay attention to where you were going if you didn't want to end up with a knife in your belly.

An enormous space station located deep in the Terminus Systems, Omega was unlike any other facility in the known galaxy. Built from the remains of a massive, irregularly shaped asteroid, the heavy-metal-rich core had been mined until the asteroid was almost completely hollow, providing the initial resources used to construct the facilities that completely covered every exposed inch of its surface. Its exact age was unknown, although everyone agreed the station had originally been built by the Protheans before they disappeared. However, nobody agreed on which had been the first species to resettle it once the Protheans were mysteriously wiped out.

Several groups had tried to lay sole claim to it over the station's long history, but none had been able to maintain control for more than a few years. Now it served as a meeting place and interstellar hub of commerce for those unwelcome in Citadel space, like the batarians and the salarian Lystheni offshoot, as well as mercenaries, slavers, assassins, and criminals from all races.

Despite the occasional war between occupying species, Omega had developed into a de facto capital of the Terminus Systems. Numerous factions had settled on the station over the centuries, with each new arrival building out sections of the station to suit their specific needs. Their efforts had transformed Omega into the equivalent of a massive floating city divided into numerous independent districts, each marked by mismatched architecture and haphazard design. From a distance, the exterior of the station looked uneven or even lopsided. Arms added to the main hub jutted out at all angles from the asteroid's surface, with further add-ons extending out from these arms at bizarre angles. And within the various districts the buildings seemed to have been constructed without plan or purpose; streets twisted and turned unexpectedly, and sometimes curled back on themselves to form infuriating dead-ends. Even residents of the station could quickly become lost or disoriented, and the overall effect was highly unsettling for new arrivals.

Pel had been to Omega enough times to get over the disturbing randomness, but he still hated the place. The station teemed with individuals from every alien species; even humans had become a noticeable presence. And in contrast to the ordered, harmonious—almost sterile—coexistence found on the Citadel, the streets of Omega were crowded, dirty, and dangerous. There was no law enforcement; the few rules that existed were enforced by gangs of hired thugs employed by those who controlled each section of the station. Petty crime was rampant, and killings were common.

That didn't actually bother Pel; he knew how to look after himself. He had other issues with Omega. Every corner of the station stank with the mingled odors of a dozen different alien species: sweat and pheromones poorly covered up by the gagging scent of unfamiliar perfumes; the reek of unidentifiable foods wafting from open windows and doors; the putrid stench of uncollected garbage that littered the back alleys.

As bad as the smells were, the sounds were even worse. Unlike Council space, most aliens here refused to speak the common trade language unless absolutely necessary. An endless cacophony of grunts, squawks, and squeaks assailed his ears as he made his way through the crowds, his automated translator useless in the face of obscure interstellar dialects it wasn't programmed to decipher.

The aliens couldn't even agree on a single name for the station. Each speaker called it something different in his or her native tongue. The unpronounceable asari name loosely translated as "heart of evil," the turians referred to it as "world without law," the salarians called it "place of secrets," and the krogans knew it as "land of opportunity." For the sake of convenience, the automated translator Pel wore strapped to his belt translated all these terms into the human word "Omega"—the absolute end of all things.

As much as he didn't want to be here, he had a job to do. Cerberus had sent him to broker a deal with his contact, and Pel knew better than to cross the Illusive Man. Of course, that hadn't stopped him and his team from taking on a few freelance projects over the past year that his superiors might not approve of. That's why it was so important to do things right: complete his missions as instructed; keep a low profile and don't make a mistake that might draw extra attention to his unauthorized activities.

Unless they already know, Pel thought, wondering if his tail was a Cerberus operative. Maybe the whole mission had been a ploy to get him alone on Omega's streets, where a dead human wouldn't attract any notice.

"Only one way to find out," he muttered, breaking into a run, thankful he wasn't wearing any kind of body armor that could slow him down.

He darted and dodged through the crowd, spinning and wheeling his way past startled aliens, ignoring the unintelligible threats and curses they shouted after him. He veered sharply down an empty side street lined with garbage cans, trash bins, and piles of refuse. Racing past several closed doorways, he ducked behind a large trash bin, crouching low. From his pocket he pulled out a small mirror, angling it so he could see back down the length of the alley without having to peek his head out and expose himself.

A few seconds later his pursuer skidded into view, coming around the corner from the main street into the deserted alley at a full run. The figure was small, about a foot shorter than Pel, and covered head to toe in dark clothing. His pursuer's face was completely obscured by a tightly wrapped scarf.

The figure stopped and stared down the length of the alley, head turning from side to side looking for some sign of where Pel might have disappeared to. His follower pulled out a pistol, adjusted the setting, then began to move forward cautiously, weapon ready.

Pel could have drawn a weapon of his own; he had several to choose from: the trusty Hahne-Keder pistol strapped to his hip, the knife in his belt, or the small emergency zip-gun in the heel of his boot. The figure didn't appear to be wearing any kind of combat suit that might be equipped with kinetic shields, so a single well-placed shot would be lethal. But killing his pursuer wouldn't tell him who was following him, or why. Instead, he simply waited silently for his adversary to approach.

The figure continued to advance, staying in the middle of the alley, obviously trying not to get too close to the doorways or refuse containers where an enemy might be waiting to leap out. But his pursuer's head was still turning side to side, hesitating to stare at each potential hiding spot a fraction of a second too long.

His target was close now, maybe ten feet away. Peering in the mirror, he waited until the figure's head turned away from him and then charged out, coming in hard and focusing his attack on the weapon hand of his too slow to react opponent.

Grabbing the forearm with his left hand, he used his right to bend the wrist holding the pistol inward, redirecting the weapon so it was pointed back at the owner. The whole time he kept his legs churning, using his momentum and size to drive his smaller adversary backward and off-balance.

They crashed to the street, the pistol jarring loose, and Pel heard a distinctly male grunt from his opponent. They wrestled briefly, but Pel was bigger, stronger, and had the advantage of being on top when they hit the ground. He twisted the other man so he was lying facedown, then Pel looped his forearm under his chin, applying pressure in a choke hold. His free hand still clutched his enemy's wrist, and Pel bent the arm up behind his prone opponent's back.

The man beneath him struggled and squirmed. There

was a wiry strength to his limbs, but he couldn't over-come the advantages of Pel's size and leverage.

"Who are you?" Pel hissed in his ear, using the common trade language. "Who sent you?"

"Golo," came the strained reply.

Pel loosened his choke hold slightly. "Golo sent you?"

"I *am* Golo." Pel's translator relayed the words in English, but he recognized the speaker's native tongue, and the unmistakable sound of words being spoken from behind a sealed enviro-mask.

With a grunt of disgust, Pel rolled off the quarian and stood up.

"You were supposed to meet me in the bar," he said, not bothering to help his contact up from the ground.

Golo got to his feet gingerly, checking to see if any-thing was broken. He looked pretty much the same as every other quarian Pel had meet. Slightly shorter and smaller than a human, he was wrapped in several lay-ers of mismatched clothing. The dark scarf that had covered his face had been torn away during their scuffle, revealing the smooth, reflective visor of a hel-met that obscured his features.

"My pardon," the quarian answered, switching to English. "I set up the meeting so I could watch you from a safe distance, to make sure you were alone. I've had too many meetings in the past where the per-son I was supposed to meet was only a lure to draw me out into an ambush."

"Why is that?" Pel wondered aloud, his irritation growing. "You make a habit of double-crossing people?" He was too pissed off to be impressed by Golo's excellent command of a human dialect.

"My word is my bond," Golo assured him. "But there are many who dislike quarians. They think we are nothing but scavengers and thieves."

That's because you are, Pel thought to himself.

"I was going to follow you back to your apartment," the quarian continued. "And then make face-to-face contact with you there."

"Instead you drew a weapon on me."

"Only for self-defense," Golo objected. "When you ran I knew I had been spotted. I was afraid you would try to kill me."

"I still might," Pel replied, but it was an empty threat. Cerberus needed the quarian alive.

Golo must have sensed he was out of danger, because he turned his back on Pel and retrieved his weapon from the ground.

"We can go to your home and continue our business in private," the quarian offered, securing his pistol somewhere inside the folds of his clothes.

"No," Pel replied. "Somewhere public. I don't want you to know where I'm staying." *You'll probably come back later and rob me blind.*

Golo shrugged indifferently. "I know a place not far from here."

The quarian took him to a local gambling hall located in the district. A heavily armed krogan standing at the door nodded slightly as they entered. The sign above his head said "Fortune's Den" in many languages, though Pel doubted anyone ever got rich in this place.

"You come here often?" he asked as Golo led him to a booth near the back.

"The owner and I have an arrangement. Nobody will disturb us here."

"Why didn't you just tell me to meet you here in the first place?"

"As I said before, I had to make sure you were alone. Olthar would be very unhappy if I led a group of human mercenaries to his establishment."

The inflection he put on "Olthar" made it sound like a volus name to Pel, but he couldn't be sure. Not that it mattered.

Taking the seat opposite Golo, Pel was surprised to see the place was almost empty. A pair of four-eyed batarians were throwing dice, a few rotund volus were playing some kind of game that resembled backgammon, and a handful of humans were clustered in the center of the room playing cards under the watchful eye of a shifty-looking salarian dealer. He would have preferred a strip bar—one with human or even asari dancers—but he didn't bother to complain.

"No quasar machines," he noted.

"Too easy to hack, too expensive to repair," the quarian explained.

A waitress—human—came over and wordlessly set a mug on the table in front of him, then scurried away without making eye contact. She might have been attractive once, long ago. As she left, Pel noticed she wore a small electronic locater on her ankle; a device commonly used by slavers to keep track of their property.

His jaw clenched involuntarily. The idea of a human

enslaved by alien masters sickened him, but there
wasn't anything he could do to help this woman. Not
right now anyway.

Soon a day of reckoning will come, he reassured
himself. *And justice will rain down on all these sick
alien bastards.*

"My treat," Golo told him, nodding to the glass in
front of Pel.

It looked like some alien variant of beer, but he'd
learned the hard way to avoid human food prepared
in nonhuman establishments. If he was lucky, it
would simply be flat and bitter. If he was unlucky, he
might spend half the night puking his guts out.

"I'll pass," he said, pushing the glass away. "Why
aren't you drinking anything?" he asked after a moment, suddenly suspicious.

"Germs," Golo explained, tapping the face shield
of his helmet.

Pel nodded. Since being driven from their homeworld by the geth, virtually all quarians now lived on
the Migrant Fleet, a flotilla of several thousand ships
wandering aimlessly through space. Generations of
living in such an isolated, carefully controlled environment had rendered the quarian immune system all
but useless against the viruses and bacteria swarming
over every inhabited planet in the galaxy. To avoid
exposure, they wore form-fitting enviro-suits beneath
their ragged clothes and never removed their airtight
visored helmets in public.

This had led to rumors that the quarians were in
fact cybernetic; a mix of organic and machine beneath their clothes and visors. Pel knew the truth was
much less sinister—a quarian simply couldn't survive

outside the flotilla without a hermetically sealed suit and mask.

"Let's get down to business," Pel said, turning to the task at hand. "You said you can give us transmission frequencies and communication codes for the Migrant Fleet."

The Migrant Fleet had become of great interest to the Illusive Man and Cerberus, particularly in the wake of the geth attack on the Citadel. Most thought of the quarians as nothing more than a nuisance; nearly seventeen million refugees eking out a hand-to-mouth existence on their fleet of outdated and substandard ships. For three centuries they had traveled from system to system, searching in vain for a suitable uninhabited planet they could use to establish a new homeworld.

The common belief was that the greatest threats the quarians posed to any established colony were the consumption of local resources—such as stripping a system's asteroid belts of precious metals or element zero deposits—and the disruption of communications and starship travel inevitably caused by several thousand unscheduled and unregulated vessels passing through. These inconveniences made the quarians unwelcome in any civilized region of space, but it couldn't be said anyone actually feared them.

The Illusive Man, however, was able to see past their motley garb and jury-rigged ships. Technologically, they were easily the equivalent of any other species. The quarians had created the geth, who had become a scourge upon the galaxy. And they had managed to sustain a civilization numbering nearly seventeen million individuals over hundreds of years without the benefit of any planetary resources. Who knew what else they were capable of?

The Migrant Fleet was also the largest single armada in the known galaxy: tens of thousands of ships, ranging from tiny shuttles to cruisers to the three enormous Liveships—marvels of aerospace and agricultural engineering that provided the primary source of food for the entire flotilla. It was accepted fact that a significant portion of the ships in the fleet were armed, though how many and to what extent was unknown. In fact, very little was known about the quarian flotilla at all. They were a completely insular society; no outsider had ever set foot on one of their vessels since their exodus three centuries ago.

The Illusive Man didn't trust aliens with so many ships and secrets. Getting the quarian codes and transmission frequencies would allow Cerberus to monitor communications among the vessels of the Migrant Fleet . . . provided they could somehow get one of their own ships close enough to tap into tight-beam messages without being seen. Pel wasn't sure how the Illusive Man planned to pull off that part of the plan, but it wasn't his concern. He was just here to acquire the codes and frequencies.

"I can't actually give you the transmission codes," Golo informed him. "They've changed since I was last part of the flotilla."

Pel bit his lip to keep from swearing out loud. He should have known better than to trust Golo. He was an exile from the Migrant Fleet. The quarians didn't have the space or resources on their ships to house a prison population, and therefore criminals were dealt with by expelling them from quarian society, abandoning them on the nearest inhabited planet or space station. In Golo's case, Omega.

What kind of sick, twisted deviant do you have to be to get exiled by an entire race of beggars and thieves? he asked himself, wondering if Golo was a murderer, rapist, or just a complete sociopath.

"However, I do have something to offer you," Golo continued, seemingly oblivious to Pel's barely contained rage. "I will lead you to someone who *can* provide you with the information you want. For a price."

Dirty, double-dealing son-of-a-bitch.

"That wasn't our deal."

"You need to learn to be flexible," he said with a shrug. "Improvise. Adapt. That is the way of my people. It was how I survived when I first found myself on this station."

You mean when they dumped you off here. Just another piece of garbage for someone else to clean up.

Despite his unspoken disdain, Pel had a grudging respect for Golo. Quarians were as unwelcome on Omega as anywhere else in the galaxy; the fact that he had managed to survive on the station was a testament to his cunning and resourcefulness. And a warning that he couldn't be trusted. Pel wasn't willing to report back to the Illusive Man empty-handed, but he also wasn't quite ready to trust the quarian yet. Not without knowing a little more about him.

"Tell me why you were exiled."

Golo hesitated. A sound that might have been a sigh of regret came from behind his mask, and for a second Pel thought the quarian wasn't going to respond. "About ten years ago, I tried to make a deal with the Collectors."

Pel had heard of the Collectors, though he'd never actually seen one. In fact, many people, including Pel, weren't sure they really existed. From the stories, they sounded more like the interstellar equivalent of an urban legend than a real species.

By most accounts they had first appeared on the galactic scene roughly five hundred years ago, allegedly emerging from an uncharted region of space somewhere beyond the otherwise inaccessible Omega-4 relay. And while, if the stories were true, they had been around for five centuries, almost nothing was known about the enigmatic species or their mysterious homeworld. Isolationist to the extreme, the Collectors were rarely seen anywhere but Omega and a few of the nearby inhabited worlds. Even then, decades could pass with no reported sightings at the station, only to give way to a few years marked by several dozen sporadic visits from envoys looking to barter and trade with other species.

On those rare occasions when Collectors did venture into the Terminus Systems, they reportedly made it clear that similar visits by other species into their territory would not be tolerated. Despite this, countless vessels had dared to attempt the passage through the Omega-4 relay over the centuries in search of their home planet. None of them had ever returned. The staggering number of ships, expeditions, and exploratory fleets that had disappeared without explanation into the Omega-4 relay had led to wild speculation about what lay hidden beyond the portal. Some believed it opened into a black hole or the heart of a sun, though this didn't explain how the Collectors could use the relay themselves. Others claimed it led to the futuristic equivalent of paradise: those who passed through were now living lives of decadent luxury on an idyllic planet, with no desire to return to the violent struggles of the lawless Terminus Systems. The most widely accepted explanation was that the Collectors had some manner of defensive technology, unique and highly advanced, that utterly destroyed any foreign vessel passing through the relay.

But Pel wasn't sure he believed any of the stories.

"I thought the Collectors were just a myth."

"A common misperception, particularly in Council Space. However, I can assure you from personal experience that they are very real."

"What kind of deal did you make with them?" Pel asked, his curiosity piqued.

"They wanted two dozen 'pure' quarians: men and women who had spent their entire lives on the fleet, uncontaminated by visits to other worlds."

"I thought every quarian had to leave the fleet during their Pilgrimage," Pel remarked, referring to the quarian right of passage into adulthood.

"Not all quarians make the Pilgrimage," Golo explained. "Exceptions are made for those too sick or infirm to survive outside the colony. And in rare cases an individual with a valuable skill or talent can receive a dispensation from the Admiralty.

"I knew from the start I'd probably get caught," he added, almost regretful, "but the terms of their offer were too good to pass up."

Pel nodded: this fit with the stories he'd heard. When the Collectors came to barter, they typically sought to exchange merchandise or technology for living beings. They were, however, far more than simple slavers. The tales of their requests were always unusual or bizarre: two dozen left-handed salarians; sixteen sets of batarian twins; a krogan born of parents from feuding clans. In return, the Collectors would offer incredible technology or knowledge, such as a ship with a new mass drive configuration that increased engine efficiency, or a cache of advanced targeting VI mods to radically improve weapon accuracy. Eventually this technology would be adapted by galactic society as a whole, but for several years it would provide a significant edge for anyone smart enough to take the deal. Or so the tales told.

In the absence of any true name for the species, their willingness to pay so extravagantly to have their odd but highly specific requests satisfied had earned them the generic title of Collectors. Similar to the conjecture spawned by the mystery of what lay beyond the Omega-4 relay, numerous theories had evolved attempting to explain the motivation behind their illogical demands. Some believed there was a religious significance to the requests, others saw it as evidence of deviant sexual predilections or gruesome culinary appetites.

If the Collectors actually did exist, as Golo claimed, then Pel tended to support the most generally accepted belief that they were conducting genetic experiments on other species, though he couldn't even begin to guess at their exact nature or purpose. Certainly it was enough to make any reasonable person suspicious.

"If the Collectors are real, why hasn't more been done to try and stop their activities?" he wondered aloud.

"As long as you can profit from the deal, who cares?" Golo replied, his rhetorical question encapsulating the general attitude of the entire Terminus Systems in a single breath. "They show up and offer something worth a few million credits, and all you have to do is give them a couple dozen prisoners in exchange. They're no worse than the slavers, but they pay a lot better."

Slavery was illegal in Council Space, but here in the Terminus Systems it was an accepted—even a common—practice. However, it wasn't the morality of what the Collectors were doing that concerned Pel.

"Isn't anyone worried about what they're doing behind that relay? They could be making powerful new genetic weapons. What if they're studying species to learn our weaknesses and vulnerabilities so they can invade?"

Golo laughed, the sound reverberating off his mask with a distant, hollow timbre.

"I have no doubt they are up to something *unpleasant*," he admitted. "But they've been doing this for five hundred years. If they were planning an invasion, it would have happened by now."

"But aren't you even curious?"

"The curious try to go through the Omega-4 relay," he reminded his human companion. "And they don't come back. The rest of us here on Omega are more worried about getting killed by our neighbor than what's happening on the far side of the galaxy. You need to stay focused to survive out here."

Good advice, Pel thought. The Collectors were definitely intriguing, and he wouldn't be surprised to learn that the Illusive Man already had agents looking into them somewhere. But that wasn't his mission.

"You said you could lead me to people who can give me those transmission codes."

Golo nodded eagerly, glad the subject had turned back to their current business.

"I can set up a meeting with a crew from one of the scout ships from the Migrant Fleet," he promised. "Just make sure you take one of them alive."

FIVE

The flight attendant greeted him with a cheerful smile, her voice warm and inviting. "Welcome aboard, Mr. Grayson. My name is Ellin."

He didn't recognize her, but she could have been a recent hire; he didn't use the corporate shuttle very often. Ellin had striking green eyes—probably tinted—and long, lustrous golden hair—probably dyed. She looked to be in her early twenties, though of course there was no guarantee she was anywhere close to that young.

"Pleased to meet you, Ellin," he replied with a nod. He realized he was smiling at her with a goofy grin. *Always was a sucker for blondes.*

"We won't be leaving for a few minutes yet," she informed him, reaching out to take the briefcase from his hand, "but your room is ready. Please follow me and we can get you settled while the pilot makes his final preflight checks."

He studied her figure appreciatively from behind as she led him down the narrow corridor toward the private VIP chamber in the aft of the vessel.

"I hope everything is to your liking," she commented on reaching their destination, stepping forward and holding the door open so he could enter.

The room bore almost no resemblance to the simple, often crowded bunks found on military vessels or the common sleeping rooms of long-distance mass-transit shuttles. Equipped with a luxurious bed, state-of-the-art vid screen, private shower and hot tub, full wet bar, and just about every other conceivable amenity, it compared favorably to any suite in all but the most expensive planet-side hotels.

"We'll be arriving at the Grissom Academy in about eight hours, Mr. Grayson," Ellin continued, setting his briefcase in the corner. "Can I get you anything before lift-off?"

"I think I just want to rest," he said. Every joint in his body ached, and his head was pounding—classic signs of red sand withdrawal. "Wake me an hour before we arrive."

"Of course, Mr. Grayson," she replied, then turned and left him alone, closing the door behind her.

He stripped off his clothes, suddenly aware of how much he was sweating. There was a faint tremor in his left hand as he unbuttoned his shirt. But the idea of dusting up never crossed his mind; he wouldn't let Gillian see him stoned. Naked, he collapsed on the bed, too hot to bother crawling under the soft, silk sheets.

He heard the deep rumble as the pilot fired up the engines. Grayson could have flown himself, of course . . . he still knew how to handle a vessel like this. But Cerberus needed him to play a different role now. His cover was that of a high-level executive with Cord-Hislop Aeorospace, a midsized starship manufacturer based on Elysium. This allowed him to travel across the galaxy in private vessels without drawing undo attention, and offered a reasonable way to explain the large donation he'd given to the board of the Grissom Academy in order to get Gillian accepted into the Ascension Project.

The days of pretending to be a private pilot for up-and-coming politicians were long gone; now he was the one enjoying the luxurious room and service from a personal flight attendant. The Illusive Man looked after those who pleased him.

I bet Menneau thought that, too. Right before Pel killed him.

Grayson sat up in bed, his mind going back to Pel's recent visit. Maybe his old friend had told the Illusive Man about the red sand after all. Cerberus wouldn't just sit by if they felt his addiction jeopardized the mission.

Was Ellin really just a flight attendant? Thousands of everyday people worked ordinary jobs for Cord-Hislop without ever suspecting it was a corporation controlled by a shadowy paramilitary group. Hardly anyone at the company—or anywhere else, for that matter—even knew an organization like Cerberus existed. But hidden within the rank and file of employees, scattered across all rungs of the corporate ladder, were dozens of the Illusive Man's agents. Maybe Ellin was one of them. Maybe she was waiting outside the door to stick an ice pick in his neck, just like he'd done to Keo.

He rolled out of bed and pulled on the terry-cloth bathrobe hanging on the wall, then pushed the call button. A few seconds later there was a gentle rap on the door. Grayson hesitated, then waved his hand in front of the access panel. He resisted the urge to jump back as the door slid open.

Ellin was standing there, armed only with her relentlessly cheery smile and perky attitude.

"Is there something you need, Mr. Grayson?"

"My clothes . . . can you have them cleaned and pressed for me?"

"Of course, sir."

She stepped into the room and collected his discarded garments, picking them up with a cool, practiced efficiency. There was a confidence about her; a professionalism that could be a sign of specialized military training . . . or it could have simply been part of her job. He tried to watch her without being seen, hoping to catch her surreptitiously watching him. If she was working for Cerberus, she'd have been instructed to keep close tabs on her passenger.

Ellin stood up and turned to face him, the bundle of clothes in her arms. The well-practiced smile fell away from her face, and Grayson realized he was still staring at her intently.

He shook his head to clear away the dark thoughts. "Sorry. My mind was somewhere else."

Her smile reappeared, though her eyes looked nervous. "Is there anything else, Mr. Grayson?"

He picked up the slightest waver in her voice. *Either she's just a scared little stewardess, or she's very, very good at pretending to be one.* The thought was quickly followed by another: *The red sand's making you paranoid.*

"Thank you, Ellin. That will be all."

The relief on her face as he stepped aside to let her

exit was obvious. Once she was safely outside the door, she hesitated, then turned back.

"Do . . . do you still want me to wake you an hour before we land?"

"That will be fine," he said abruptly, closing the door before she could see the flush of embarrassment creeping up his neck and into his face.

Get it together, he chided himself, removing the robe and falling back onto the bed. *Quit jumping at shadows. This mission's too important to screw up.*

The sound of the engines had changed. Staring up at the ceiling, he could feel a slight pressure on his chest pushing him down into the soft mattress. The ship was taking to the sky, battling gravity and atmosphere as it headed for the stars. The room that had seemed so hot before was suddenly cold; he shivered and crawled in under the blankets.

The artificial mass effect fields generated inside the ship's hull dampened the turbulence and g-forces of their lift-off, but his pilot's instincts could still feel the motion. It was familiar, reassuring. Within minutes it had rocked him to sleep.

"We have a new assignment for you," the Illusive Man said, and Grayson realized he was dreaming once again.

They were alone in Grayson's apartment, just the two of them . . . and the infant sleeping quietly in the Illusive Man's arms.

"I was impressed with your work on the Eldfell-Ashland job. I know it was a difficult mission."

"It was for the greater good," he replied.

Even if he wanted to, there was nothing else he could say. He had believed it back then, with every fiber of his being. He still believed it, though the part of his mind that knew he was dreaming realized things weren't as simple as they used to be.

"I have a special assignment for you," the Illusive Man said, handing over the child. "She's biotic."

Grayson took the little girl in his arms. She was warm and soft, and lighter than he'd expected. Disturbed by the transfer, her eyes popped open and she began to fuss. Grayson shushed her gently, rocking her in his arms. Her eyelids drooped, she blew a small bubble, and then she was asleep again.

Based on her age he had no doubt as to how she had been exposed to element zero.

"You're going to be working for Cord-Hislop as part of your cover," the Illusive Man informed him. "Sales for now, but you'll climb to the executive ranks over the next few years. We want you to raise the girl as your own."

"Who's my partner?"

"None. Your wife died when your daughter was born. You never remarried."

Grayson wondered what had happened to the girl's real mother and father, but he wasn't foolish enough to ask.

"Do you understand how important this mission is?" the Illusive Man asked. "Do you see what biotics can ultimately mean to humanity?"

The younger man nodded. He believed in what he did. He believed in Cerberus.

"We went to a lot of trouble to find this particular girl. She's special. We want her to look up to you. To trust you. Treat her as if she is your own flesh and blood."

"I will," he promised.

He had offered the vow without understanding the consequence of what it really meant. Had he known the true cost, he might not have been so quick to reply . . . although in the end the answer would have been the same.

The baby gurgled softly. Grayson stared down at her scrunched-up little face, fascinated.

"You won't be alone in this," the Illusive Man assured him. *"We have top experts in the field. They'll make sure she gets all the proper training."*

Grayson watched, transfixed, as the girl fidgeted in her sleep, her hands balling up into tiny fists that traced tight little circles in the air.

The Illusive Man turned to go.

"Does she have a name?" Grayson asked without looking up.

"A father has the right to name his own daughter," he said, closing the door behind him.

Grayson woke, as he always did, with the echo of the closing door from his dream still in his ears.

"Lights—dim," he called out, and a faint glow from the bedside lamps cast the dark shadows from his room. Only an hour had passed; seven more until they reached the Academy.

He climbed out of bed and pulled on the robe, then picked up his briefcase. He carried it over to the small desk in the corner of the room and set it on top, then settled into the accompanying chair and punched in the access code. A second later the case opened with a soft, depressurizing hiss.

Inside were several dummy documents to help with his cover as a Cord-Hislop executive—contracts and sales reports, mostly. He pulled them out and dumped them on the floor, then lifted up the case's false bottom to reveal the contents underneath. Ignoring the vial Pel had given him—he wouldn't need that until he actually saw Gillian—he reached for the small cellophane bag of red sand.

Grayson wondered how much the Illusive Man had actually known about the girl on that night he'd given him Gillian. Did he know about her mental condition? Did he know the Alliance was one day going to start a program like the Ascension Project? Had he given the little girl to Grayson, fully aware he was one day going to order him to give her up again?

He opened the baggie and carefully poured out a small pile of the fine dust. Enough to take the edge off, nothing more. Besides, he had plenty of time to come down before they reached the Academy.

It was easy in the beginning. Gillian seemed like any other normal young girl. Every few months she was visited by Cerberus experts: taking blood samples and alpha-wave readings; checking her health; testing her reflexes and responses. But even with all the doctors, Gillian had been a happy, healthy child.

Her symptoms began to manifest sometime between the ages of three and four. An unnamed dissociative disorder, the experts told him. Easy to diagnose but difficult to treat. Not that they hadn't tried, unleashing a barrage of drug and behavior therapies on the young girl. Yet their efforts had been in vain. With each year she grew more distant, more closed off. Trapped inside her own mind.

The growing emotional gulf between them should have made it easier on Grayson when Cerberus decided to give her over to the Ascension Project. It hadn't.

Grayson didn't have much he could cling to, apart from his dedication to Cerberus and his devotion to his daughter. The two were inextricably linked; after Gillian had been given into his care he had been pulled from active-duty missions so he could better focus on raising his daughter. Caring for the helpless infant had filled the void in his life. And as she had grown—as he had raised her from a baby to a beautiful, intelligent though troubled young girl—she had become the center of his world . . . just as the Illusive Man had wanted.

Then, two years ago, they had ordered him to send her away.

He resealed the plastic bag, stashing it safely away in the false bottom of his case. Then he got up, went into the bathroom and returned with the blade from his Ever-Sharp razor. Using the edge, he divided the pile of red sand into two long, thin lines.

The Illusive Man had wanted Gillian to join the Ascension Project so Cerberus could piggyback their own research on the Alliance's cutting-edge work. And whatever the Illusive Man wanted, he got.

Grayson knew he had no choice in the matter, but it was still hard to let her go. For ten years she had been an integral part of his life. He missed seeing her in the mornings and tucking her in at night. He missed the rare moments when she broke through the invisible walls that separated her from the outside world and showed him genuine love and affection. But, like any parent, he had to put his child's welfare above his own.

The program was good for Gillian. The scientists at the Academy were pushing the boundaries of biotic research. They had made advances that went far beyond anything Cerberus could have achieved on its own, and it was the only place Gillian could be properly fitted for the revolutionary new L-4 amps.

Sending his daughter away was also necessary for the greater cause. It was the best way for Cerberus to study the absolute limits of human biotics; a powerful weapon they would one day need in the inevitable struggle to elevate Earth and its people above the alien races. Gillian had to play her part in the Illusive Man's plans, just as he did. And one day, he hoped, people would look back on his daughter as a hero of the human race.

Grayson understood all this. He accepted it. Just as he accepted the fact that he was now merely a go-between; a proxy who allowed the Cerberus researchers to get access to Gillian whenever they needed it. Unfortunately, acceptance didn't make it any easier.

If it was possible, he would have visited her every week at the Academy. But he knew constant visits were hard on Gillian; she needed stability in her life—she didn't deal well with disruptions and unexpected surprises. So he stayed away, and did his best not to think about her. It made the loneliness easier to bear, turning the constant pain into a dull ache hovering in the background of his thoughts.

Sometimes, however, he couldn't help but think about her—like now. Knowing he was going to see her made him acutely aware of how much it would hurt when he had to leave her behind again. At times like these, he couldn't dull the pain. Not without help.

Bending forward in the chair, he pinched his left nostril closed and inhaled the first line of red sand. Then he switched nostrils and snorted the second. The dust burned his nasal cavities and made his eyes water. Sitting up straight, he blinked away the tears. He grabbed the arms of the chair, clenching so tightly his knuckles went white. He felt his heart beating, slow and heavy: *thump . . . thump . . . thump*. Three beats was all it took before the euphoria washed over him.

For the next several minutes he rode the wave, eyes closed, his head lolling back and forth. Occasionally he would make a soft *ngh* sound in the back of his throat, an inarticulate moan of pure pleasure.

The initial rush began to fade quickly, but he fought against the urge to take another hit. He could sense the unpleasant emotions—fear, paranoia, loneliness— lurking in the dark corners of his consciousness, still there but momentarily kept at bay by the narcotic's warm glow.

He opened his eyes, noting everything in the room had taken on a rosy hue. This was one of the side ef- fects of red sand . . . but not the most significant one.

Giggling softly at nothing in particular, he leaned back in his chair, balancing it on the two rear legs. His eyes cast about the room, searching for a suitable target before finally noticing the documents he had scattered across the floor.

Careful not to tip over in his seat, he reached out with his left hand and twiddled his fingers. The pa- pers rustled, as if fluttering in the breeze. He struggled to focus—never easy when floating in the red clouds. A second later he swiped at the empty air with his hand, and the papers leaped from the floor and swirled wildly about the room.

He kept them in the air as long as he could, his temporary, drug-induced biotic ability making the papers dance like leaves before a storm.

By the time Ellin knocked on the door seven hours later, he was sober once again. He had slept for a few hours, showered and shaved, and cleaned up the room, careful to leave no evidence of the red sand behind.

"One hour until we touch down, Mr. Grayson," she reminded him, handing him his cleaned and pressed clothes.

He took them with a nod of thanks, then closed the door. Alone in the privacy of his room he made one final check to make sure he hadn't missed anything incriminating.

That's the difference between an addict and a junkie, he reminded himself as he began to dress, his hands now steady as they buttoned up his shirt. *Both need their fix, but an addict still makes an effort to hide what he's doing.*

SIX

Kahlee couldn't sleep. She told herself it was partly because she preferred her own bed, and partly because Jiro was snoring loudly in her ear. She didn't bother to wake him, though—she was used to it. Their lovemaking usually ended this way, despite the fact that he was almost two decades her junior. He always started strong, full of passion and fire, but he didn't know how to pace himself.

"You'll learn eventually," she whispered, patting him lightly on his bare thigh. "And all your future girlfriends will thank me for it."

Moving quietly so as not to wake him, she rolled out from under the covers and stood, naked, by the side of the bed. Now that they weren't generating body heat, the air in the room felt cool enough to make her shiver.

She began to hunt around for her clothes, no easy task. In his exuberance, Jiro tended to toss each piece haphazardly about the room as he undressed her. She located her shirt and pulled it over her head, then heard Jiro mumble something. Glancing over, she realized he was still asleep, his words nothing but unintelligible dream-talk. Kahlee stared at him for a long, lingering moment—he looked so young when he was curled up in his bed, and she felt a momentary twinge of guilt and embarrassment.

There was nothing illegal about what they were doing; they were both of age, and even though she was technically his boss, there was nothing in either of their employment contracts specifically forbidding their relationship. It was, as Jiro liked to say, an ethically gray area.

Kahlee sometimes got the impression that Jiro was only using her to advance his career, though there was a chance this was her own guilty conscience trying to suck all the fun out of the relationship. If he actually did believe sleeping with the boss would somehow help him, he was sadly mistaken. If anything, she tended to be harder on Jiro than the other researchers. But he was good at his job; the staff respected him, and the students all liked him. That was one of the things that had attracted her in the first place.

That plus his fine ass, she thought with a wicked grin.

She'd had other sexual partners over the years, of course—probably more than her fair share, to be honest. But like Jiro they were all just flings. Not that she'd ever been looking for anything serious. While she was in the military the Alliance had always come first, and once she became a civilian she'd focused on building her career rather than a long-term relationship.

Fortunately, there was still plenty of time. Thanks to medical advances over the last century, women no longer had to start their families before forty. If she really wanted to, she could wait another twenty years and still give birth to a perfectly healthy child.

Kahlee still wasn't sure *what* she wanted, though. It wasn't that she didn't like kids; the opportunity to work closely with biotic children was one of the reasons she'd accepted the position with the Ascension Project. She just couldn't see herself settling into a life of domestic bliss.

Get over yourself, she thought, *and find your damn clothes.*

She pushed the thoughts away. Spotting her pants dangling over the back of a chair, she pulled them on. She was still looking for a missing sock when Jiro woke with a sputtering yawn.

"You're leaving?" he asked, still groggy.

"Just back to my own room. I can't sleep here with you snoring like a sick hippo."

He smiled and sat up, propping his pillow behind him and leaning back against the headboard.

"You sure this doesn't have anything to do with Grayson's visit?"

She didn't bother to deny it, instead saying nothing as she continued to look for her missing sock. Finding her prize, she sat down on the edge of the bed and pulled it on. Jiro watched her silently, patiently waiting for her to speak.

"I'm more worried about Gillian," she finally confessed. "Nothing we do seems to help her. Maybe the program isn't right for her."

"Whoa, just a minute!" Jiro exclaimed, suddenly very awake. He crawled across the mattress quickly and put a hand on her shoulder. "Gillian's got more biotic potential than . . . well, than anybody! The Ascension Project was meant for someone like her."

"But she's not just a biotic," Kahlee objected, voicing the arguments that had been running through her mind. "She's a girl with a serious mental condition."

"You're not thinking of asking the board to expel her, are you?" he asked, looking horrified.

She turned and scowled at him. "That's a decision her father needs to make."

"So you're going to talk to Grayson about it?" Much of the anxiety had left his voice.

"I'll let him know what his options are. Gillian might be better off if she wasn't trying to develop her biotic abilities at the Academy. He could get her a private tutor; someone trained to deal with her condition. Lord knows he can afford it."

"What if he doesn't want to pull her out of the program?"

"Then I'll have to start wondering if he really has his daughter's best interests at heart." She regretted the words as soon as she said them.

"Now you're starting to sound like Hendel," he chastised her.

The remark stung more than it should have; Nick's comparison of her and the security chief yesterday was still fresh in her mind.

"Sorry," she apologized. "I'm just tired. I can't keep coming here night after night." Trying to make light of it, she added, "When you get to be my age, you need your sleep."

"You're kidding, right?" he asked, incredulous. "I hardly ever get to see you. You're always working . . . or spending time with Hendel."

"He likes to keep tabs on the students," she explained. *Especially Gillian.*

"I'm starting to think you two are more than just friends," Jiro said darkly.

Kahlee actually laughed out loud. She saw Jiro stiffen, and he turned away from her.

"I'm sorry," she said, wrapping a comforting arm around his shoulder. "I didn't mean to laugh. But trust me, I'm not Hendel's type. You might be, though."

For a second he seemed puzzle, a look of confusion on his boyish face. "Ohhh," he said a moment later, grasping what she meant.

The phone in the bedroom beeped before either of them could say anything else. Jiro looked at the ID on the display, and his eyes went wide.

"It's Hendel!"

"So?" Kahlee said with a shrug. "Answer it."

He reached over and hit the button for the speaker phone.

"Hendel?"

"Grayson's shuttle just pinged us," the voice on the other end of the line snarled. "He'll be here in an hour.

"Figures the son-of-a-bitch would be running on his own clock," Hendel added.

Kahlee rolled her eyes. It was common for people visiting a planet or space station to schedule their visits so they would arrive at a convenient hour by the local time. But Grayson traveled a lot for his job, and constantly adjusting to different time zones could take its toll on a person. Gillian's father wasn't the only parent to show up in the middle of the night; he was just the only one Hendel complained about.

"Uh, yeah, okay," Jiro answered. "I'll get ready."

"I tried Kahlee's room, but she wasn't there," Hendel added. "I assume she's with you."

Jiro turned to her with a shrug and a look that seemed to say, *What should I tell him?*

"I'm here," she answered after a long, awkward silence. "I'll come down with Jiro to the landing bay to meet him."

"Meet you both there in forty-five minutes." The phone call ended with a click.

"How did he know about us?" Kahlee wondered out loud. She didn't think anyone knew; she and Jiro had always been discreet.

"Wouldn't be much of a security chief if he didn't," Jiro chuckled, getting out of bed and heading for the small shower in his en suite.

Hendel was gruff and surly, and he tended to be overprotective toward his charges, but no one could ever accuse him of being bad at his job. Still, Kahlee wasn't satisfied.

"What do you think tipped him off?" she called out, stripping off her shirt.

Jiro popped his head out from the bathroom. "You, probably. I bet he can read you like an open book. You're not that great at keeping secrets."

"Maybe it was you," she countered as she unbuttoned her pants. "You're not much good at keeping secrets either."

"I might be better than you think," he said mysteriously. Then he laughed and disappeared back into the bathroom. A second later she heard the shower running.

Now completely naked, Kahlee crossed the room and entered the en suite. Jiro raised his eyebrows suggestively when she opened the shower stall door and squeezed in with him.

"Forget it," she told him. "We need to get there before Grayson's shuttle touches down. I'm afraid of what might happen if we leave him alone with Hendel."

"Why does he hate Grayson so much?" Jiro asked, rubbing shampoo into her hair from behind.

Because he thinks Grayson is so prejudiced against biotics that he can only bear to see his own daughter twice a year. Because Hendel's own parents dumped him off with the BAaT program when he was a kid, basically disowning him. Because part of him thinks helping Gillian learn to cope with her biotics might get rid of the memories of his own abandonment and childhood isolation.

"It's complicated" was all she said.

"Maybe Hendel's got a crush on him," Jiro teased.

Kahlee let out a disapproving sigh. "I just pray to God you aren't stupid enough to ever make that joke where he can hear you."

SEVEN

Grissom Academy was a medium-sized space station with half a dozen small docking bays built along its exterior, each capable of accommodating small- to medium-sized vessels. Most of the arrivals were supply ships bringing in necessary resources from Elysium to keep the Academy running, along with twice-daily runs of the public passenger shuttle down to the surface of the planet below.

When Kahlee and Jiro arrived, Hendel was waiting for them, staring intently out the observation window toward the docking bays. She was disappointed to see that the station was currently oriented with the observation window looking out away from the planet they orbited; she always found the image of Elysium hovering below them in space to be particularly awe-inspiring.

Most visitors to the Academy—parents and friends of staff, typically—would come through Elysium, booking passage to the planet and then transferring to the passenger shuttle. Only those important or wealthy enough to have access to personal shuttles had the option to dock their vessels right on the station itself, eliminating the time and hassle necessitated by going through the public spaceports.

This direct access also allowed them to bypass the customs and security checks found planet-side, so by law there had to be a security officer on hand to clear them on arrival. This was more a formality than anything else, and Hendel normally delegated the task to one of his underlings. But on those rare occasions when Grayson arrived, the security chief was always there to greet him in person. Kahlee knew it was Hendel's none-too-subtle way of letting Grayson know he was being watched.

Fortunately, Grayson's shuttle hadn't shown up yet. Hendel turned to look at them as they approached, breaking his vigil.

"I was starting to wonder if you were going to make it in time."

His comment was directed at Kahlee; it almost seemed as if he was intentionally ignoring Jiro's presence. She decided to let it slide.

"How long before they arrive?"

"Five, maybe ten mintues. I'll sign Grayson in, then he's yours to deal with. Take him to the cafeteria for a few hours or something."

"He's going to want to see his daughter right away," Jiro protested.

Hendel glared at the younger man as if he had interrupted a private conversation, then shook his head. "These surprise visits are hard enough on Gillian. I'm not going to wake her up in the middle of the night just because her father's too selfish to wait until morning to see her."

"Wanting to see his daughter right away isn't being selfish," Kahlee countered.

"The last few months she's been getting up early anyway," Jiro added. "She only sleeps a few hours a night. The rest of the time she just sits up in bed with the lights off and stares at the wall. I think it has something to do with her condition."

A sour grimace crossed Hendel's face. "Nobody told me that." He took his job seriously, and he didn't like it when other people knew more about the habits and behaviors of the students than he did.

He's looking for a fight, Kahlee thought. She'd have to keep a close eye on him; she wasn't about to let him ruin this visit for Grayson or Gillian.

"There wasn't anything you could do about it," Kahlee answered coolly. "Besides, Dr. Sanchez said it's nothing to worry about."

Hendel picked up on the unspoken warning in her tone and let the matter drop. For a few minutes they stood without speaking, just staring out the window. Hendel broke the silence with a seemingly innocent comment.

"So, it sounds like your old friend is in the running for one of the Council seats," he noted.

"Old friend?" Jiro asked, curious.

"Captain David Anderson," the security chief explained, seemingly oblivious to Kahlee's reflection in the window, scowling at him. "They served together in the Alliance."

"How come you never mentioned him before?" Jiro wondered, turning to her.

"It was a long time ago," she replied, trying to sound blasé about it. "We haven't talked in years."

There was an uncomfortable silence, and Kahlee could only imagine the questions running through Jiro's head. He was a confident young man, but it still must have been unsettling to realize his girlfriend had a previous relationship with one of humanity's most well-known military heroes. When he finally spoke again, she was caught completely off-guard by what he said.

"I'd rather see Ambassador Udina on the Council."

"Interesting to see how that all plays out," Hendel replied, though he did raise a curious eyebrow.

Further conversation was cut off by a sharp beep emanating from the intercom above their heads, warning of an incoming vessel. Through the observation window they could see red lights flashing outside, on the perimeter of one of the docking bays. A few seconds later Grayson's ship—a small, high-end corporate shuttle—drifted into view.

The shuttle maneuvered into position, moving silently in the vacuum of space. It settled into one of the hangars, and Kahlee felt the slightest bump under her feet as a pair of large, automated docking clamps locked the ship into place. A fully enclosed platform extended out from the station to connect with the shuttle's doors, latching tight. The pressurized, oxygen-filled tunnel allowed passengers to go from vessels docked at the exterior landing bays directly into the confines of the station without having to go through the bother of putting on spacesuits.

"All right, let's go down and meet our guest," Hendel muttered, making no effort to hide his displeasure.

Passengers exiting their vessels would come down the tunnel into the waiting room, a large antechamber with transparent, bulletproof walls. Several waist-high poles linked at the top by heavy red rope snaked their way back and forth through the room, creating an area where visitors lined up when they arrived en masse. At the end of the queue a yellow line had been painted on the floor. Beyond the line stood a pair of Alliance guards, both armed—a reminder to anyone coming aboard that the Grissom Academy was a joint military-civilian operation.

Behind the guards, a single door led from the waiting room into the reception area beyond, where another Alliance soldier sat at a computer to register all arrivals and departures. The door was kept closed until the soldier working the registration desk was satisfied that the individuals in the waiting room had authorization to come onto the station.

Grayson was already in the waiting room when they reached reception, pacing impatiently back and forth just behind the yellow line. The guards inside the room with him simply stood at attention, seeming not to notice his urgency.

The young woman behind the registration desk glanced up as Hendel approached, her face brightening when she recognized the Ascension Project's security chief.

You're wasting your time, sister, Kahlee thought.

"One visitor, as scheduled," she said, her voice a little too light and breezy to sound completely professional. "Just waiting for clearance."

"Let him through," Hendel said with a sigh.

She smiled, and punched some buttons on her keyboard. A small green light above the glass door flickered on and there was an audible click as the lock disengaged. A moment later the door swung silently open.

"Go on in, Mr. Grayson," Kahlee heard one of the guards inside the waiting room say, but Grayson was practically through the door already anyway.

He looks like hell, Kahlee thought.

Grayson was wearing a simple business suit and carrying an expensive-looking briefcase; his clothes were clean and freshly pressed, and it was obvious he had recently shaved. Despite these efforts, there was an unhealthy, almost desperate look about him. Always a thin man, he looked positively skeletal now; his clothes seemed to be hanging off him. His face was drawn and haggard, his eyes sunken and bloodshot, his lips dry and cracked. She still wasn't willing to completely concede to Hendel's accusation that he was a drug addict, but he certainly looked like a duster.

"Good to see you again, Mr. Grayson," Kahlee said, stepping forward and offering her introduction before Hendel could say something inappropriate.

"It's been a long time," the security chief added, undeterred by her efforts. "We were starting to think you'd forgotten where to find us."

"I'd come more often if I could," Grayson replied, shaking Kahlee's hand but looking at Hendel as he spoke. He didn't seem angry. If anything, he sounded almost apologetic. Or guilty. "Things have been . . . complicated . . . lately."

"Gillian was very excited when we told her you were coming, sir," Jiro chimed in from over Kahlee's shoulder.

"I'm looking forward to seeing her, Dr. Toshiwa," he replied, smiling. Kahlee noticed his teeth were discolored, as if covered with a faintly luminous sheen—another telltale sign of a duster.

"Do you want me to take your case?" Hendel asked, almost grudgingly.

"I'd prefer to keep it with me," Grayson replied, and Kahlee noticed a faint look of disapproval cross Hendel's features.

"Come on," she said, taking Grayson by the forearm and gently turning him away from Hendel. "Let's go see your daughter."

"I'm sorry about the poor timing of my arrival," Grayson said to her as they made their way through the Academy toward the Ascension Project dorms. "I always have trouble adjusting my schedule to local time."

"It's not a problem, Mr. Grayson," she assured him. "You're welcome to come see Gillian anytime, day or night."

"I feel bad about waking her up," he continued. "But I have to leave again in a few hours."

"We'll just let her sleep through her classes tomorrow," Hendel remarked, walking a few steps behind them.

Grayson didn't acknowledge him, and Kahlee wasn't sure if he'd even heard the comment. But it put an end to the conversation until they reached Gillian's room.

Kahlee waved her hand in front of the access panel, and the door slid open.

"Lights—on," she said softly, and illumination filled the room.

Gillian wasn't sleeping. As Jiro had warned them, she was sitting cross-legged on her bed, on top of the covers. She was wearing a faded pink pair of pajamas that looked to be a size too small; Kahlee remembered they had been a gift from Grayson on her birthday a few months ago.

"Hey, Gigi," Grayson said, stepping forward into the room, calling her by his pet name.

Her eyes lit up and she held out her arms toward him, but didn't move from her sitting position. "Daddy!"

Grayson came to the side of the bed and leaned in, but pulled up short of hugging her. Instead, he clasped his daughter's hands tightly in his own, which was what she had been expecting.

"You're getting so big!" Grayson said in amazement, releasing one of her hands to take a half-step back and get a better look at her. After a long moment of silence, he added softly, "You look just like your mother."

Kahlee tapped Hendel and Jiro on their elbows, then nodded toward the door, indicating they should leave. The three of them slipped out of the room, and the door *swoosh*ed shut behind them.

"Come on," Kahlee said once they were out in the hall. "Let's leave them alone."

"All visitors have to be attended by someone on staff while at the Academy," Hendel objected.

"I'll stay here," Jiro offered. "He said he can only stay a few hours, so I don't mind hanging around. Plus I know Gillian's files. In case he has any questions."

"That'll work," Kahlee answered.

Hendel looked as if he were going to argue, but instead he only said, "Make sure you sign him out and let me know when he leaves."

"Come on," Kahlee said to Hendel. "Walk me down to the cafeteria and I'll buy you a coffee."

The cafeteria was empty—it would still be several hours before the staff and students made their way down for breakfast. Hendel settled himself at one of the tables by the door while Kahlee made her way over to the beverage dispensers. She swiped her employee card through the slot and ordered up two cups of coffee, both black, then carried them back over to the table and offered one to Hendel.

"Son-of-a-bitch looks worse than ever," the security chief said, taking the cup from her hand. "Might be high right now."

"You're too hard on him," she said with a sigh, settling into the seat across from Hendel. "He's not the first parent of a biotic child to experiment with red sand. It's a way for us ordinary people to understand what it's like to be biotic."

"No," he said sharply. "Getting high and flinging paper clips around with your mind for a few hours isn't anything like being a biotic."

"But it's the closest someone like Grayson can ever get. Put yourself in his shoes. He's just trying to connect with his daughter."

"Then maybe he should come see her more than twice a year."

"This can't be easy on him," she reminded Hendel. "His wife died during childbirth. His daughter has a mental condition that makes her emotionally distant. And then he finds out she has this incredible ability, and he has to send her away to a private school.

"He's probably on an emotional roller coaster every time he sees her: love, guilt, loneliness. He knows he's doing what's best for her, but that doesn't mean it's easy on him."

"I just get a bad vibe off him. And I've learned to trust my gut."

Rather than answer, Kahlee took a long drink from her cup. The coffee was nice and hot, but it had a mildly bitter aftertaste.

"We need to petition the board for better coffee," she muttered, hoping to change the subject.

"How long have you and Jiro been together?" Hendel asked her.

"How long have you known?"

"A couple months."

"Then it took you about two months to find out."

"Be careful with that kid, Kahlee."

She laughed. "I'll make sure I don't break him."

"That's not what I meant," he said, his voice serious. "There's something I don't trust about him. He's too slick. Too smooth."

"Your gut again?" she asked, holding her cup up close to her face to hide the smile on her lips. Apparently Hendel wasn't just protective of the students.

"You saw how he reacted when I mentioned your history with Anderson."

"Thank you very much for that, by the way," she said, arching her eyebrows.

"It didn't seem to rattle him," Hendel continued, ignoring her verbal jab. "Like he already knew."

"So what if he did?"

"Well, it was pretty obvious you didn't tell him. So how'd he find out? The records from that mission were sealed. Hell, even I only know because you told me."

"People talk. Maybe I mentioned it to someone on staff who mentioned it to him. You're making too much of this."

"Maybe," he conceded. "Just be careful. I've learned to trust my instincts."

Grayson spent the next four hours with Gillian. He let her do most of the talking, cycling between extended bursts of eager, almost frantic conversation and long stretches of silent withdrawal where she almost seemed to forget he was there. He liked listening to her voice, but he didn't mind the silences, either. It was good just to see her again.

When she did talk, it was mostly about school and the Academy: which teachers she liked and which ones she didn't; her favorite subjects; new things she'd learned in her courses. Grayson noticed that she never mentioned the other students, or anything to do with her biotic training. He decided not to push her. He'd get all the information he needed soon enough.

It was almost time for him to go. He'd learned the longer he stayed the harder it was to leave. So he always set himself a limit for each visit; having a mission parameter made it easier to do what he had to do.

"Gigi?" he said softly.

Gillian was staring at the wall, lost inside herself again.

"Gigi?" he said a little louder. "Daddy has to go. Okay?"

Last time he had left, she hadn't even acknowl-edged him when he said good-bye. This time, however, she turned her head slightly and nodded. He didn't know which was worse.

He stood up from her bedside and leaned in to kiss her on the top of her head.

"Get into bed, honey. Under the covers. Try to sleep."

Moving slowly, like some kind of automaton powered by his words, she did as instructed. Once she was settled and had closed her eyes, he crossed the room and opened the door.

"Lights—off," he whispered. The room went dark as he closed the door behind him.

Jiro was waiting for him out in the hall.

"Is it safe here?" Grayson asked him, his voice gruffer than he'd intended.

"Should be," the young man answered, speaking quietly. "Everyone's still in bed. We can go back to my room if it's going to take awhile."

"Let's just get it over with so I can get the hell off this station," Grayson said, dropping to one knee and laying his briefcase on the floor.

He released the lock, opened the false bottom, and removed the vial Pel had given him. Then he stood up and handed it to Jiro. The scientist took it from him, holding it up to the lights in the corridor ceiling.

"Looks like they switched compounds again. The Man must want to try something different." He slipped the vial into his pocket. "This isn't going to show up on any of her medicals, is it? I mean, it's untraceable, right?"

"What do you think?" Grayson asked him coolly.

"Yeah, okay. Same doses as before?"

"They didn't give me any new instructions," Grayson replied.

"Any idea what this new stuff is supposed to do to her?"

"I don't ask questions like that," Grayson answered sharply. "Neither will you, if you're smart."

Christ, he thought, as soon as the words were out of his mouth. *Now I sound like Pel.* He honestly didn't know if that was good or bad, though he figured his old partner would find something humorous about it.

"They're not going to do anything to harm her," Grayson added, though he wasn't sure if he was trying to convince Jiro or himself. "She's too valuable."

Jiro nodded. "Here are the latest results on all the students in the Ascension Project," he said, pulling an optical storage disk from the pocket of his lab coat and handing it to Grayson. "Plus my private research on our star pupil in there." He nodded his head toward Gillian's door.

Grayson took the OSD without a word and hid it away inside his briefcase.

"Are you sleeping with Sanders?" he asked once the disk was secured.

"Figured it fell within my mission parameters," Jiro answered with a grin. "I'm supposed to pump her for info, so I'm pumping her every chance I get."

"Just watch you don't get emotionally involved," Grayson warned him. "It makes things messy."

"I've got it under control," the kid assured him with an infuriatingly cocky grin.

Somewhere Grayson imagined Pel was laughing his ass off.

EIGHT

Feda'Gazu vas Idenna adjusted the pistol hanging from her belt as she climbed down from the land rover. She never wore a weapon back on the flotilla, but every quarian who left the safety of the Migrant Fleet was armed at all times.

Lige and Anwa, the two members of her crew she had picked to accompany her to this meeting, climbed out of the vehicle to stand on either side of her. She could sense their nervousness. It mirrored her own.

She didn't trust Golo. He was a fellow quarian, but he was also a criminal so vile and dangerous he had been exiled from the Fleet. That was why she had refused to meet with him at Omega: too many places for an ambush. He had objected at first, but in the end he'd agreed to meet her here on Shelba, a desolate, uninhabited world in the nearby Vinoss System.

The atmosphere on Shelba was breathable—barely— but the temperature was always well below freezing, making it unsuitable for habitation or farming. And the crust consisted of only common, low-value metals and minerals, making it uneconomical for mining. The world was ignored—undeveloped and empty. If

Golo was going to try and double-cross her, setting up their exchange here might make him reconsider whether it was worth the trouble.

Feda shivered, despite the fact that her enviro-suit protected her against the worst of the chill. Part of her wanted to forget this deal; just turn around and leave. But Golo had promised to sell her a shipment of air-filtration coils and reaction catalyzers, and several of the ships in the flotilla were in desperate need of replacement parts. Despite her personal reservations, she couldn't in good conscience turn his offer down.

"There," one of her companions called out, pointing across the vast, open expanse of blue plain and glittering green rock formations that made up the barren planet's surface.

A small rover was approaching in the distance, throwing up clouds of turquoise dust as it sped toward them. Feda took another look at their surroundings, scanning the horizon for signs of other vehicles. To her relief, she saw nothing.

Perched atop a tall outcropping of emerald-hued rock over a mile away, Pel watched the quarians arrive through the scope of his Volkov sniper rifle. He'd had his doubts about whether they'd even show up, given Golo's reputation among his own kind. But the quarian had assured him they'd be there.

Looks like the little bastard was right.

The quarians stepped down from their vehicle. "We have three targets," a voice said over the headset built into the helmet of his enviro-suit.

"Alpha squad take the one on the right," he responded flatly. "Beta squad take the one on the left. Leave the one in the middle to me."

"Alpha squad—target acquired," the voice answered back.

"Beta squad—target acquired," a second voice confirmed, this one female.

Peering through the scope, he was confident his team could hit their targets, even from this range. But the quarians were all wearing armor, and the odds of a round penetrating the kinetic barriers of their shields before they could make it back into the safety of the vehicle were low. Golo still had to do his part if the plan was going to work.

"Hold fire until my signal," he ordered, taking a bead on the quarian in the center.

The quarians waited patiently as their contact approached. Soon Feda could hear the whine of the rover's engine and the crunching of its tires over the rough, uneven terrain, the thin atmosphere giving everything a sharp, brittle sound.

Once the rover had come within fifty meters, Feda held up her hand, palm forward. The vehicle rolled to a stop. A few seconds later a quarian emerged and began to walk slowly toward them, hands held above his head. He stopped ten meters away, just as she had instructed when setting up the details of the meeting. Lige and Anwa had drawn their assault rifles, pointing them at the newcomer.

"Golo?" she asked, confirming the identity of the man behind the mask.

"Are you here to rob me?" he said by way of reply, nodding toward the weapons pointed at his chest. He kept his hands high. Unlike Feda and her crew, he wasn't wearing any armor.

"I'm not taking any chances," she answered. "Not with you."

There were several crimes that could result in exile from the Fleet: murder, repeated violent offenses, vandalism or sabotage directed at the Liveships or the food supplies. But Golo's offense—attempting to sell quarians to the Collectors—seemed particularly heinous. Loyalty was a cornerstone of quarian culture; survival on the Migrant Fleet required every member of the community to work together. Trying to sell another quarian for personal profit was a betrayal of everything Feda believed in; an unforgivable sin.

"You came alone?" she asked.

Golo nodded. "The parts are in the back of the truck, if you want to see."

Feda pulled her pistol and used it to cover Golo, nodding at Lige to go check out the vehicle. He approached slowly, weapon still drawn. The rover was a simple cargo carrier, with a small two-person cab and a freight trailer on the back. The trailer was little more than a rectangular box, with a vertical sliding door for loading and unloading.

Lige pressed the panel on the side of the trailer, but instead of the door rising up the panel beeped sharply and flashed red.

"It's locked."

"What's the access code?" Feda demanded, waving her pistol menacingly in Golo's direction.

"Seven two six nine," he answered, and Lige punched the numbers in.

Then all hell broke loose.

"Get ready," Pel muttered into his transmitter as one of the quarians approached Golo's vehicle.

An instant later there was a bright flash as the bomb inside the back of Golo's rover exploded. The blast threw the quarian standing beside the vehicle through the air and knocked the others, including Golo, to the ground.

"Fire," he said, his voice calm as he pulled the trigger of his sniper rifle with a smooth, even pressure.

Feda was thrown from her feet by the explosion. She hit the ground with a jarring thump, but quickly rolled to her feet and brought her pistol up to fire at Golo, who was still on the ground, cowering with his hands over his head.

She squeezed the trigger, but nothing happened. Glancing down, she saw the status indicator on her weapon flashing red—the automated targeting system had overloaded. Cursing, she slapped the manual override on the handle, knowing full well the pulse that had disabled her weapon had probably scrambled her kinetic shields as well.

A flash of agonizing fire erupted in her shoulder as a hyperaccelerated projectile no bigger than a pin sheared effortlessly through the ablative plates of her body armor before exploding in the flesh and bone underneath. The impact spun her around and sent the pistol flying from her hand. She felt her kneecap disintegrate and she collapsed to the ground, her scream rising up to meet the unmistakable *zip-zip-zip* of high-powered rounds slicing through the thin air.

She could see Lige's body, laying where the blast had thrown it. His mask had been shattered by the close range impact of the detonation, turning his face into a bloody mess. She could see one eye clearly; it stared at her, lifeless and unblinking. The body jerked and jumped as it was struck by enemy bullets, rounds wasted on a corpse.

Get to the vehicle! her mind screamed at her, and in response she began to crawl on her belly toward the rover. She never felt the round that entered the back of her skull and ended her life.

Pel continued firing, pumping round after round into the motionless body until he heard Golo's voice in his helmet.

"I think you can stop now. They're all dead."

Standing up, Pel collapsed his weapon and snapped it into the quick-release clasp on his back.

"Beta squad, meet me down at the rendezvous point. Alpha squad, keep an eye out for reinforcements."

The gravity on Shelba was .92 Earth standard, so he was able to make good time, even with the restrictions of the enviro-suit. It took him just over five minutes to get down to the scene of the massacre. Golo was there waiting for him, as were the two women from Beta squad. They were already stripping the clothes and gear from the dead quarians. The dark clothes were torn with bullet holes and stained with blood, but it was unlikely anyone would notice these details until it was too late.

Pel was too big to pass as a quarian, but the women were about the right height and build. With their faces obscured by helmets and bundled up in cloth and rags, it would be difficult to tell them apart from their victims.

"Did you locate their ship?" Golo asked him as he approached. Like the women, he was using strips of clothing from one of the bodies to obscure his identity.

"We spotted them when they touched down," Pel told him. "Maybe ten clicks from here."

"Probably three or four more on board," the quarian informed him. "They'll most likely be armed, but they won't be wearing combat suits. Remember, you want to take one of them alive. The pilot, if possible."

Hilo'Jaa vas Idenna, the pilot of the scout ship *Cyniad* of the fleet ship *Idenna,* was surprised to see Feda's rover coming toward them from over the edge of the horizon.

He reached out and flicked the transmit button on the radio.

"Feda? This is Hilo. Do you read me?"

A second later the reply came through, but it was obscured by static so thick he couldn't make anything out.

"I can't hear you, Feda. Is everything okay?"

This time the answer was a piercing shriek of radio feedback that made Hilo wince as he shut off the transmitter.

"Get ready," Hilo said over the shipboard intercom. "Feda's on her way back."

"Why didn't she call ahead?" a voice responded over the speaker a few seconds later.

"Sounds like the rover's got some radio trouble."

"I just fixed it last week!" the voice objected.

"Guess you need to fix it again," Hilo replied with a smile. "Be alert, just in case."

It wasn't uncommon for things to break down on the *Cyniad*. Like all ships, vessels, and vehicles associated with the Migrant Fleet, their rover had seen better days. Most species would have decommissioned it long ago, or relegated it to the scrap heap. The quarians, short of materials and resources, had no such luxury.

Hilo wondered how much longer their makeshift repairs could keep the rover running before they'd finally have to admit defeat and strip it down for parts. Hopefully a few more months at least. Maybe another year if they were lucky.

Lucky's not a concept usually associated with us quarians, he thought as the rover rolled to a stop beneath the loading doors.

Three figures jumped out. One was using hand gestures, signaling to the ship to open the loading bay doors so they could drive the cargo container inside. Hilo got up from his chair and made his way down to the hold so he could help get everything stored away. He was halfway there, squeezing his way past the table and chairs of their tiny mess hall, when he heard the sounds of gunfire and screaming.

Grabbing the pistol at his belt, he kicked aside the chairs in his way and raced to the aid of his crewmates. He half-climbed, half-slid down the ladder leading to the cargo hold, his mind never stopping to think that he might get there too late.

He burst into the hold and froze, boggled by the scene before him.

The cargo container was open, but there was nothing inside. The crew were dead, scattered about the hold where they had been gunned down. Several armed and armored figures, too large to be quarian, were searching the room, looking for other survivors. All of this his mind registered in an instant. What threw him, however, was the sight of Feda, Lige, and Anwa standing with their weapons drawn and pointed at him. Even up close, it took him a second to realize they were imposters.

By then it was too late. One fired, the bullet shredding the meat of the muscle as it tore through his thigh. He screamed and dropped his weapon. Then they were on him, two of the figures pinning him to the floor while the third loomed above him, gun drawn and ready. Hilo thrashed wildly against them, his grief-numbed mind oblivious to the agonizing pain shooting up from his thigh or the implied threat of the pistol pointed at his head.

"Stop and we'll let you live," the figure standing over him said in flawless quarian.

Even in his agitated state, his mind was able to piece together who was speaking. Feda had warned them about the man they were going to meet: an exile who had betrayed his own people. Now the crew of the *Idenna* had fallen into his trap. Hilo's body went limp as his mind gave in to hopelessness and despair.

The quarian leaned down close to him, his gun held casually in his hand. "Who are you?"

He didn't answer.

"I asked your name," he repeated, slamming the butt of his pistol against the side of Hilo's head. His vision filled with stars.

"Who are you?" Again, he didn't answer.

The pistol slammed his head again, and his teeth bit down on his tongue. He tasted blood in his mouth, but he didn't lose consciousness.

"I am Golo'Mekk vas Usela. I will ask you one last time. Who are you?"

Golo, crew of the Usela.

"You have no right to that name!" Hilo shouted, his words echoing inside his helmet. "You are vas Nedas! Golo nar Tasi!"

Crew of nowhere; Golo child of no one. Outcast. Alone. Reviled.

This time the pistol smashed into the faceplate of his helmet, hard enough to crack the glass. The unfamiliar, terrifying scent of unfiltered air—air infected with bacteria and germs—flooded in.

An adrenaline surge of pure, instinctive fear gave new strength to Hilo's limbs, and he bucked himself free of his captors. He spun to his knees and tried to stand and run, but the bullet he had taken in his thigh had turned the muscle into a useless mass of pulp and tissue. He fell forward instead, slamming face-first into the steel deck of the landing bay.

Someone landed on his back, hard enough to knock the wind out of him. A second later he felt a sharp pinprick of pain in the back of his neck, and then his mind was drowning in a warm, blue haze.

He felt himself being rolled over, but he was powerless to resist. He lay on the ground, staring up into the overhead lights, unable to move or speak. The blue haze was growing thicker, swallowing him up as the world slipped away. The last thing he heard before he slid into unconsciousness was a human speaking.

"You cracked his mask. If he catches something and dies, my boss won't be happy."

NINE

Gillian made her way through the cafeteria with slow, uncertain steps. The other children were talking and laughing; a wall of overwhelming, terrifying, nonsensical sound she did her best to ignore.

She held her lunch tray out in front of her, carefully balancing it with each trembling step as she advanced cautiously to the empty table in the back of the room. She sat there every day, alone, as far away from the sound and fury of the other kids as possible. Occasionally a particularly loud noise—a shrill laugh, the clatter of a lunch tray falling to the floor—would cause her head to twitch abruptly, as if she had been slapped. Yet she was always careful not to drop her tray when this happened.

When she was younger she had stayed behind in the classroom when the lunch bell rang while the others ran off to the cafeteria. Hendel or Miss Sanders would bring lunch to her and she would eat at her desk in the blessed silence of solitude. But she didn't do that anymore. She was trying to fit in.

Gillian was painfully aware that she was different, and more than anything, she wanted to be normal. But the other kids scared her. They were so quick. So loud. They were always touching. The boys slapped one another on the back or traded punches in the shoulder; sometimes they pushed and shoved each other, laughing loudly at jokes she didn't understand. The girls would lean in close together, cupping a hand to their lips then pressing it against a friend's ear to whisper secrets. They would squeal and giggle, clutching one another's wrist or forearm, or clasping a friend's hand between their own. Other times she saw them braiding each other's hair. She couldn't imagine what that was like; to live in a world where physical contact didn't cause the flesh to erupt with burning fire, or sting with freezing cold.

At least nobody teased her or made fun of her—not to her face, anyway. They mostly avoided her, keeping their distance. Yet Gillian couldn't help but notice their expressions when they looked in her direction— confusion, mistrust, bewilderment. She was some kind of freak, best left alone. But she was trying. Every day she suffered the ordeal of walking across the cafeteria, carrying her tray slowly and carefully to her table in the corner. She hoped it would get easier over time, become more bearable through repetition and routine. So far it hadn't.

Reaching her destination, she sat down in the same chair she sat in every day, with her back against the wall so she could look out over the cafeteria. Then she began to eat with slow, deliberate bites, staring out at the other children with terror and yearning, unable to comprehend their world, yet hoping she could one day be like them.

* * *

Nick watched Gillian as she made her way down the central aisle of the cafeteria. As she passed by their table, he let out a sharp, yelping bark, like a dog that had been stepped on. The girl flinched, but otherwise didn't acknowledge him. And, much to his dismay, she didn't drop her tray.

"Ha! Told you!" Seshaun gleefully cackled.

Glumly, Nick handed over his chocolate cake, the forfeiture for losing the bet.

"What's her problem, anyway?" he asked, a general question thrown out to the half-dozen boys assembled at the table.

"She's got like a mental condition or something," one offered. "I heard Hendel talking about it once."

Nick grimaced at the name. He was still mad at Hendel for putting him into lockdown.

"Why is she in our class if she's retarded?" he wanted to know.

"She's not retarded, jack-wad," Seshaun answered. "She's just weird."

"I bet she's not even biotic," Nick continued, staring at her.

She was staring back, though he couldn't actually tell if she was looking at him or someone else in the room.

"She comes to all the training sessions," one of the boys countered.

"Yeah, but she just sits there. She never does any of the exercises."

"That's because she's *weird*!" Seshaun repeated.

He was pretty sure she was staring at him now. He waved his arm wildly above his head, but it elicited no reaction.

"Waving to your girlfriend?"

Nick replied by flipping Seshaun off, a gesture he had only recently learned.

"Why don't you go over and give her a kiss?" Seshaun taunted him.

"Why don't you lick my nut-sack?"

"Just go sit down and talk to her. See what she does."

"Hendel said nobody's allowed to bother her," one of the others chimed in.

"Screw Hendel," Nick replied automatically, though he did glance back over his shoulder to the front of the cafeteria, where the security chief was sitting with some of the teachers.

"Okay, then," Seshaun pressed him. "Go over there. Talk to her."

Nick looked around the table at the faces of the other boys, grinning eagerly as they waited to see if he'd accept the dare.

"Do it and I'll give your cake back," Seshaun offered, literally sweetening the deal.

Nick hesitated, uncertain. Then his stomach grumbled, making the decision for him. He pushed himself away from the table and jumped to his feet before he could change his mind. He glanced back quickly to make sure Hendel was still busy talking with the other teachers, then ran down the aisle to Gillian's table.

Skidding to a stop, he plopped himself down in the chair across from her. She looked straight at him but didn't say anything. Suddenly he felt awkward and embarrassed.

"Hey," he said.

She didn't reply, but merely kept chewing the food in her mouth. He noticed her plate was still mostly full: a bowl of soup, two sandwiches, an apple, a banana, a piece of vanilla cake, and half a quart of milk.

The amount of food on her plate wasn't unusual—one of the first things the kids learned was that biotics needed to eat more than other people. But Nick couldn't believe the manner in which she was consuming her meal. Every item on her plate had a bite taken out of it, even the cake.

He watched in fascinated disbelief as she took a bite from one of her sandwiches, set it down, chewed her food slowly and deliberately, swallowed, then picked up the second sandwich to repeat the process. After a single bite she moved on to the apple, then the banana, then the cake, then a drink of milk, then the soup, then back to the first sandwich again. She didn't say a word the entire time.

"Why are you eating like that?" he finally asked, bewildered.

"I'm hungry," she replied. Her voice was flat and toneless, leading Nick to believe she hadn't meant it as a joke.

"Nobody eats like that," he told her. When she didn't reply he added, "You're supposed to eat the soup and sandwiches first. Then the fruit. The cake comes last."

She stopped mid-bite, the apple poised halfway between her lips and the table. "When do I drink the milk?" she asked in the same monotone voice.

Nick just shook his head. "You *cannot* be for real."

The nonanswer seemed to satisfy her, because she

resumed eating, holding to the familiar pattern of one bite from each item before moving on.

Turning around, Nick looked back at the table with Seshaun and the others. They were laughing and making obscene gestures at him. He turned back to Gillian; she hadn't seemed to notice.

"How come you never do anything in biotic class?" he asked her.

She looked uncomfortable, but didn't answer.

"Do you even know how? I'm pretty good at biotics. I can show you a trick, if you want."

"No," she said simply.

Nick scowled. He felt like there was something going on that he didn't quite understand, like she was making fun of him somehow. Then he got an idea.

"Careful with your milk," he said, a nasty grin spreading across his face. "Looks like it's going to spill."

As the words left his mouth, he reached out with his mind and *pushed*. The milk toppled over, drenching the sandwiches and slopping over the tray onto the table before running off the edge to spill on Gillian's lap.

And then Nick found himself flying backward.

Jacob Berg, the Academy's math professor, was in the middle of telling a joke about an asari and a volus who walked into a krogan's bar when, out of the corner of his eye, Hendel saw something that was simultaneously incredible and terrifying.

Near the back of the cafeteria, Nick was hurtling across the room. He flew twenty feet through the air before slamming down on one of the tables. The force of the landing launched lunch trays into the air and snapped the table's legs, sending it crashing to the floor. Several students seated at the table screamed in surprise, and then a stunned hush fell over the room as everyone looked to see who was responsible.

Hendel was as shocked as any of them to see Gillian standing in the back of the room, her hands raised to the sky and her face twisted into a mask of rage and fury. And then, to his horror, he realized that she wasn't done.

The table in front of her flipped over, the empty chairs surrounding it cartwheeling away like they had been kicked by some invisible giant. Lunch trays all around the cafeteria shot straight up to the ceiling, sending a shower of food and cutlery over the students as they came back down.

Panic set in. Screaming students leaped from their seats and raced to the exit at the far end of the cafeteria, knocking one another down in their scrambling haste to escape. Their now-empty chairs were swept up and tossed haphazardly about the room, adding to the chaos.

Hendel was on his feet, moving against the tide of the crowd in a desperate attempt to get closer to Gillian. As big as he was, it was still difficult to wade through the sea of bodies trying to flee the scene.

"Gillian!" he shouted, but his voice was drowned out by the screams of the mob.

Nick was still lying on the floor amid the ruins of the table on which he had landed. Hendel dropped to one knee to check on him: he was unconscious, but breathing.

Leaping back to his feet, he continued to press forward, shoving kids roughly aside in his desperation until he broke free of the crowd. Less than thirty feet now separated him from Gillian.

The space between them looked like a tornado had passed through: overturned tables and chairs were strewn about, the floor was slick with spilled food, milk and juice. Gillian still stood at the back wall, her hands still raised up. She was shrieking; a high-pitched, keening wail that sent a shiver down Hendel's neck.

"Gillian!" he cried out, running toward her. "Stop this right now!"

He jumped over a downed table, his feet almost sliding out from under him when he landed on the slick remains of someone's lunch on the other side. He pinwheeled his arms for balance, only to be knocked down by a flying chair that struck him from his blind side.

The blow stung but it wasn't disabling. He scrambled back to his feet, his sleeve and knees covered in milk and bits of crushed, soggy bread.

"Gillian!" he shouted again. "You have to stop!"

She didn't respond, didn't even seem to know he was there. He started moving forward again, his hand dropping down to the stunner at his belt. But he hesitated, and instead of drawing it, he tried one last time to reach her.

"Please, Gillian! Don't make me—" his words were cut off as he was struck by an invisible wave of biotic force. It hit him in the chest like an anvil dropping from on high, knocking the breath from his lungs. He was lifted off his feet and shot straight back like he was on a rope being pulled from behind. He crashed through toppled tables and chairs, banging his head and slamming his elbow so hard it made his right hand go numb.

He came to rest twenty feet later, amid a pile of chairs and lunch trays. Groggy, he struggled to his feet. The effort made him cough, and he tasted blood in his mouth.

Hendel took a moment to gather himself, then drew upon his own biotic abilities, releasing them a second later as he threw up a powerful high-gravity barrier to shield him from flying furniture and further biotic attacks from Gillian.

Crouching behind the shimmering wall of the barrier, Hendel fumbled with the stunner at his belt. His right hand was still numb from the blow to his elbow, and he had to reach across with his left to grab the weapon.

"Please, Gillian, don't make me do this!" he called out one more time, but the girl couldn't hear him above the sound of her own screams.

There was a sudden burst of light and heat a few feet to his side. Snapping his head around, he saw an astonishing sight: a swirling vortex of concentrated dark energy was launching vertically in a pillar toward the ceiling, building to a critical threshold before collapsing in upon itself.

A biotic with advanced military training, Hendel instantly recognized what had happened: Gillian had created a singularity—a subatomic point of nearly infinite mass, with enough gravitational force at the center to warp the fabric of the space-time continuum. The nearby tables and chairs began to slide across the floor, drawn inexorably toward the epicenter of the cosmic phenomenon that had suddenly manifested in the middle of the space station's cafeteria.

Moving on instinct, Hendel popped up from behind the barrier, fighting to aim his weapon against the rapidly mounting gravitational pull emanating from the singularity. Locking on his target, he fired. The stunner found its mark and the singularity vanished with a loud clap and a sharp outrush of trapped air. The girl's screams cut off instantly as electrical impulses shot through her. She appeared to stand up on her toes, her head thrown back as her muscles went rigid. Then her body convulsed, sending her limbs into a brief spastic dance before she collapsed unconscious to the floor.

Hendel rushed to her side, calling on his radio for medical backup.

Gillian muttered something in her sleep. Kahlee, sitting on the edge of her hospital bed, instinctively reached out to place a comforting hand on her brow, only remembering at the last second to pull it back.

She wondered if the girl was waking up. Nearly ten hours had passed since she'd unleashed her biotic powers in the cafeteria, and the doctor said it would take six to twelve hours for her to regain consciousness after being hit with the stunner.

Kahlee leaned in and softly whispered, "Gillian? Can you hear me?"

The girl responded to her voice, rolling over from her side onto her back. Her eyes fluttered then snapped open wide, taking in the unfamiliar surroundings with confused terror.

"It's okay, Gillian," Kahlee assured her. "You're in the hospital."

The girl sat up slowly, looking around, her brow wrinkled in confusion.

"Do you know how you got here?" Kahlee asked her.

Gillian folded her hands in her lap and nodded, her eyes lowered so she wouldn't have to look at Kahlee.

"The cafeteria. I did something bad. I hurt people."

Kahlee hesitated, uncertain of how much detail the girl could handle. There had been a lot of property damage, and a number of twisted ankles and swollen fingers from people in the fleeing crowd who had fallen and been stepped on. The most serious injuries were to Nick, who had suffered a concussion and a bruised spine, though he was expected to make a full recovery.

"Everybody's okay now," Kahlee assured her. "I just want to know what happened. Did someone make you angry?"

"Nick spilled my milk," she answered, though Kahlee already knew this from talking to the boy.

"Why did that make you so angry?"

The girl didn't answer. Instead, she said, "Hendel was yelling at me." She frowned and crinkled up her brow. "He was mad at me."

"Not mad. Just scared. We were all scared."

Gillian was silent, then nodded, as if to say she understood.

"Do you remember anything else about what happened, Gillian?"

The girl's face went blank, like she was slipping deep inside herself, trying to dig up the answers.

"No," she finally answered. "I only remember Hendel yelling at me."

Kahlee figured as much. They'd taken readings from Gillian while she was unconscious, pulling the data from her smart chips to see if it could tell them anything. But what they'd seen didn't make any sense. There was a sudden spike in her alpha wave activity in the days leading up to her outburst, but no logical explanation for the increase. Personally, Kahlee thought it could have been some emotional trigger: her alpha levels had climbed the day after her father's visit.

"How come Hendel's not here?" Gillian asked, her voice guilty.

Kahlee answered with a half-truth. "He's very busy right now."

As the security chief, he was still dealing with the fallout of what had happened in the cafeteria. All attempts were being made to downplay the incident: a statement had been released to the media, staff and students were being debriefed, and parents were being notified. As a further precaution, Grissom Academy was still in full emergency lockdown. Yet as busy as he was, she knew there was something else keeping him away right now. It could have been anger, disappointment, or even guilt . . . quite likely it was a mix of all three. However, she wasn't about to try and explain all that to a twelve-year-old.

"When will he come see me?"

"Soon," Kahlee promised. "I'll tell him you're waiting."

Gillian smiled. "You like Hendel."

"He's a good friend."

The girl's smile broadened even further. "Will you two get married some day?"

Kahlee laughed out loud in spite of herself. "I don't think Hendel wants to get married."

Gillian's smile slipped, but didn't disappear completely. "He should marry you," she insisted, matter-of-factly. "You're nice."

This wasn't the time to explain why that would never happen, so Kahlee decided to change the subject.

"You have to stay in this room for a few days, Gillian. Do you understand?"

This time the smile vanished completely and she nodded. "I want to sleep now."

"Okay," Kahlee told her. "I might not be here when you wake up, but if you need anything you push that red button over there. A nurse will come help you."

The girl glanced over at the call button dangling from the side of her bed and nodded again. Then she lay back down and closed her eyes.

Kahlee waited until Gillian was asleep before she stood up and left her alone in the room.

TEN

Kahlee remained seated at the desk in her room and ignored the knock at the door. She continued to stare at the computer screen trying to make sense of the numbers they'd pulled from Gillian's implants. There was going to be fallout from what had happened in the cafeteria. Over the next few days people would be screaming for answers. They'd expect Kahlee to tell them what had happened, and why nobody had seen it coming. So far, she hadn't found any explanation to give them.

The knock came again, more insistent.

"Door—open," she said, not bothering to get up.

She expected to see Hendel, but it was actually Jiro who had come calling. He was dressed casually, in a blue, long-sleeved button shirt and black slacks. He had a bottle of wine and a corkscrew in one hand and a pair of long-stemmed glasses in the other.

"Heard you had a rough day," he said. "Thought you could use a drink."

She was on the verge of telling him to come back later, but at the last second she nodded. He stepped in, waving the bottle in front of the access panel so the door slid shut behind him. Setting the glasses down on the table, he set about using the corkscrew to open the wine.

"Any idea what happened?" he asked as the cork broke free with a soft but audible pop, his question a preview of the endless inquiries to come.

"I really don't want to talk about work right now," she answered, getting up from her chair and crossing the room as he poured the wine.

"Whatever my lady desires," he said with a wink, handing her a glass.

She took a small sip, letting the wine's flavorful bouquet fill her palette. She tasted fruit, though it was more earthy than sweet.

"That's nice," she said, taking another, somewhat larger sip.

"I picked it up last time I was groundside on Elysium," he replied with a mischievous smile. "I thought it might be a good way to loosen up my boss."

"This could get me pretty loose," she confessed, downing the rest of the wine and holding out her glass for a refill. "Now that the bottle's open, no sense letting it go to waste."

Jiro obliged by refilling her glass. As he turned to set the bottle down, Kahlee leaned in and gave him a quick kiss. He responded by wrapping his arm around her waist and pulling her in close, so their hips pressed tight against each other.

"I didn't know this stuff would work so fast." He laughed.

"I can't help it if I'm a quick study," she answered, deftly undoing the top button of his shirt with her free hand.

"They say you should let wine breathe before you drink it," he whispered, nuzzling her earlobe.

"Works for me," she answered, setting her glass down on the table then leaping up to wrap her legs around his waist as he carried her over to the bed.

Their lovemaking didn't last long. Kahlee set the pace, fast and fierce as she tried to work off the stress and tension of the day, and Jiro was happy to follow her lead. When it was over they simply lay intertwined atop the sheets, naked and sheened with sweat as they tried to catch their breath.

"You really know how to make a girl work up a thirst," she panted.

Taking the hint, Jiro disentangled himself and rolled from the bed. He returned a few seconds later with the wine.

"Ready to talk about it now?" he asked as he handed over her glass and crawled back into bed beside her. "It might make you feel better."

"I wasn't actually there," she reminded him, taking the wine and snuggling up close against his body. "I only know what I've heard."

"Did you talk to Hendel?"

As he spoke he ran his fingers along her shoulder and up the side of her neck. The soft caresses caused tiny goose bumps of pleasure to form on her flesh.

"He didn't have much time. I only spoke to him for a few minutes."

"Then you know more than me. So what happened?"

"Gillian tore up the cafeteria," she said simply. "Hendel had to disable her with his stunner."

"Any idea how it started? What set her off?"

"We think Nick was teasing her."

Jiro shook his head. "Always looking for trouble, isn't he?"

"Got more than he bargained for this time. Hendel figures Gillian threw him twenty feet."

"Was he hurt?"

"Roughed up. Nothing too serious."

"That's good," he replied, but the words seemed hollow, an automatic response. "Did you run Gillian's numbers?"

Kahlee nodded. "Her alpha waves began to rise the day after Grayson came to see her. They're completely off the charts."

"Do you know what caused the increase?"

Something about his tone made Kahlee uncomfortable. He seemed more excited than concerned.

"Not a clue," she admitted. After a moment's hesitation she added, "Hendel said she created a singularity."

"Jesus," he gasped in amazement. "That's incredible!"

She sat up quickly, shaking his tender hand from her shoulder and glaring down at him as he lay on the bed.

"What's wrong with you?" she snapped. "You sound like you're glad this happened!"

"It's pretty exciting," he admitted, with no hint of shame or apology. "A girl with no advanced training unleashes one of the most powerful biotic abilities? Damn. I knew she had potential. But nothing like this."

"You realize what kind of a PR nightmare this is going to be for the Academy, right?"

"Let the board worry about that," he told her. "We have to look at this as an opportunity. We've always wondered what Gillian could do if she learned to tap into her power. This could be the kind of breakthrough we've been waiting for!"

Kahlee scowled at him, then realized he was just being honest. And he was only giving voice to the idea a small part of her was already thinking. She was worried about Gillian, of course, but the scientist inside her was already trying to figure out what this could mean for their research.

She let the scowl slip from her face, and took another drink from her glass before settling back down against Jiro's bare chest. She couldn't get mad at him just because he had been honest with her. He was passionate about his work; still young and impulsive. The people running the Grissom Academy, however, were older and wiser.

"Don't get too excited," she cautioned him. "After all this, the board will probably decide it's too dangerous to keep her in the program."

"You're not going to let them kick her out, are you? Not when she's finally beginning to show progress!"

"Gillian's not the only student in the Ascension Project. We were lucky this time, but another outburst and someone could get seriously hurt. Or killed."

"That's why we have to keep her here," Jiro insisted. "Where else can she go to get the kind of help she needs? Who else is going to teach her to control her power?"

"Her father can afford to hire private biotic tutors," she countered.

"We both know it's not the same," he answered, his voice getting louder. "They won't have access to the kinds of staff and resources we have here."

"You don't have to convince me," she told him, her voice rising to match his. "I don't get to make this decision. It's up to the board. And her father."

"Grayson will want to keep her in the program," he answered with absolute certainty. "Maybe he could make another donation to convince the board to let her stay."

"This comes down to more than money."

"You can talk to the board," he continued, still pressing the issue. "Tell them the Ascension Project needs Gillian. Her numbers are so far ahead of every other kid here it's like she's a whole different species. We need to study her. If we can identify the source of her power we could advance the science of human biotics to places we can't even imagine!"

Kahlee didn't answer right away. On some level, everything he said was true. But Gillian was more than just a test subject; she had an identity beyond the numbers on their charts. She was a person; a young girl with a developmental disorder, and Kahlee wasn't convinced that keeping her in the program was the best thing for her in the long run.

"I'll talk to the board," she finally promised, choosing her words carefully. "But I can't guarantee what my recommendation will be. And they might not listen to me, anyway."

"You could always get your father to talk to

them," he said with a wry smile. "I think they'd listen to him. After all, they named the school after him."

"I'm not bringing my father into this," she said with cold finality.

For several minutes they sat there in silence, but then Jiro spoke again, not quite willing to let the topic of Gillian die.

"I heard they're keeping her in the quarantine ward."

"Just for a few days. Hendel thought it would be safer until he's had a chance to sort this all out."

There was another long silence, broken when Jiro said, "She's probably scared. I'd like to go see her."

This was the other side of Jiro: the compassionate young man who was worried about the feelings of a twelve-year-old girl rather than his research. Kahlee rolled over and kissed him on his bare chest.

"She'd like that. You can go tomorrow. I'll make sure you have clearance."

When Kahlee woke the next morning her head was pounding from the aftereffects of the wine. Jiro was gone, and she was shocked to see from her bedside clock that she had overslept by a full hour.

You know you're getting old when half a bottle of wine makes you sleep through your alarm, she thought as she slowly rolled out of bed and stood up.

It was then she noticed a note on the table, held in place by the empty bottle of wine. Pressing her hands against her throbbing temples, she staggered over to read it.

Gone to see Gillian. Turned off your alarm. Figured you could use the sleep. J.

She crumpled up the note and dropped it into the recycling bin as she made her way to the bathroom.

By the time she was showered and changed, the last of her hangover was gone. She wanted to speak to Gillian again and see if she remembered anything else, but first she needed to check on Hendel. Glancing at her watch, she knew she'd find him in his office.

"How you doing, kiddo?" Jiro asked, poking his head into Gillian's hospital room.

She was wearing a hospital gown and sitting up in her bed, staring straight ahead at an empty wall. But when she heard his voice, she turned toward the door and smiled.

Early on, when he'd first started treating her, Jiro had worried she'd get a bad vibe off him. Her condition made her more perceptive than other children, and he was afraid she might sense the ulterior motive behind his interest in her. As it turned out, however, Gillian's reaction was just the opposite—she genuinely seemed to like him.

Jiro had developed his own personal theory to explain her reaction. He was fascinated by the research Cerberus was conducting in the field of human biotics; he couldn't wait to see what results their latest serums would have on Gillian. As a result, he was always upbeat when he came to check her numbers. He suspected she was feeding off this energy and excitement, making her more responsive to him than most of the other techs.

"Nice place you got here," he said, coming over to stand by the side of her bed.

"I want to go back to my own room," she answered in her familiar monotone.

He studied her carefully as she spoke, looking for signs she was somehow different now. *No visible changes in alertness,* he noted silently.

"You can't go back to your own room quite yet," he told her out loud. "Everybody's still trying to figure out what happened to you in the cafeteria." *Including me.*

When Grayson had given him the vial of unfamiliar fluid last week, he'd had a feeling something major was going to happen. He couldn't explain it, but somehow he'd known they'd made a breakthrough. Something they wanted to test on Gillian right away. But he hadn't expected anything this soon . . . or this big.

There was no doubt in his mind that the girl's remarkable display was linked to the mysterious Cerberus elixir. Unfortunately, the incredible success of the treatment had thrown a wrench into the experiment. He was supposed to give Gillian another dose of medication today, but he couldn't give it to her here. Too many people, and too many security cameras.

"I hate this room," Gillian informed him.

"Would you like to go for a walk?" he suggested, seizing on the opportunity to get her out of the quarantine wing and somewhere more private. "We could go to the atrium."

She pondered the offer for a good five seconds, then nodded once, definitively.

"You get dressed," he told her. "I'll tell the nurse where we're going."

Leaving the room, he made his way over to the admissions desk. He recognized the nurse on duty from seeing her around the facility, but he didn't know her name. However, that hadn't stopped him from flirting with her when he'd first arrived and signed in.

"Leaving so soon?" she asked, smiling brightly. She was small, with dark skin and a round, pretty face.

"I'm going to take Gillian down to the atrium. A little break from that room will be good for her."

She frowned slightly, wrinkling her nose. "I don't think we're supposed to let her leave," she said, apologetically.

"I promise to bring her back when I'm done," he joked, flashing his most charming grin.

The frown fell away, but she still looked uncertain. "Hendel might not like that."

"Hendel's as bad as an overprotective mother," he told her with an easy laugh. "Besides, I'll have her back before anyone even knows we're gone."

"I don't want to get in trouble." She was wavering, but she wasn't quite there yet.

He reached over the admissions desk and set a reassuring hand on her arm. "Don't worry, Hendel and I are good friends. I'll protect you from him," he said with a sly wink.

After a moment's hesitation, she relented and handed him the patient register. "Just don't be too long," she warned as he signed Gillian out.

Handing the register back, he gave the nurse one last smile, then turned to see Gillian standing silently at the threshold of her room, watching them intently.

"Time to go," he told her, and she obediently moved forward and fell into step beside him.

*   *   *

Kahlee wasn't surprised to find the door to Hendel's office closed when she got there. She could only imagine all the things he'd had to deal with over the past twenty-four hours.

"Door—open," she heard him call out in response to her knock.

When he saw her standing there he motioned for her to come in before saying, "Door—close."

Hendel's office was a mess, but that in itself wasn't unusual. He didn't like paperwork, and it tended to pile up quickly. He always had stacks of printed reports piled on his desk, with a few more piles stacked on the floor beside it, waiting for his review. The tops of the tall metal cabinets along the back wall were covered with all manner of forms, requests, and waivers needing signatures or waiting to be filed in the proper folder.

The security chief was seated behind his desk, staring intently at his computer screen. She crossed the room and took one of the two chairs across from his. He reached out and flipped off the monitor as she sat down, let out a long, weary sigh, then leaned back in his chair.

He'd changed his soaked, food-stained clothes since she'd seen him yesterday outside Gillian's hospital room, but it looked like he hadn't taken the time to shower. She could still see tiny bits of bread caught in his hair and clinging to the short, reddish brown whiskers of his beard. There was a day's growth of stubble on his cheeks, and his eyes were bloodshot and baggy.

"Were you working all night?" she asked him.

"Damage control," he answered. "Some anonymous jackoff on staff already leaked the story. I've got calls coming in from media, school administrators, government officials, and angry parents. The parents are the worst."

"They're just worried about their kids."

"Yeah, I know." He nodded. "But if I find out who leaked the story I'll make damn sure their ass gets fired." He sat forward in his chair, thumping his hand hard on the desk to punctuate his words.

"Did you get in touch with Grayson yet?"

Hendel shook his head disapprovingly. "I left a message, but he didn't call back."

"Maybe he's not available."

"An emergency contact number's no damn good if you're not there during an emergency," he snapped back at her, then immediately apologized. "Sorry. I've got a lot of things on my mind."

"Anything you want to talk about?"

"No," he said, resting his elbows on the desk and placing his head in his hands.

Kahlee stayed silent, waiting patiently. A few seconds later he looked up at her and said softly, "I think we might have to pull Gillian out of the program."

"I was thinking that myself," she said with a sympathetic nod.

Hendel leaned back in his chair again and put his feet up on the desk, tilting his head back to stare up at the ceiling.

"I'm thinking of offering the board my resignation," he said, the casualness of his voice at odds with the bombshell he'd just dropped.

"What?" Kahlee exclaimed. "You can't quit! The children need you!"

"Do they?" he wondered out loud. "Yesterday I let them down when they needed me the most."

"What are you talking about? Nick and Gillian were the only ones hurt, and they'll both be fine in a few days. You did everything right!"

He swung his feet down from the desk and sat up, leaning forward intently.

"No, I didn't," he told her, his voice gravely serious. "When I realized Gillian wasn't going to stop, I should have hit her with my stunner without a second thought. But I hesitated."

"I think that's a good thing," Kahlee protested. "I'd be more worried if you didn't think twice about it."

"Everyone in that cafeteria was in danger," he explained, speaking slowly. "Every second I let her keep going there was a chance someone else could get hurt. Or worse."

"But that didn't happen. There's no point beating yourself up over it."

"You don't understand," he said, shaking his head in frustration. "I put the safety of Gillian ahead of every other student at this Academy. I can't afford to do that in my position. I'm trained to react in emergency situations, and I can't let my personal feelings get in the way."

Kahlee didn't say anything right away, her mind reeling as she processed the information. She thought he was overreacting, but he wasn't a man prone to empty comments; she had no doubt he was serious about leaving.

"What will you do?"

"I was thinking of asking Grayson to hire me as a private tutor for Gillian."

Suddenly everything made sense. Kahlee realized this wasn't about Hendel feeling guilty over what had happened. Not really. Hendel cared about all the kids in the program, but Gillian was different. She needed more help than the other children. She needed more time and attention. Because of this, Hendel had grown more attached to her than the others. It wasn't fair, but who ever said life was fair?

Gillian was special to him. Hendel cared for her. He loved her. And he was willing to do whatever it took to stay in her life, even if it meant throwing away his career.

"Hold off on that resignation for a while," Kahlee said, reaching out to pat him gently on the hand. "At least until we know for sure if the board will let Gillian stay."

"They're not going to let her stay. We both know that."

"Probably not," she admitted. "But there's always a chance." Her mind went back to her conversation with Jiro from the night before. "If I have to, I could get my father involved."

"Your father?" Hendel asked, confused.

"Admiral Jon Grissom."

Hendel's jaw gaped. "Grissom's your dad? I . . . I didn't know that."

"I don't like to talk about him," she said. "Jiro's probably the only one who knows."

"What did he say when you told him?" Hendel asked, still stunned.

"I . . . I don't remember," Kahlee answered uncertainly, trying to think back. *Funny. I should remember telling him something like that.* "I actually can't remember telling him. But he knows. We were talking about it last night." *But if I didn't tell him, then how does he know?*

Hendel's expression changed from disbelief to one of concern. "Kahlee? What's the matter? What's wrong?"

"Nobody knows who my father is," she said slowly, still trying to work out the implications for herself. "It's not even listed in my Alliance personnel file. There's only one document that mentions my father: the classified report Anderson filed twenty years ago. Top secret clearance required."

"And you're positive you never mentioned it to him? Why the hell would one of your lab techs have top secret clearance?" Hendel asked, worried. "Something doesn't add up."

Kahlee could only nod, numb from the possibility that the man she'd been sleeping with had been lying to her all along. *Lying about how much? And why?*

"I need to talk to Jiro. Now!" Hendel told her, yanking open the drawer of his desk and pulling out a pistol. "Where is he?" he demanded, strapping the pistol onto his hip.

"He went to see Gillian."

Hendel slammed the buttons of the speaker-phone on his desk, moving quickly, but still staying calm and focused. Kahlee was upset as well, but even so, Hendel's urgency surprised her. Perhaps he was eager to get back to being in control, anxious to focus on something other than the events of the past day.

"Quarantine ward," the nurse's voice answered.

"This is Security Chief Mitra. Has Dr. Toshiwa come to see Gillian yet?"

"Yes, sir. He took her to the atrium. Would you like me to—"

Hendel killed the call, barking out, "Door—open!" as he sprinted from the room. He moved so fast it took Kahlee a full second before she reacted and took off after him.

ELEVEN

"We're almost there," Jiro said encouragingly. "Just a little farther and then we can sit down."

Gillian was moving slowly, taking one painfully measured step at a time as they made their way down the walking path of the Grissom Academy's atrium. He should have anticipated this. She was distracted by all the trees and plants; leaves in a myriad of shapes and flowers in a kaleidoscope of colors were too much for her limited sensory perception to process all at once.

They hadn't seen anybody else in the atrium so far; not surprising as most of the staff and students were in class. But the trails that wound their way through the wooded park were popular spots for runners looking to get in some exercise during their free time. He didn't want to start giving her the medication only to have some off-duty Alliance soldier come jogging around the corner and catch him in the act. So he was doing his best to hurry her along, careful not to touch her or upset her by getting overly anxious.

"We can rest over by the waterfall, Gillian. Come on. Not much farther."

The atrium was a five-acre woodland that had been

carefully constructed at the heart of the space station to provide a place for faculty and students to commune with nature. The glass roof was equipped with adjustable mirrors to reflect and redirect light from Elysium's sun down onto the trees below, mimicking the duration of the day-night and seasonal cycles found on the planet.

Local flora made up the majority of the plant life, though a few exotic species imported from other human colonized worlds were found in specially tended gardens scattered throughout the park. It was also home to carefully monitored populations of insects, birds, and small mammals indigenous to Elysium, as well as numerous fish species in the small streams that wound their way through the landscape.

The streams were artificial, the water pumped through them in a continuous circuit that both began and ended at a large pond atop a grassy knoll that rose up from the center of the park. At the base of the knoll was a small clearing where water spilled down from the pond in a makeshift waterfall—a popular place for picnics and lunches. This early in the day, though, Jiro suspected the clearing would be empty . . . and it was located safely out of sight of the running trails.

"That's good, Gillian," he cooed when she started moving again, her head turning slowly from side to side in bemused wonder at the spectacle surrounding her.

"Okay, let's turn right now," he said to her when they reached a branch in the trail. It was warm beneath the artificial sunlight; he was sweating under his lab coat.

She stumbled once as he led her down the path toward the waterfall: unlike the carefully tended running trails, the ground here was allowed to grow over with roots, making it rough and uneven. He reached out to grab her elbow to keep her from falling. Fortunately her attention was focused on what he guessed to be the Elysium equivalent of a chipmunk chattering at them from a branch above their heads, and she didn't seem to react to his touch.

Still keeping his grip on her elbow, he propelled her quickly down the path until they reached their destination. Half a dozen benches were situated around the edges of the clearing, each positioned so that anyone seated on them could watch the water tumbling off the fifteen-foot-high ledge into the pool below. He was relieved to see the benches were empty.

Lunch was still over an hour away, and it wasn't likely anyone would arrive before then. But he didn't want to take any more of a chance than he had to. Still gripping Gillian by the elbow, he led her over to one of the benches in the shade and helped her sit down, letting go of her arm.

Then he waited, giving her time to adjust to her new surroundings. He hoped the gentle splashing of the waterfall would have a soothing effect on her.

After a few minutes she muttered, "Why did you bring me here?"

He realized she must have picked up on his sense of urgency. He chose his next words carefully. He didn't want to scare her or upset her; not after what she'd shown she was capable of.

"I need to check your readings, Gillian," he said, keeping his tone professional.

She frowned, and his heart began to beat a little faster.

"Miss Sanders checked them yesterday."

"I know you don't like it, but I need to check them again," he explained. "Because of what happened yesterday."

Gillian chewed her lip, then nodded and bowed her head forward, exposing the nape of her neck.

He reached into the pocket of his lab coat and pulled out the vial Grayson had given him. From another pocket he produced a long syringe.

"This might hurt," he warned her as he filled the syringe.

Pulling the back collar of her T-shirt down slightly, he eased the long needle into the flesh between her shoulders, carefully sliding the tip between the vertebrae.

As per the instructions from Cerberus, he had administered the last dose to her orally, mixing it in with a glass of water he had brought to her room. However, as part of their ongoing experiment, every alternate dose was to be administered through direct injection into the cerebrospinal fluid.

Gillian whimpered softly as he pressed his thumb down on the top of the syringe.

Jiro didn't know exactly what kind of drugs Gillian was being given, but he understood enough to guess they were some kind of neurological stimulant. The previous dose would have been diluted by passing through her digestive system before being absorbed into her circulatory system and then finally transferring across the blood-brain barrier. In contrast, an injection directly into the cerebrospinal fluid should have more immediate, and dramatic, effects.

"All done," he said as he pulled the needle free.

Gillian brought her head back up, her gaze fixating on the waterfall. One hand absently went up to rub the back of her neck where he had injected her.

Strange. She's never done that before.

"Does it hurt?" he asked.

The girl didn't answer, though her hand fell away from her neck. It dangled at her side, limp and useless.

"Gillian? What's wrong?"

Her head lolled to the side, her eyes rolling back into her skull. Her body began to shiver, then tremor, then bucked hard enough to throw her from her seat. She toppled forward, Jiro just managing to catch her before her head struck the ground.

He turned her onto her side as her arms and legs began to twitch, gripped by the spasms of a full-blown seizure.

"Oh, Jesus!" he swore as her mouth began to foam.

Hendel's feet pounded hard on the dormitory floor, the sound echoing down the hall as he raced toward the atrium. Even as he ran, his mind was trying to evaluate the situation.

Jiro may not be who we thought he was.

That didn't necessarily make him an enemy, but until Hendel knew what was going on he had to assume the worst. He pulled his gun as he ran, his hand snapping it free from the holster on his hip in one quick motion without ever breaking stride.

He debated calling for backup, then quickly dismissed the idea. Jiro didn't know his cover was blown; Hendel didn't want anyone sounding an alarm and tipping him off.

Why did he take Gillian to the atrium?

He didn't know how Jiro was connected to Gillian, or if he was somehow responsible for what had happened in the cafeteria. But he intended to find out . . . one way or another.

Skidding around a corner, Hendel slammed into the wall, absorbing the blow with his hip and shoulder so that he lost almost no momentum.

Too many people in the quarantine ward. He wanted privacy. But for what?

He rounded another corner, sprinted down a short hallway, then took the corridor branching off to his left that led into the wooded serenity of the atrium. If Jiro needed privacy, he'd have to get Gillian somewhere off the paths. But he couldn't just drag her out into the woods: she'd freak out every time a branch brushed against her.

The clearing by the waterfall.

With Gillian in tow, Jiro would have to stay on the trails, following the long, winding path that eventually led to the clearing. Hendel didn't have to worry about that. Trusting his sense of direction, he veered off the trail, crashing through the brush as he carved his own direct path.

Branches slashed at his face and tore at his clothes. He swatted away a wiry limb from an Elysium fir, only to have it spring back so that the needles scratched across his cheek, leaving bright red furrows.

Hendel simply blocked out the pain, charging forward until he exploded in the clearing. Jiro was kneeling on the ground, over Gillian's body.

"Get away from her!" Hendel shouted, aiming his pistol at the young scientist.

The other man looked up, fear and confusion on his face.

"Stand up and back away!"

Jiro did as he was told, moving slowly, his hands raised. "I don't know what happened. She just started having a seizure."

Hendel dared a quick glance down at Gillian, who was convulsing on the ground.

"Over there," Hendel said, gesturing with his weapon. "On your stomach. Facedown. Don't move."

Jiro did as he was told, moving quickly. When he was in position, Hendel stepped forward and dropped to his knees beside Gillian, his attention focused entirely on her.

Daring to shift his head slightly, Jiro could see the security chief huddled over the unconscious girl. Slowly, quietly, he reached down and unclipped the stunner from his belt. When Hendel set his pistol on the grass beside Gillian to check her vitals, Jiro aimed his stunner and fired.

The shot took the security chief square between the shoulder blades, causing him to arch his back and cry out before slumping forward across Gillian's body.

Jiro scrambled to his feet and ran forward, crouching down to pick up Hendel's gun with his left hand, his stunner still clenched tightly in his right. As his fingers closed around the butt of the pistol, the security chief's hand shot out and seized him by the wrist.

Crying out in surprise, Jiro tried to pull away. Hendel—disoriented but somehow still conscious after a direct hit from 100,000 volts of electrical current—held on, twisting Jiro's wrist up and in, forcing him to drop the pistol.

Jiro kicked at his prone opponent. The first blow hit him squarely in the ribs, causing the bigger man to grunt in pain and roll onto his side, releasing Jiro's wrist. A second kick caught him in the stomach, but Hendel managed to wrap his arms around Jiro's leg.

Thrown off-balance, Jiro fell to the ground. Then Hendel was on him. They wrestled briefly, grappling at close quarters as they rolled away from where Gillian lay. The security chief was bigger, stronger, and better trained. But Jiro still had his stunner.

He jammed the weapon against the other man's ribs and fired again, just as Hendel brought his elbow up hard into the side of Jiro's temple.

Jiro recovered first, woozily scrambling to his feet. Swaying to keep his balance, he saw that Hendel, unbelievably, was struggling to rise. The younger man still had the stunner clutched in his hand, and he used it for a third time, completely draining the battery. Hendel fell face forward on the ground, where he lay motionless.

Unwilling to take the chance his enemy might not be out completely, Jiro turned and ran into the surrounding trees. Tossing aside the now useless stunner, he ran with an uneven, stumbling stride through the trees, still trying to shake off the lingering effects of the sharp elbow to his head.

* * *

Kahlee's lungs were burning by the time she reached the entrance to the atrium. She had tried to keep up with Hendel in the race from his office, but with each of his long, powerful strides she'd fallen farther and farther behind. Within seconds he was out of sight, and a minute later even the sound of his footsteps had vanished.

She'd continued on, racing through the halls and stairwells until she reached the atrium . . . and now she didn't know where to go. So she simply stopped and waited, trying to catch her breath and wondering what to do next.

Calling for backup was an option; there was an emergency call box at the entrance to the atrium. But if Hendel was the security chief, and if he wanted backup, he would already have called for it.

You're probably overreacting, she told herself. *All you know for sure is that Jiro lied to you. It might piss you off, but that doesn't mean you should call in security.*

She began to pace back and forth, frustrated by her inactivity, but still not having any useful plan. She could go look for them, but there were several paths and trails; she could easily choose the wrong one and miss them. However, there was only one entrance to the atrium, so as long as she stayed put they would all eventually come to her.

And when they do, I'm going to get some answers!

Hendel couldn't feel his body. He didn't know if he was asleep, awake, alive, or dead. His head was a bubbling cauldron of disconnected, incoherent thoughts and sensations. And then one clear image came bubbling to the surface.

Gillian.

He took a deep breath and held it for three seconds, then slowly let it out. The action was pure instinct; an exercise to calm and focus the mind ingrained by years of biotic training. Another deep breath and the world around him became still, the fragmented pieces of his awareness settling into position.

He was lying facedown on the ground. Every muscle in his body burned with lactic acid, exhausted and utterly spent.

He hit you with a stunner. The son-of-a-bitch hit you with a stunner.

He was tired. He needed to sleep it off. Nothing else he could do.

Don't you dare black out, you worthless son-of-a-bitch!

The words were his own, but the voice in his head was that of his first drill sergeant from basic training. Whenever he faltered during his Alliance career—pushed to the limits of endurance by a 20k run, or exhausted after hours of biotic training—he would hear that voice, relentlessly driving him onward. But those days were over. He'd retired. He wasn't a soldier anymore.

Don't give me that BS! Once a soldier, always a soldier! Now get your lazy ass up off the ground and move!

Somehow he found the strength to push himself up onto his hands and knees. That's when he saw Gillian, still lying on the grass. She wasn't convulsing anymore. She wasn't moving at all. She wasn't even breathing.

He reached down and pressed the emergency alert button on his belt. Security and medical teams would dispatch immediately, homing in on the signal. Response time to the waterfall in the atrium was seven minutes.

Too slow. She can't wait that long.

He started crawling toward Gillian, his muscles screaming in agony, too weak to even attempt to stand.

Jiro uttered a prolonged string of profanities in his native tongue, cursing the thorn-covered branches that were tearing at his clothes as he tried to pick his way through the atrium's forests. But he didn't stop; he didn't know how long Hendel would be down, and he needed to find a way off the station before the security chief woke up.

There was an emergency shuttle at the docking bay that could take him down to the planet's surface. If he thought up a good excuse he might be able to charm or bribe the pilot into making the trip. Failing that, he'd need to hijack or steal it. It was a crazy, desperate plan, but he was a desperate man. He had known from the moment Hendel found him in the clearing that his only option was to get clear of the facility.

He burst from the undergrowth back onto the running trails, less than twenty feet from the atrium's exit. He didn't notice Kahlee standing off to the side until she called out to him.

"Jiro? What happened to you?" she asked, coming down the path toward him.

She was staring with guarded curiosity at his torn shirt, the scratches on his face and hands, the welt on the side of his head from where Hendel had elbowed him.

"Jiro," she said again, her voice stern. "I want some answers. Where's Hendel?"

"How should I know?" he said, with an easy laugh. "He's your friend, remember?"

If she came just a little closer he might be able to grab her, overpower her before she could run for help. Instead, she stopped just out of reach.

"You signed Gillian out of her room. Where is she?"

Hearing the accusation in her voice he realized he wasn't going to talk his way out of this one.

"Get out of my way," he said coldly, dropping all pretense. "Or you're going to get hurt."

"You're not going *anywhere,*" she told him, setting her feet and dropping into a fighting crouch. "Not until I know what's going on."

Jiro quickly weighed the situation. He had shaken off the effects of his fight with Hendel; he was young, fit, and he outweighed Kahlee by fifty pounds. He knew she'd had combat training in the military, but he figured the odds were still in his favor. He smiled and shrugged, pretending to give in. Then he leaped at her.

He'd hoped to catch her off-guard, but she hadn't fallen for his simple ruse. Instead, she met his charge with a hard kick to the knee as she spun out of the way. Staggering and off-balance, he swung at her with a fist but caught only air as she slid under his clumsy blow. He whirled to face her, preparing to lunge once again.

He never got the chance. Kahlee shot forward, her left fist jabbing toward his face. He ducked to the side, into the path of an uppercut delivered with her right. It caught him on the side of his jaw, and he grunted in pain, stumbling backward.

His opponent wasn't about to let him get away that easily. She followed up with a flurry of short, quick kicks and punches, deftly blocking and redirecting his ham-fisted counterattacks. A chop to his throat left him gagging for air, a leg sweep sent him crashing to the ground. As he attempted to rise to his feet she landed a knee to his groin, ending the savage, one-sided confrontation.

Kahlee stepped forward and stared down at him where he lay crumpled on the ground, curled up into a fetal ball and clutching at his wounded privates. He tried to beg for mercy, but when he opened his mouth all that came out was a long, low moan of unintelligible pain.

She knelt down beside him, reached out with two fingers, hooked them into his nostrils and gave a slight pull. The pain was excruciating, and he whimpered in terror.

"Now, darling," Kahlee said in a tone dripping with mock sweetness, her fingers still hooked into his nostrils, "I'm going to ask some questions. And you're going to give some answers."

Pain is a good thing, maggot! Lets you know you're still alive!

Reaching Gillian's body, Hendel tilted her head

back and forced two hard puffs of air down her throat, then compressed her chest ten times in rapid succession, pressing hard with the heels of his palms just above the bottom of her breastbone. He forced two more puffs of air down her throat, then resumed compressions.

He knew CPR wouldn't start her heart or get her breathing again—those kind of miraculous recoveries only happened on the vids. All he was trying to do was keep the blood circulating and oxygen reaching her brain until real help arrived.

Just keep her alive. Keep her here.

The compressions were exhausting; anything less than one hundred per minute was too low to save her. It was nearly impossible to keep up the grueling pace for more than a few minutes, even under normal conditions. In his present condition it was hopeless.

Don't you dare quit on me! Nobody quits in my army!

His breath was coming in wet, ragged gasps. Beads of sweat from his brow were crawling down his forehead to sting his eyes. The muscles in his arms twitched and trembled, threatening to cramp up with each compression. The world around him dissolved into a hazy cloud of pain and exhaustion as he pumped Gillian's heart for her.

One Two Three Four Five Six Seven Eight Nine Ten—Breathe-Breathe

One Two Three Four Five Six Seven Eight Nine Ten—Breathe-Breathe

One Two Three Four Five Six Seven Eight Nine Ten—Breathe-Breathe

And then hands were on his shoulders, pulling him

away. He fought them for a second, feebly, before realizing they were there to help. As soon as he was clear, the two EMTs dropped down by Gillian's side. The first ran his omnitool over her, taking her vitals.

"Code Twelve," he noted, his tone clipped and efficient.

His words spurred both men into action, their efforts perfectly coordinated through hundreds of hours of training. The first snapped open his medic's kit, yanked out a syringe and injected Gillian with a hyperoxygenating compound to replenish the dwindling supplies in her bloodstream.

The other pulled a small, palm-sized device from his belt—even in his hazy condition, Hendel recognized it as a portable defibrillator—and then pressed it against her chest. The EMT hesitated just long enough for his partner to finish injecting the needle and pull clear before flipping the switch, jolting Gillian's heart with a series of concentrated electrical impulses in an effort to restart it.

"I've got a pulse," his partner said a second later, announcing the readings coming off his omnitool. "Oxygen levels look good. I think she's going to pull through!"

Hendel, still half-sitting, half-lying on the ground where the EMTs had dragged him away from Gillian's body, didn't know whether to laugh with joy or cry with relief. Instead, he collapsed onto his side and slipped into unconsciousness.

TWELVE

Grayson staggered into his living room. He was wearing only his housecoat, with nothing on beneath. His head was still floating from the lingering effects of the red sand he'd taken last night, but when he tried to make the pen on the coffee table dance it just sat there motionless, mocking him.

You're coming down. Can't even move a pen. You'll be sober in another hour if you aren't careful.

He wanted another hit, but instead he forced himself to check for incoming messages. He wasn't surprised to see that Grissom Academy had tried to contact him yet again while he was sleeping.

Or maybe you were so stoned you just didn't hear the call.

This was the fourth time they'd called. He didn't want to listen to the message; the first three had all been about the same thing. Something had happened to Gillian, some kind of accident in the cafeteria. Something to do with her biotics.

The news hadn't come as a surprise. He'd been expecting something like this ever since Pel had shown up with the new dosage. The Illusive Man was patient, but Cerberus had poured too much time and too many resources into Gillian with too few results. The new drugs were evidence that they were escalating the program. Someone had made the decision to push the envelope, to test his daughter's limits in the hopes of forcing a breakthrough. It was inevitable *something* would happen, good or bad.

You're pathetic. You knew this could harm her, but you went along with it anyway.

He'd accepted the decision because he believed in Cerberus. He believed in what they stood for. He knew there were risks, but he also knew that Gillian might be critical to the long-term survival of the race. The ability to unlock new and amazing biotic potential could be the advantage humans needed to rise above the other species.

Risks had to be taken. Sacrifices had to be made. The Illusive Man understood this better than anyone, which was why Grayson had followed his orders without question. This morning, however, he couldn't help but wonder if that made him a patriot, or just a coward.

That all depends on who gets to write the history books, doesn't it?

He made his way over to the vid screen on the far wall, then reached down and pressed the button to activate the message playback.

"Mr. Grayson? This is Dr. Kahlee Sanders from the Grissom Academy."

By default he had video conferencing capabilities disabled; he preferred the privacy of audio-only communications. But even without visual cues, he could tell from her tone something else had happened. Something bad.

"I'm not sure exactly how to tell you this, Mr. Grayson. Gillian was in the hospital, recovering from her episode in the cafeteria when . . . well, we think there may have been an attempt on her life. We think Dr. Toshiwa tried to kill her.

"She's alive," Kahlee's voice quickly added. "Hendel got to her in time. She had a seizure, but she's okay now. We're keeping her under medical observation. Please, Mr. Grayson, contact the Academy as soon as you get this message."

The recording ended with a click. Grayson didn't move or react, but merely stood frozen in place as his mind tried to wrap itself around the implications of her words. *We think Dr. Toshiwa tried to kill her.*

Jiro's only contact with Cerberus was through Grayson; they had no way of reaching him directly . . . at least, none that he knew of. This was standard operating procedure: fewer operatives with direct access meant less chance of a security breach. And if one of their own people compromised the mission it was easier for Cerberus to figure out who the traitor was.

Jiro's not dumb enough to turn on the Illusive Man. And even if he did, trying to kill Gillian doesn't make any sense.

There was another possible explanation: the new medication. If it had caused the seizure, and if they caught Jiro giving it to her, then they might think he was trying to kill her. But did that mean they had Jiro in custody now? And if they did, how much had he already told them?

He pushed the button to play the recording again.

"Mr. Grayson? This is Dr. Kahlee Sanders from the Grissom Academy. I'm not sure exactly how to tell you this, Mr. Grayson. Gillian was in the hospital, recovering from her episode in the cafeteria when . . . well, we think there may have been an attempt on her life. We think Dr. Toshiwa tried to kill her.

"She's alive. Hendel got to her in time. She had a seizure, but she's okay now. We're keeping her under medical observation. Please, Mr. Grayson, contact the Academy as soon as you get this message."

All the other calls had come from the security chief. He didn't know if it was significant that this one was made by someone else.

Did Jiro rat you out? Are they setting a trap? Trying to lure you in?

He couldn't put it off any longer; he had to make the call. And this time he'd need to reactivate visual communication. He made a quick scan of the room to verify he hadn't left a needle or a baggie of red sand in view of the vid screen. Then he checked himself in the mirror—he looked tired and disheveled, his eyes bloodshot. But if he sat in the chair on the far side of the room it shouldn't be noticeable. At least, that's what he hoped.

With everything in position he sat down and placed the call. A few seconds later the image of the Illusive Man appeared, filling the vid screen. He had a face born for the screen: his silver gray hair was cut short, framing and accentuating his perfectly symmetrical features, which were highlighted by the sharp line of his clean-shaven jaw and a perfectly proportioned nose.

"Grayson," he said by way of greeting, his voice smooth. If he wondered about the fact that Grayson was sitting on the far side of the room for the call, rather than the customary six to ten feet away from the screen, he didn't show it.

"Something's happened with Gillian," Grayson said, studying the Illusive Man's reaction carefully. *Is this new information? Is he surprised, or does he already know?* Of course the Illusive Man's steely-blue eyes gave nothing away; his face was an emotionless, unreadable mask.

"Is she all right?" he asked, his voice showing just the slightest hint of concern, though that could have been for Grayson's benefit. It was possible he already knew everything that had happened.

"She had a seizure. The new medication was too much for her."

"Is that what Jiro said?" His face showed just enough care and worry to make the question not seem callous. Again, Grayson wasn't sure if it was an act.

"The Academy called to tell me. Jiro's been compromised."

There was a flicker of emotion across the Illusive Man's face, but it was gone too quickly for Grayson to identify it. *Anger? Surprise? Disappointment?*

"How much has he told them?"

"I don't know. The message came in last night. I called you as soon as I heard it."

"We need to play this out," the Illusive Man told him after a moment's consideration. "Assume he hasn't blown your cover yet."

It was a reasonable assumption. Jiro was new to Cerberus—they'd only recruited him a few years ago—but he understood how things worked. Two things would help ensure his silence, for a while at least: his loyalty to their cause, and his fear of the Illusive Man's retribution.

It was inevitable he'd tell them something—sooner or later the Alliance would break him. But the longer he could hold out, the more time he gave for someone to clean up the mess. If he held out long enough for the mission to be salvaged then he didn't have to worry about Cerberus coming after him to extract its revenge. As long as he kept his mouth shut, he could even cling to the hope that the Illusive Man might send someone to rescue him. It had happened with key operatives in the past, though Grayson figured Jiro would ultimately be deemed expendable.

"Contact the Academy," the Illusive Man instructed him. "Tell them you're coming to take Gillian out of the program. We've gotten everything we can from the Ascension Project. It's time we took direct control of her training."

"Yes, sir." He'd hesitated only a split second before answering, but this was enough for the Illusive Man to pick up on it.

"What happened at the Academy was an accident. A mistake," he said, his face morphing into an expression of sincere apology and regret. "We don't want Gillian to get hurt. She's too valuable. Too important. We care what happens to her."

Grayson didn't answer right away. "I know," he finally replied.

"We always feared there could be side effects with the new treatment, but we didn't think anything like this would happen," the Illusive Man continued to explain. "Monitoring her from a distance, analyzing all the results after the fact . . . it increases the risks of something going wrong. Once you bring her in, we'll keep her under constant observation. We can be more cautious with our tests. Bring her along slowly."

He was saying all the right things, of course. And Grayson knew there was at least some element of truth in his words.

He's just telling you what you want to hear! He's playing you!

"I give you my word this won't happen again," the Illusive Man vowed.

Grayson wanted to believe him. He *needed* to believe him. Because if he didn't, what options were left? If he didn't turn Gillian over to Cerberus, if he tried to take her and run, they'd find him. And even if they somehow managed to stay hidden, what then?

Gillian needed order and routine to function. He couldn't even imagine how she would cope if she had to live the life of a fugitive, constantly fleeing from one location to another in an effort to stay one step ahead of their pursuers. And what would happen as her power continued to grow? Could she ever learn to control her abilities? Or would she always be some kind of biotic time bomb, waiting to go off?

"I know Gillian is different," the Illusive Man added, as if he was reading Grayson's thoughts. "I don't know if we can cure her condition, but the more we learn about it the more we can help. We won't turn our backs on her. She means too much to us. To me."

"I'll call the Academy," Grayson answered, "and tell them I'm on my way."

Gillian needs expert help. Cerberus understands

her condition better than anyone. This is what she needs.

You're rationalizing, a bitter voice from the dark corner of his mind chimed in. *Just admit the truth. What the Illusive Man wants, the Illusive Man gets.*

The bag Pel was carrying was heavy; he kept switching it from hand to hand but he couldn't deny his arms were beginning to get sore. Fortunately, he was only a block away from the small two-story warehouse Cerberus was using for their base of operations on Omega. It was conveniently located along the edges of a small, unregulated spaceport in a district controlled by the Talons, a predominantly turian mercenary band.

On principle Pel didn't like dealing with any non-human group, but the Talons were one of the best options for freelancers looking to gain a foothold on Omega. The warehouse was in a prime location: their proximity to the spaceport allowed small ships to come and go without drawing undue attention, and they were within walking distance of a monorail linked to several other sections of the city. The Talons charged high rates for rent and protection, but they didn't ask any questions or stick their beaks in where they didn't belong. They were also one of the few factions strong enough to keep a firm hold on their territory, reducing the chances of riots or uprisings that sometimes swept through Omega's less stable districts.

Although the district was officially classified as turian, there was a smattering of other species on the streets as well. A pair of batarians walked toward and past him, casting a wary glance at the hated human and the bag he was carrying. A single hanar floated up from behind and brushed by his shoulder, moving quickly. He instinctively shied away from its long, trailing tentacles. There were even a handful of humans scattered about, though none of them worked for Cerberus. The five men and three women assigned to Pel's team tended to stay inside the warehouse; especially now that they had a prisoner to interrogate.

He was only a few feet from the door to the warehouse when a familiar figure stepped out of the shadows.

"What's in the bag, friend?" Golo asked.

"How did you find this place?" Pel demanded, setting the bag down and letting his hand rest casually on his hip, just above his pistol.

"I have been keeping tabs on you," the quarian admitted. "It wasn't all that hard to discover this location." He didn't know if quarians smirked, but Pel imagined a smug look on the alien's face beneath his visor.

He wasn't really that concerned; Golo didn't pose much of a threat to what they were doing. But he didn't like being spied on. Especially not by the alien equivalent of a gypsy-thief.

"Why are you here?"

"I have another business proposal for you," Golo replied.

Pel grimaced. "I'm still pissed off about the last deal we cut with you," he told him. "That pilot we captured on the quarian ship isn't giving us the codes we need."

"You have to understand the culture of the Migrant Fleet," Golo explained. "Quarians are reviled by almost every other race. They can only rely on each other to survive. Children learn at a young age to value family and community, and loyalty to your home ship is prized above all else."

"No wonder they kicked you out."

Pel couldn't tell if his jab stung or not; the quarian's reaction was hidden behind his mask. When he spoke, he continued on as if he hadn't heard the insult.

"I'm surprised you haven't been able to pry the information out of him. I assumed you would be well versed in getting prisoners to talk."

"Torture's not much good if your subject is delusional and hallucinating," Pel answered, a little more defensive than he intended.

"He caught some kind of virus or something. Now he's mad with fever," he continued, his voice becoming dark and dangerous. "Probably happened when you cracked his mask."

"Allow me to make amends," Golo replied, unfazed. "This new offer is one I don't think you'll want to turn down. Perhaps we can go inside and talk?"

"No chance," Pel shot back. "Wait here. I'll be back in five minutes."

He picked up the bag again, then stared pointedly at the quarian until he turned away. Once he was sure the alien wasn't looking, he punched in the access code for the door and stepped inside.

It was actually closer to ten minutes when he reemerged, but Golo was still waiting for him. Pel was half hoping he would have grown frustrated and left.

"I'm still curious, friend," the quarian said by way of greeting. "What was in the bag?"

"None of your business. And we're not friends."

In actuality, the bag had contained nothing more than ordinary groceries. There was a full stock of rations and emergency supplies inside the base, and while they were nutritionally adequate for survival, they were bland and tasteless. Fortunately, Pel had discovered a shop in a nearby district that stocked traditional human cuisine. Every three days he took the monorail to the store and bought enough food to keep his team well fed and happy. It wasn't cheap, but it was an expense he had no trouble justifying to Cerberus. Humans deserved real human food, not some processed alien mishmash.

There was no harm in sharing this information with the quarian, of course, but Pel wanted to keep their relationship adversarial. It was to his advantage if Golo wasn't sure where he stood.

"You said you had some kind of proposal," he prompted.

Golo looked around, clearly nervous. "Not here. Somewhere private."

"What about that gambling hall you took me to last time? Fortune's Den?"

The quarian shook his head. "That particular district is currently under an ownership dispute. The batarians are trying to push the volus out. Too many shootings and bombings for my taste."

Par for the damn course, Pel thought to himself. "Violence is inevitable when different species try to live side by side," he said aloud, spouting a common Cerberus axiom. *If the Alliance could ever figure that out we wouldn't need someone like the Illusive Man to watch out for us.*

"This opportunity is quite tempting," Golo assured him. "Once you hear the terms I'm sure you'll be interested."

Pel just crossed his meaty arms and stared at the quarian, waiting.

"It involves the Collectors," Golo whispered, leaning in slightly.

After a long pause, Pel sighed and turned back to the warehouse door. "All right. Let's go inside."

THIRTEEN

"You are cleared for approach on dock four. Over."

Grayson made a slight course adjustment to comply with the traffic control tower's instructions, and brought his shuttle in to the Grissom Academy's exterior landing bay. The medium-range passenger vessel he was piloting on this visit was slightly smaller, and far less luxurious, than the corporate shuttle he normally used for his visits. But these were hardly normal circumstances.

For this journey he had come alone, in the guise of a frantic father rushing to the side of his gravely ill child. It wasn't a hard role for him to play, given how he felt about Gillian. His concern for her was genuine. But depending how much Jiro had told them, it might not matter.

He waited impatiently at the shuttle doors for the docking platform to connect, then went quickly into the large, glass-walled waiting room. There were no other passengers waiting for clearance, and the two Alliance guards posted by the exit signaled him to come forward. He could see Dr. Sanders and the Project Ascension security chief waiting for him on the other side of the transparent, bulletproof wall.

"Go on in, Mr. Grayson," one of the guards told him in a sympathetic voice, not even bothering with a cursory search as he waived him through.

Grayson chose to take that as a good sign.

"Are you sure you're up for this?" Kahlee whispered to Hendel as Grayson made his way through the security screening room. "You still look a little unsteady on your feet."

"I'm fine," he whispered back. "Besides, I want to see how he reacts when we tell him the news."

Kahlee wanted to say something back to him, like, *You can't seriously think Grayson won't care about his daughter almost being killed!* But Grayson was through security now, and he would have heard her. So she bit her tongue and prayed that Hendel would have the good sense to treat his arrival with the proper courtesy.

"Mr. Grayson," Hendel said with a curt nod.

"Where's Gillian?" he asked immediately. "I want to see my daughter."

Not surprisingly, he looked much worse than the last time they had seen him. He wasn't wearing a suit this time, but was dressed in a pair of denim pants and a simple short-sleeved shirt, revealing his thin, sinewy arms. He had what looked to be at least a few days worth of stubble growing on his chin. There was a desperate gleam in his eye and an air of nervous apprehension hung about him . . . not surprising, given what had happened.

"Of course," Kahlee said quickly, before Hendel could offer any objections. She wasn't about to let Grayson wait around here in the hall. There would be time enough for discussion later, after he had seen Gillian.

Hendel cast her an annoyed glance, but all he said was "Follow me."

Nobody spoke as they made their way to the hospital room, though she could see the muscles along Hendel's throat flexing as he clenched and unclenched his jaw.

When they reached the hospital room Grayson stopped. One hand slowly came up to cover his mouth at the sight of the young girl lying in bed, hooked up to half a dozen machines.

"Oh, Gigi," he whispered, and the pain in his voice wrenched at Kahlee's heart.

"What are all those machines for?" he asked a moment later, his voice shaky.

"They're just monitors," Kahlee explained, trying to keep her voice professionally optimistic. "So we can keep an eye on her."

Grayson stepped into the room, moving slowly, as if he was suddenly underwater. He knelt down at the side of her bed and reached out with a hand, placing it not on her head but on the sheets just above her shoulder.

"Oh, Gigi . . . what did they do to you?" he muttered.

At the sound of his voice Gillian's eyes fluttered open and she turned her head to face him.

"Daddy," she said, her voice weak but obviously happy to see him.

Hendel and Kahlee kept their distance, giving him time with his daughter.

"I heard what happened," he told her. "I was so scared."

"It's okay," she assured him, reaching over to pat him on the hand. "I'm okay now."

It was hard to say which of the adults was more stunned by the simple gesture. In all the years Gillian had been at the Grissom Academy, Kahlee had never seen her actually initiate physical contact with another person. Gillian herself seemed oblivious to their reaction, as she let her hand drop back down to her side and closed her eyes.

"I'm tired," she mumbled. "I need to sleep now."

A few seconds later she was snoring softly. Grayson stared at her for several long moments before standing up and turning to face them. An awkward silence hung in the air.

Kahlee broke it by saying, "The doctors say she's going to make a complete recovery. They just want to keep her here for a few days to monitor her. Because of her condition."

"You said Dr. Toshiwa did this to her?" Grayson's face had lit up when Gillian patted his hand. Now, however, his expression was one of dark, barely contained anger.

Kahlee nodded with her head toward the door, indicating they should step outside to continue the conversation so their words wouldn't disturb the sleeping girl. The two men took the meaning and the three of them went out into the hall, far enough that they were out of earshot. She did notice, however, that both Hendel and Grayson stopped just before they rounded the corner that would have taken them out of sight of the room.

"Jiro was conducting some kind of unauthorized experiment on her," Hendel explained, picking up where they had left off. "We have him in custody."

Grayson nodded slightly. "Good."

"He was working for a group called Cerberus," Hendel suddenly shot out, firing the words quickly. Kahlee could see he was looking to provoke some kind of reaction.

"Cerberus?" Grayson said quizzically after a moment, turning his head slightly to the side.

"A radical pro-human terrorist group," Hendel replied. "Well funded. Jiro was one of their agents. We think he infiltrated the Ascension Project to get close to Gillian."

"Never heard of them. Was he working alone?"

Hendel hesitated before answering, and Kahlee worried he might be trying to play some kind of game with Grayson. To her relief, when the security chief finally replied he did so honestly.

"We don't know yet. Interrogations take time. He's giving it up bit by bit. Probably figures he can negotiate a better deal on his prison time by holding something back."

"You should try torture instead of negotiation." Grayson's voice was flat and cold, but the anger was impossible to miss—the primal rage of a father defending his only child.

"That's not how the Alliance does things," Kahlee told him.

"We'll get the answers soon enough," Hendel added, though Kahlee wasn't sure if he meant it as comfort to a concerned parent, or a threat.

Grayson began to pace back and forth in the narrow confines of the hospital corridor, one hand reaching up to scratch at the stubble on his chin.

"So for all you know, there could still be more of these Cerberus agents working in the facility."

"That's not likely," Hendel assured him. "I had some run-ins with Cerberus during my years with the Alliance. I picked up a few things about their methods. Their undercover operatives tend to work alone."

"But you don't know for sure," Grayson pressed, stopping directly in front of him. "Dr. Toshiwa worked here for years, and you had no idea he was with them."

The security chief didn't reply, but shifted his feet uncomfortably.

"Anyone could be working for them. Another researcher. A teacher. One of the nurses. Even you!"

He punctuated his accusation by jabbing his finger in Hendel's muscular chest. The bigger man bristled, but held his tongue. Kahlee stepped forward and put a hand on Grayson's wrist, gently lowering his hand.

"Hendel saved Gillian's life," she reminded him.

The father dropped his head, chagrined. "I forgot. I'm sorry."

He looked up again and extended his hand. "Thank you, Chief Mitra." Hendel shook it without comment.

"I appreciate everything you two have done for Gillian," Grayson told them, his voice taking on a more businesslike tone. "Not just now, but in all her years here at the Academy. And I'm grateful she had the opportunity to be part of the Ascension Project.

"But after all this, I can't let her stay here. She

needs to be with me. It's the only way I can be sure she's safe."

Kahlee nodded. "We're sorry to lose her, Mr. Grayson, but we understand. We'll find a place for you to stay here on the station until she's well enough to travel."

"I don't think you understand," Grayson said, shaking his head. "I'm leaving. Now. And I'm taking my daughter with me."

"I . . . I'm sorry, sir," Kahlee replied, momentarily caught off-guard. "But that just isn't possible. She needs medical attention. Until we release—"

"You said there's nothing physically wrong with her," he protested, cutting her off.

"She's still weak from her ordeal," Hendel countered, his voice rising. "Biotics require an extremely high caloric intake to—"

"I've got food on my ship."

"She needs a specially balanced diet because of her condition," Hendel stressed.

"I'd rather have her miss out on a few optimally nutritious meals than leave her here with you people!" Grayson shouted, his anger boiling over. "The last time she was in this hospital somebody tried to kill her!"

Kahlee held her hand up to cut off Hendel before he responded. "We'll make sure there's a guard posted outside her room at all times," she assured Grayson.

"What if the guard is working for this Cerberus group?" he shot back. "What about the nurses who check on the monitors? Or the people who fix the meals? Don't tell me she'll be safe here!"

"She won't be safe anywhere!" Hendel shot back. "Do you have any idea who you're dealing with? Cerberus probably has agents on every Alliance world and colony. They've got operatives in every level of the government and the military! If you take her away from here, they'll find you!"

"Damn it, Hendel!" Kahlee shouted, smacking him hard on the shoulder to shut him up. He looked over at her angrily, but kept quiet when he saw the expression on her face.

"Why don't you go tell Gillian you're leaving," she suggested to Grayson. "We'll find someone to unhook the machines."

"Thank you," Grayson replied, with a small nod of acknowledgment. Then he turned and made his way back toward Gillian's room.

Kahlee waited until he disappeared inside the door before wheeling on Hendel.

"What the hell is wrong with you?" she demanded. "Did you really think you could scare him into letting Gillian stay?"

"He should be scared," the security chief replied. "Cerberus is dangerous. You can't let them leave."

"We don't have any other choice," she told him. "Gillian's not a prisoner here. If her father wants to take her, we can't stop him."

"Then stall him," he insisted. "At least until we learn more from Jiro."

"And how long is that going to take?" she asked, incredulous. "An hour? A day?"

"That little punk wasn't calling the shots," Hendel told her. "We've got to keep Grayson around until we find out who was giving Jiro his orders."

"You can't possibly think he's involved?" Kahlee asked in disbelief.

"I get a bad vibe from him," the security chief told her. "There's something off about that guy. And even if he isn't working for Cerberus, he's still a drug addict! I'm not turning Gillian over to him without a fight."

She knew Hendel well enough to realize he wasn't going to back down. She also knew Grayson was scared for his daughter's life, and he wasn't going to let Hendel bully him. If she didn't come up with a solution, something bad was going to happen. Her mind was racing, shuffling through ideas, trying to sort out some way to resolve the situation.

As if on cue, she saw Grayson and Gillian, still wearing her hospital gown, exiting the room. Hendel saw them, too, and headed straight for them.

And that's when a wild plan hatched in Kahlee's frantic brain.

Grayson's heart was pounding as he waited in the hospital room for a nurse to come and disconnect the machines monitoring Gillian's status. He had played his part well enough so far, but he knew it was only a matter of time before the Alliance interrogators got Jiro to cough up the name of his contact. He needed to be well away from the station before that happened.

He began to pace anxiously in the room, back and forth at the foot of Gillian's bed.

The nurse isn't coming. The security chief is on to you. He's stalling. You're out of time.

He made a quick turn, breaking off his pacing, and

stepped quickly over to the bed so he could lean in close to Gillian's ear. "Come on, Gigi. Wake up, honey. It's time to go."

She stirred and sat up, her eyes bleary and still half-asleep.

"Where are we going?"

He didn't answer, but instead turned his attention to the machines. Everything looked straightforward enough.

"We have to hurry, Gigi," he said, turning back to his daughter. "I need to unhook the machines, okay?"

She looked concerned, the anxiety on her face mirroring his own, but she nodded. It only took him a minute to disconnect her: he just had to remove a few simple electrodes taped to her head, a monitor strapped to her wrist, and another strapped to her abdomen. She flinched each time his fingers touched her bare skin, her face twisting into a grimace of discomfort. The moment when she had reached out and voluntarily touched his hand now seemed long, long ago.

"All done," he said when he was finished.

He cast around the room frantically until he located a pair of sandals in the corner. Picking them up, he brought them over to the side of the bed and set them on the floor.

"Put your shoes on. Quickly, now."

Gillian did as she was told, and a few seconds later the two of them were out in the hallway. They didn't get more than ten feet before Grayson felt a heavy hand come down on his shoulder, hard enough to make him wince.

He spun around, not at all surprised to see it was

Hendel who had stopped him. Kahlee was standing just behind the big security chief, looking confused and uncertain.

"You were supposed to wait for the nurse," Hendel said in an angry voice.

Grayson shrugged his hand off. "Every second we stay here Gillian could be in danger. I'm done waiting."

"Where are you going to go?" Hendel challenged. "Where do you think you can take her that Cerberus won't find you?"

"I know people in the Terminus Systems," he answered quickly, knowing he had to tell them something. "People I trust."

"Who's that? Your dust dealer?"

Grayson didn't answer, but simply turned away. Hendel grabbed him again and spun him around, grabbing his shirt and slamming him up against the wall. Pinned there, he saw Gillian watching the confrontation with a look of pure terror.

"Wait!" Kahlee said, stepping in to separate them. "What if we came with you?"

Both men just looked at her like she was crazy.

"You want to get Gillian out of here," she said to Grayson, speaking quickly. "What if we come with you? I can monitor Gillian's implants, and Hendel has basic medical training."

Neither man replied, though Hendel did let go of Grayson's shirt and took a step back.

"If you're really hiding from a terrorist group then you'll need all the help you can get," Kahlee added.

"How do I know I can trust you two?" Grayson asked in a guarded tone.

"Hendel already saved Gillian's life once," Kahlee reminded him. "As for me, you'll just have to go with your instincts."

Grayson nodded, this unexpected scenario already playing out in his head. It wasn't the ideal situation, but every second he was still on the station brought him closer to being exposed. All he needed to do was get clear of the Academy, then he could deal with these two on his own terms.

But first he had to sell it. "You understand what this means, right? You'll probably both lose your jobs."

Kahlee exchanged glances with Hendel. She turned back to Grayson and nodded solemnly.

"Fine. You two can come," he said. "But we have to leave right now, and we don't tell anyone where we're going. If there are other Cerberus agents here at the Academy, I don't want to give them a chance to follow us."

"Fair enough," Kahlee agreed, then turned to Hendel. "Are you in?"

He hesitated before responding. "If I'm going to keep an eye on Gillian—and you—then it looks like I don't have a choice." He met Grayson's glare. "I'm in."

Grayson turned back to Gillian, crouching down slightly so that their eyes were level. She still looked terrified.

"It's okay, Gigi," he said softly. "Nobody's mad anymore. Now we're all going to go on a trip together, okay?"

It took several seconds for her mind to process the

situation, then the fear slipped away, replaced with her typical neutral expression. She nodded.

The four of them made their way through the hospital and down the corridor toward the landing bays. Five minutes later they were at security. Despite several curious looks from the guards on duty, they got through with a quick word from Hendel. Ten minutes after that they were on board the ship and pulling away from the station, Grayson at the controls while Hendel, Kahlee, and Gillian were strapped into the passenger seats near the back.

He had Gillian, and he was away from the Academy. And as soon as they accelerated to faster-than-light speed, it would be impossible for anyone to track them. Of course he still had to figure out a way to deal with his two unwanted tagalongs, but he was already working on a plan for that.

A physical confrontation was out of the question. Not only was the security chief bigger than him, he was also a biotic with a pistol strapped to his hip. And he knew from the personnel files he'd studied that both Mitra and Sanders had advanced hand-to-hand combat training.

If you hadn't been half-stoned when you started this trip you might have been smart enough to pack a weapon of your own up here in the cockpit.

He didn't have anything to drug them with, and even if he did he doubted Hendel would let down his guard long enough to take any offered food or drink without making sure it hadn't been tampered with.

Fortunately, Grayson wasn't alone in this. He typed in a quick coded message, then sent it off before plotting a course for Omega.

Let's see how Hendel deals with Pel and his team, he thought, feeling the faint push of g-forces pressing him into his seat as the ship accelerated to FTL.

Only then did he allow himself a long, slow sigh of relief.

FOURTEEN

Six standard weeks ago Lemm'Shal nar Tesleya had chosen, like many young and naïve quarians before him, to visit Omega during his Pilgrimage. Foolishly romanticizing what life must be like outside the rigid confines of the Migrant Fleet, he had been fascinated by the idea of millions of inhabitants from all the different species and cultures living in such close proximity, unfettered by laws or government. He'd expected to find adventure and excitement around every corner, as well as the freedom to do whatever he wanted.

It hadn't taken him very long to discover the harsh reality: Omega was a cesspool of violence and depravity. Pointless, random death lurked in the shadows and alleys. The station was a haven for slavers, and he witnessed firsthand weeping men, women, and children being bought and sold like chattel. Within a week he'd come to understand that the so-called freedom of Omega was a perversion of the word. With no laws or government, Rule of Force was the order of the day; the strong thrived and the weak suffered horribly. But nobody can stay strong forever, and he knew that even those on top would one day find themselves brought low.

He had also learned that the inhabitants of Omega lived in constant fear, wrapping themselves in cloaks of anger and hate to keep it at bay. Driven by selfishness and greed, their lives were brutal, short, and miserable. He pitied their wretched existence, and gave thanks to his ancestors for the strong sense of belonging and community fostered among his own people. And so he had left Omega behind, continuing his journey across half a dozen worlds in the Terminus Systems.

He realized now that the new appreciation he had gained for quarian society, and its underlying tenets of altruism and sacrifice for the greater good, was at the core of the Pilgrimage. Many left the Migrant Fleet as children, inexperienced and rebellious. After seeing how other societies lived, most returned as adults: wiser and dedicated to upholding the cherished ideals of quarian culture. Of course, there were always a few who chose not to return, rejecting the flotilla's collectivism for the trials and tribulations of a lonely, solitary existence.

Lemm had no intention of being one of those, but he couldn't go back to the Fleet yet. For though he had learned an important lesson, his Pilgrimage was not yet complete. In order to return he first had to find something of significant value to quarian society, then present it as a gift to one of the ship captains. If his gift was accepted, he would lose the surname of nar Tesleya, and take the vas surname of his new captain's vessel.

That was why he had come back to Omega, despite

his contempt for the place. That was why he was here prowling the streets, looking for a quarian named Golo.

The name was infamous among the inhabitants of the Migrant Fleet. Unlike those who chose to leave the flotilla of their own accord, or those who never returned from their Pilgrimage, Golo had been banished by the Admiralty. Branded a traitor to his people, Golo had gone to the one place in the galaxy that most mocked everything the quarians stood for and believed in. Somehow he had survived and even profited during his exile, though in Lemm's mind this only reaffirmed the decision to banish him. Anyone who could carve a life for themselves out of the vile fabric of Omega's tattered society had to be cruel, ruthless, and completely untrustworthy.

Lemm was traveling light. He wore a simple armored enviro-suit equipped with standard kinetic barriers, and a backpack of supplies slung over his shoulder. His most prized possession—a gift bestowed upon him before embarking on his Pilgrimage by the captain of the *Tesleya*—was his shotgun: a turian manufactured Armax Arsenal high-caliber weapon, customized with advanced autotargeting and reduced kickback mods.

His shotgun wasn't all he was armed with, however. Before leaving the flotilla, all quarians were given a rigorous, six-month program to prepare them for the weeks, months, or even years they might need to survive on their own before their rite of passage came to an end. The varied curriculum included weapons and combat training; lessons in the history, biology, and culture of all major known species; basic

first aid; rudimentary instruction on piloting and navigation for a wide variety of common spacecraft; and
specific technological skills such as decryption, elec-
tronics, and computer hacking.

Every quarian who left the safety of the Fleet was
well prepared to face the dangerous situations they
would encounter. More important, they were taught
that the best way to survive trouble was to avoid it
whenever possible. So when Lemm heard the sound
of gunfire coming from several blocks away, his first
instinct was to whip his shotgun off his back and dive
for cover.

Crouched in the darkened doorway of what he
hoped was a deserted building, he thought back to
the last time he had come to this world. The streets of
Omega had been busy and crowded everywhere he
went, despite the constant threat of robbery, beatings,
and even murder. Here, however, in a district caught
in a bloody war between two rival factions, the
streets were virtually empty. He had only seen a handful of people, scurrying from one building to another,
hunched over and crouching low in the hopes of
avoiding notice.

Their apprehension was understandable. Lemm
himself had already been shot at twice by snipers hidden away in the upper floors of buildings lining the
streets. The first had missed him completely, striking
the ground near his feet. The second had launched a
bullet that would have pierced his skull had it not
been deflected by his armor's kinetic barriers. In both
cases Lemm had responded with the only sane course
of action—he'd ducked around the nearest corner,

then fled the scene in search of a new route to his destination.

Doubling back through the twisting, confusing streets of Omega was a good way to end up lost; it was all too easy to accidentally wander down the wrong back alley and never come out again. Fortunately Lemm, like most quarians, had an excellent sense of direction. The haphazard, almost random way in which the city had been built up over the centuries was similar to the environment of his home. Many of the ships in the Migrant Fleet had evolved into convoluted mazes where every inch of available space was valued and exploited. Temporary walls were often used to transform halls or corridors into rooms, and everything was held together with makeshift repairs and jury-rigged materials.

The sound of gunfire continued, but to his relief it grew softer as the tide of battle drew the conflict to streets and buildings in the opposite direction of where he was headed. Stepping warily back out into the open street he continued on his way, weapon still drawn. A few minutes later he arrived at his destination.

The entrance to the Fortune's Den gambling hall showed evidence of several recent battles. The sign above the door was scorched with burn marks and hung at an awkward angle, as if someone had quickly replaced it after it had been shot down or blown off by an explosion. The door, made of reinforced metal, was stuck half-open. Pockmarked from the impact of stray rounds, it had been warped and twisted, probably by the same explosion that had dislodged the sign.

As a result it had jammed halfway between open and shut, unable to travel freely on its tracks.

He slid his pack off, letting it fall to the ground just outside the entrance. Taking a deep breath, and still clutching his shotgun, he turned sideways and slipped through the partially obstructed doorway. There were five batarians inside—one behind the bar, the other four seated around a table playing cards. He noticed they all had weapons either strapped to their sides or resting on the table within easy reach. On the back wall someone had mounted the head of a krogan and a volus. They looked fresh.

Every one of the batarians turned to stare at him, though none made a move for their weapons. Holding his shotgun casually in one hand, Lemm crossed the room toward the bar, trying to ignore the twenty eyes watching his every move.

"I'm looking for the owner. Olthar."

The bartender flashed a cruel grin, and nodded in the direction of the heads on the wall. "We're under new management." Behind Lemm, the other batarians laughed loudly.

"I need to find a quarian named Golo," Lemm said, unfazed, offering no reaction to the gruesome joke. He did bring his shotgun up and set it on top of the bar, keeping one hand casually resting on the stock, inches from the trigger.

The last time he'd been on Omega, he'd noticed that an air of cold certainty and unshakable confidence could make others think twice before allowing a situation to escalate into violence. It didn't always work, of course, but that was why he had brought out the shotgun.

"Golo doesn't come here anymore."

"I'll give you two hundred credits if you tell me where to find him," he offered.

The batarian tilted his head to the right—a gesture of contempt among that particular species. His two upper eyes slowly blinked, while the bottom pair continued to stare at the interloper.

"You sound young," the bartender noted. "Do you want Golo to help you on your Pilgrimage?"

Lemm didn't answer the question. Despite all their training and preparation, quarians on their Pilgrimage were generally regarded by other species as inexperienced or vulnerable. He couldn't afford to show any weakness.

"Do you want the credits or not?"

"How about instead of telling you where to find Golo, we just take your credits and that fancy weapon of yours, and mount your head up on the wall with Olthar and his pet?"

He heard more laughter behind him, and the sound of sliding chairs as the batarians rose to their feet in anticipation. Lemm didn't even bother to move; there was no way he could survive a fight in the bar. None of the batarians were wearing armor, but it was still five against one. His kinetic shields might keep him alive for a few seconds, but under a hail of gunfire they'd be drained before he even made it back out the door. He had to be smart if he was going to make it out of here alive.

Fortunately, batarians could be reasoned with. They were merchants by nature, not warriors. If this had been a room full of krogan, he'd have been dead the moment he walked in.

"You could kill me," he admitted, staring straight at the bartender's unblinking lower eyes while tapping his fingers gently on the stock of the shotgun resting on the bar. "But I'd make sure to take at least one of you down with me.

"The choice is yours. Give me Golo's location and let me leave quietly. Or everyone starts shooting and we see if you can survive a shotgun blast to the face from point-blank range. Either way, all you end up with is two hundred credits."

Both sets of the batarian's eyes drifted slowly down to the shotgun, then back up to Lemm.

"Check the markets in the Carrd district," he said.

Lemm reached into one of the exterior pockets of his enviro-suit, moving slowly so as not to startle anyone into thinking he was going for a hidden weapon, and pulled out two one-hundred-credit chips. He dropped them onto the bar, picked up his shotgun, and slowly backed out the door into the street, keeping his eyes on the batarians the entire time. There he retrieved his pack and headed back the way he had come, toward the monorail that, if it was still operational, would take him where he needed to go.

Golo wasn't surprised to find the markets in the Carrd district far busier than usual. With the ongoing war between the volus and the batarians in the neighboring district, merchants and customers alike had moved their business over to the nearby section of the station controlled by the elcor.

The extra crowds were an inconvenience, but there were few other places he could go. Quarian food was a rarity on Omega. While it was possible for him to safely consume a variety of turian products—the two species shared the same dextro-amino-acid-based biology—he still had to be wary of contamination. Bacteria and germs that were completely harmless to turians could be fatal to his own virtually nonexistent immune system.

Quarians leaving the flotilla had the option of packing travel rations: containers of highly concentrated nutrient paste they could ingest through a small, sealable feeding tube on the underside of their helmet. The paste was bland and tasteless, but it was possible to store a month's worth of rations in a single backpack, and it was commercially available throughout both the Terminus Systems and Council Space.

However, Golo, an exile with no hope of ever returning to the Fleet, didn't relish the idea of consuming nothing but tubes of paste for the rest of his life. Fortunately, he had struck a long-term deal with an elcor shopkeeper willing to bring in regular shipments of purified turian cuisine.

He had to fight his way through the crowd for several more minutes before he finally made it to the shop. Stepping inside, he was surprised to see another quarian on the premises. He was wearing armor over his enviro-suit—a surefire way to attract unwanted attention, in Golo's mind—and he had what appeared to be a very expensive shotgun strapped to his back. It was impossible to tell his age beneath his clothing and mask, but Golo suspected he was young. It wouldn't be the first time he'd encountered another of his own species who had come to Omega as part of their Pilgrimage.

He nodded by way of greeting. The other didn't speak but returned the nod. Golo proceeded to pick up his order at the counter. When he turned back he was surprised to see that the other quarian was gone.

Golo's finely honed survival instincts began to sound an alarm. His species were highly social beings. Their first inclination when seeing a fellow quarian on an alien world would be to initiate a conversation, not vanish without saying a word.

"I'll come back for these later," he said, handing his sack of groceries to the elcor shopkeeper.

"Genuine concern: is something wrong?" the elcor asked him in the deep, toneless voice common to the species.

"Mind if I leave through the back door?"

"Sincere offer: You are welcome to do so if you wish."

Golo moved to the rear of the store and slipped out the emergency exit into the alley. He hadn't gone five steps when he heard someone speaking in quarian from directly behind him.

"Don't move or I blow your head off."

Knowing the shotgun he'd seen earlier could literally decapitate him from this range, Golo froze.

"Turn around, slowly."

He did as instructed. As he'd suspected, the young quarian from inside the shop was standing in the center of the alley, pointing the shotgun squarely at his chest.

"Are you Golo?"

"You wouldn't be holding a gun on me if I was someone else," he answered, seeing no hope in trying to lie his way out of the situation.

"Do you know why I'm here?"

"No," he answered truthfully. Over the past decade he had committed dozens of acts that might have caused another quarian to hunt him down in search of vengeance. There was no point in trying to guess which one had set off this particular young man.

"A scout ship from the *Idenna* was brokering a deal here on Omega last week. The *Cyniad*. They disappeared. I think you know what happened to them."

"Who are you? Are you part of the *Idenna* crew?" Golo asked, stalling until he could come up with a plan.

"My name is Lemm'Shal nar Tesleya," the other replied.

Golo wasn't surprised to get an answer to his question. Even on the flotilla, quarians tended to wear their enviro-suits at all times: an extra layer of protection against hull breaches and other disasters that could befall their rickety ships. As a result, exchanging names at every meeting was a deeply ingrained habit. He'd been counting on this, and knowing his adversary's name gave him something to work with.

He didn't recognize his Shal clan name, but the nar in Lemm's surname marked him as technically still a child, which meant he was most likely here on his Pilgrimage. Furthermore, he was associated with the vessel *Tesleya*, not the *Idenna*, which meant he didn't know the crew personally. He must have heard about them secondhand, possibly from another quarian he had run into during his recent travels.

Golo quickly formed a likely scenario in his head.

Someone had mentioned the disappearance of the *Cyniad* to him in passing. Now Lemm believed that if he could locate the missing scout ship and its crew—or at least discover their fate—then he could give this information to the *Idenna*'s captain. In return, he would be accepted into the *Idenna*'s crew and his Pilgrimage would be over.

"What makes you think I know anything about the *Cyniad*?" he asked, hoping to bluff the young man into backing down.

"The Migrant Fleet doesn't do business with Omega," Lemm answered, not lowering the barrel of his shotgun. "Somebody must have initiated contact with the *Cyniad* to propose the deal that made them come here. Only another quarian would know how to do that. And you're the most infamous quarian on this station."

Golo frowned behind his mask. The kid was simply playing a hunch; it was only dumb luck that it happened to be right. He briefly considered denying his involvement, then realized he had an easier way out.

"I guess my reputation proceeds me," he admitted. "I contacted the *Cyniad*, but I was only the middleman. The individual actually behind the deal was a human."

"What human?"

"He told me his name was Pel," he said with an indifferent shrug. "He was willing to pay me to contact the *Cyniad*, and I was happy to take his money. I didn't really want to know more than that."

"Weren't you worried he was setting the crew of the *Cyniad* up? Luring them into a trap?"

"The Fleet turned its back on me. Why should I

care what happens to any of them as long as I get paid?"

It was the best kind of lie; one spun with a thread of unpleasant truth. By honestly owning up to his callousness and greed it made his denial of direct involvement seem more believable.

"You sicken me," Lemm said. If he hadn't been wearing his visor, Golo suspected he would have spit on the ground. "I should kill you where you stand!"

"I don't know what happened to the crew of the *Cyniad*," Golo said quickly, before Lemm could work up his anger enough to actually pull the trigger, "but I know how you can find out." He hesitated, then added, "Give me five hundred credits and I'll tell you."

Lemm brought the shotgun up so he could sight down the barrel, then stepped forward until it was pressed hard against the other quarian's mask.

"How about you tell me for free?"

"Pel's renting a warehouse in the Talon district," Golo sputtered out. Lemm took a half step back, lowering the shotgun.

"Take me there. Now."

"Don't be stupid," Golo snapped, emboldened now that the weapon was no longer pointing directly at him. "What if he has lookouts? What do you think they'll do when they see two quarians strolling down the street toward their hideout?

"If you want to do this, you have to be smart," he said, his voice slipping into a slick merchant's patter. "I can tell you where the warehouse is, but that's the easy part. You'll need to scout it out. Figure out what's going on before you try to get inside. You need a plan, and I can help."

"I thought you didn't care what happened to the Migrant Fleet. Why do you suddenly want to help?" Lemm asked, clearly suspicious.

"I could pretend it's because I feel guilty that I might have accidentally led the *Cyniad* into a trap," Golo explained, spinning another half-truth. "But honestly, I just figure this is the best way to keep you from shoving that shotgun in my face again."

Lemm seemed satisfied with the explanation. "Okay, we'll try it your way."

"Let's get off the street," Golo suggested. "Find somewhere more private. Like my apartment."

"Lead the way," Lemm answered, collapsing his shotgun and slapping it once again into the clip on the small of his back.

Golo smiled under his mask as he led the young man from the alley.

Pel and his team will rip you apart, boy. Especially when I warn them that you're coming.

FIFTEEN

"Are you ever going to tell us where we're going?" Kahlee asked, startling Grayson from a fitful doze.

With the adrenaline rush of their escape fading, his body had crashed and he'd fallen asleep in the pilot's chair. Not that it really mattered; once the course was plotted there was nothing for him to do during FTL travel. Knowing an alert from the ship would wake him once they got within range of the mass relay that would take them from Council Space into the Terminus Systems, he had simply let his mind drift away.

"Sorry," he mumbled, his mouth dry and his tongue thick and woolen, "guess I drifted off."

Kahlee sat down in the seat beside him, and he saw her nose wrinkle as if assailed by a pungent odor. Grayson looked down at his shirt and realized he was soaked in sweat; the sour perspiration of a duster going into the first stages of withdrawal. Embarrassed, he did his best to lean away from her without being obvious about it.

"I was just wondering where we're going," Kahlee said, tactfully pretending not to notice the smell.

"I was wondering that, too," Hendel added from behind him.

Twisting in his chair, he saw the security chief standing at the cockpit doorway, his broad shoulders almost completely blocking the view into the passenger cabin beyond.

"I thought you were watching Gillian," Kahlee said, pointedly.

"She's sleeping," Hendel replied gruffly. "She's fine."

"I have a contact on Omega," Grayson said, turning his attention back to Kahlee.

"Omega?" Her voice was a mixture of alarm and surprise.

"We don't have any other choice," he said grimly.

"Maybe we do. I have friends who can help us," Kahlee assured him. "I know Captain David Anderson personally. I trust him with my life. I guarantee he can protect you and your daughter."

To Grayson's relief, Hendel actually shot the idea down. "That's not an option. Cerberus has people in the Alliance. Maybe we can trust Anderson, but how are we supposed to get in touch with him? He's an important man now, we can't just show up on the Citadel and walk into his office.

"Cerberus probably has agents reporting on every move people like the captain make," he continued. "If we send a message, they'll know we're coming long before he ever will. We'd never reach him."

"I never thought you'd take my side," Grayson said, studying the other man carefully as he tried to figure out what angle he was playing.

"I just want what's best for Gillian. Right now, that means getting her out of Council Space. But Omega wouldn't have been my first choice. There are plenty of other places to hide in the Terminus Systems."

"We can't go to any of the human colonies," Grayson insisted. "The Alliance has people stationed there, and they track all incoming vessels. And we'll stick out like sore thumbs on any of the alien-controlled worlds. Omega's the one place we can go to blend in."

Hendel considered his arguments, then said, "I still want to know who your contact is." It appeared to be the closest he would come to admitting Grayson was right.

"A customer of mine named Pel," Grayson lied. "I've sold him almost two dozen vessels over the past twenty years."

"What kind of business is he in?" Kahlee asked.

"Import, export" was his evasive reply.

"Drug runner," Hendel grunted. "Told you he was taking us to his dealer."

"How do we know he won't turn us over to Cerberus?" Kahlee wanted to know.

"He doesn't know anything about Gillian being biotic, or why we're really coming," Grayson explained. "I told him I was caught with a stash of red sand during a trip to the Citadel. He thinks I'm on the run from C-Sec."

"And how do the rest of us fit into this?" Hendel asked.

"He already knows I have a daughter. I'll tell him Kahlee's my girlfriend, and you're the crooked C-Sec officer I bribed to get me off the station."

"So he's expecting us?" Hendel asked.

Grayson nodded. "I sent him a message when we left the Academy. I'll log into the comm network when we drop out of FTL at the next mass relay to see if he sent a reply."

"I want to see the message he sends you."

"Hendel!" Kahlee objected, offended at the violation of Grayson's privacy.

"I'm not taking any chances," Hendel answered. "We're putting our lives in his hands. I want to know who we're dealing with."

"Sure," Grayson said. "No problem." He took a quick peek at the readouts to get a sense of where they were on the journey. "We should reach the relay in another hour."

"That gives you time to take a shower," Hendel told him. "Try to wash the stink of the drugs off before your daughter wakes up."

There really wasn't anything Grayson could say to that. He knew Hendel was right.

Sixty minutes later he was back in the pilot's chair, cleaned and wearing a fresh set of clothes. He'd stopped sweating, but now there was a slight tremble in his hands as he adjusted the controls. He knew it would only get worse the longer he went without another hit.

Kahlee was still sitting in the passenger seat, and Hendel was once again standing behind him, leaning on the cockpit's door frame. Gillian continued to sleep peacefully in the back; Grayson had checked on her before and after his shower.

A soft electronic chime from the navigation panel warned them a second before the ship dropped from FTL flight. They felt the faint surge of deceleration, and then the navigation screens came alive as their vessel began picking up nearby ships, small asteroids, and other objects large enough to register on the sensors.

The enormous mass relay showed up as a blinking blue dot near the center of the monitor. Despite the muscle tremors, Grayson's hands moved with a quick confidence over the controls as he plotted their approach.

"You going to check the messages?" Hendel asked, the question a none-too-subtle reminder of his suspicion.

"Just need to locate a comm buoy . . . okay, got one. Linking in."

There was a short beep, and one of the monitors flickered to indicate a new message had been downloaded from the interstellar network of communication buoys used to transmit messages across the vast expanse of the galaxy.

"Play it," Hendel told him.

Grayson punched a button, and Pel's face appeared on the screen, his voice filling the cockpit.

"Got your message. Sorry things fell apart, but I warned you about getting sloppy," he said, raising one eyebrow. "Lucky for you I think I can help. I'm sending the coordinates for a landing pad near my warehouse on Omega. I'll be there with some of my crew to meet you when you touch down."

There was a brief pause, and then Pel laughed. "You understand this is going to cost you, right? You know how much I hate cleaning up someone else's mess."

There was another beep from the monitor, and the

image froze, the message ended. In his mind, Grayson breathed a sigh of relief, though he gave no outward indication of how he felt. He'd expected Pel's message to be discreet; Cerberus operatives were well versed in the art of ambiguous double talk when using nonsecure bandwidth. But with Hendel looming over him, he'd still felt a tingle of apprehension when he'd pushed the playback.

"Pretty vague," the security chief muttered.

"This is a public channel," Grayson snapped back at him, his nerves still on edge and begging for a quick hit of red sand. "Did you really think he'd admit to being a drug baron?"

"I think that's as much confirmation as we're going to get," Kahlee told her partner.

Hendel considered for a long moment, then nodded. "Okay, but I still don't like it. Take us through the relay."

Grayson bristled at being given what sounded like a direct order; this was his ship, after all. But he did as he was told, initiating the course he had programmed before picking up the message.

"You look like you need some sleep," Kahlee said to the security chief. "You go lie down. I'll keep an eye on Gillian."

And on me, I'll bet, Grayson thought. But he wasn't about to try anything now. He could simply wait until they landed at Omega, and Pel and his team would take care of everything.

As their ship shot forward to be snatched up by a twisting, shimmering bolt of energy unleashed from the mass relay, he couldn't help smiling at how well things were going to work out. He noticed Kahlee, unaware of what he was really thinking, smiling back.

Lemm peered through the binoculars at the nondescript warehouse. He'd been watching it for several hours now, perched atop the roof of a tall, four-story building on the next block. So far, he'd seen little to indicate anything unusual was going on, though all the windows were made of tinted one-way glass, making it impossible to see inside.

"I haven't noticed any guards on duty," he muttered.

"They're there," Golo assured him. "Heavily armed. Pel doesn't trust nonhumans."

Lemm didn't bother to ask why a xenophobe would set up operations in a place like Omega; greed could overcome almost any prejudice.

The warehouse, like most of the surrounding buildings, was a short, squat structure only two stories high.

"If I can get close enough to scale the wall, maybe I can sneak in through one of the second-story windows," he said, thinking out loud.

"They'll have security cameras on the street," Golo warned him. "You'll do better coming in from above."

He realized the other quarian was right. From their current perch he could leap over to the neighboring three-story building, dropping down one floor to land atop it. With the way the block had been laid out, he could continue on from there, hopping from rooftop to rooftop until he reached the warehouse.

"Good idea," he admitted.

He still didn't like the other quarian; Golo would always be a despicable traitor in his eyes. But he had to admit that he had been extremely helpful in planning Lemm's assault on the warehouse. It was almost enough to make him start trusting him; almost, but not quite.

Golo seemed determined to prove himself, however. He'd even managed to acquire architectural plans for the warehouse's interior: a mind-boggling mess of twisting halls and stairwells that doubled back and forth, seemingly in an effort to confuse and disorient anyone inside. Despite the convoluted layout, Lemm had already memorized the blueprints. In simple terms, the front half of the building was divided into two floors. Offices had been converted into barracks on the ground level; the second story consisted primarily of small storage rooms. The rear of the building was an open, high-ceilinged garage large enough to hold scores of shipping crates and several vehicles.

As he watched, the garage door rolled up and a pair of rovers sped out, heading toward the nearby spaceport. He didn't bother moving; there was virtually no chance they would spot him lying flat on a rooftop hundreds of yards away.

"What are they doing?"

"Picking up a shipment, maybe?" Golo suggested.

Lemm briefly considered his chances of trying to sneak in to have a quick look around before they got back. Golo had told him there were five men and three women working for Pel—nine humans in total. He had no idea how many had gone off in the vehicles, but it was likely only a few had been left behind to guard the building. If the crew from the *Cyniad* were being held as prisoners inside, as he suspected, this might be his best opportunity to rescue them.

"I'm going in."

"Don't be stupid!" Golo hissed, grabbing him by the shoulder as he tried to stand up. "It's broad daylight! They'll see you coming!"

"There's probably only two or three people in there now. I like those odds better than nine against one."

"Those vehicles could come back at any time," Golo reminded him. "Then you'd still be outnumbered, and they'd be the ones catching *you* by surprise."

Lemm hesitated. His gut was telling him to make his move, even though everything the older quarian was saying made logical sense.

"Stick with the original plan. Go in tomorrow night. You'll have more time to prepare. Plus, it'll be dark and most of them will be asleep."

With a sigh, Lemm settled back down and resumed his vigil. He didn't like sitting around doing nothing, but Golo was right yet again. He had to be patient.

The vehicles returned less than thirty minutes later. They disappeared into the garage, the heavy steel door slamming shut behind them.

"We've seen all we're going to see," Golo told him. "Let's go. You need to get some rest so you're ready for tomorrow night. You can sleep at my apartment."

Clearly sensing Lemm's hesitation, Golo added, "I know. You still don't trust me. Just keep your shotgun under your pillow if it makes you feel safer."

* * *

Grayson brought the shuttle in to land with a long, slow approach. The sensors picked up two vehicles parked just beyond the wall separating the docks from the interior of the station; he assumed they belonged to Pel and his team.

They landed with the softest of bumps. He shut down the controls, killed the engines, then made his way from the cockpit back to where the others were waiting.

Hendel and Kahlee were standing on either side of Gillian, the three of them waiting for him in the ship's airlock. Gillian had changed out of the hospital robe into one of her old sweaters and an old pair of her pants they'd found in the back of the ship. She'd obviously grown since she last wore the clothes—the sleeves stopped halfway down her forearm, and the pant cuffs stopped several inches above her ankles. She was still wearing the sandals from the hospital.

She smiled as Grayson approached, and he stepped in beside her, intentionally placing himself between his daughter and the security chief, who scowled.

"Let me do the talking," Grayson warned him as he activated the airlock.

The door behind them snapped shut, sealing them in. There was a rush of air as the ship's systems equalized the interior and exterior pressure before opening the outer door and extending the covered landing platform that would take them safely through the vacuum of the docks and into the breathable air of the station.

With Grayson and Gillian in the lead and Kahlee and Hendel following, they walked slowly down the ramp until they were standing on the level ground of

Omega's surface, where Pel and five people Grayson didn't recognize were waiting for them: three men and two women, all wearing armor and carrying guns. Despite the military gear, they seemed relaxed and at ease. A few of them were even smiling.

"How's it going, Killer?" the big man said, coming over to greet them.

"Killer?" Grayson heard Hendel mutter, but he ignored the comment as he stepped forward to shake Pel's offered hand.

"This is it?" Pel asked with a toothy grin, his hearty grip nearly crushing Grayson's fingers. "Everyone's off the ship and ready to go?"

"Just the four of us," Grayson confirmed, wincing slightly as he pulled his hand free and took a step backward. "Let me introduce . . . "

The words died in his mouth as Pel and the others all brought their weapons up simultaneously, pointing them at the new arrivals in an unmistakable gesture of hostility. Their casual attitude had vanished, replaced by one that was hard and dangerous.

Grayson swore silently to himself; he'd told Pel to act with discretion so he didn't upset Gillian. He was about to say something to this effect when he suddenly realized one of the women was pointing a weapon at him, as well.

"What's going on, Pel?"

"Everybody stay calm and nobody gets hurt," Pel warned. To one of the men on his team he said, "The big man and the girl. They're biotics. Put them out first."

The man holstered his weapon and pulled out what looked like an automated, multicartridge hypodermic. He stepped up to Hendel, moving with well-trained precision.

"Hold out your wrist," Pel ordered.

Hendel simply glared at him.

"Hold out your wrist or I shoot the woman," Pel clarified, aiming his pistol at Kahlee's face. The security chief reluctantly complied, extending his arm with his palm up.

The man grabbed the tips of his fingers and bent them down slightly, then reached out with the hypodermic and pressed it against the exposed underside of his wrist. There was the sharp sound of a high-tension spring releasing, and Hendel grunted softly as the tip of an unseen needle penetrated his skin, injecting him with some unknown drug. A second later he swooned and collapsed, unconscious.

"Hendel!" Kahlee shouted, leaping to catch him before his head smacked the ground. She staggered under his weight and fell at the feet of the man with the hypodermic, Hendel's body sprawled on top of her.

The man reached down and pressed the hypodermic against her neck. There was another sharp recoil from the spring, and a second later Kahlee slumped over unconscious.

"Daddy?" Gillian called out, her voice trembling. Her eyes were wide with fear and incomprehension.

"The girl!" Pel snapped. "Quickly!"

"Please, don't," Grayson pleaded, but his former partner wouldn't even turn to look at him. The woman holding the gun on him gave a slight shake of her head, warning him not to move.

The man grabbed Gillian's wrist and roughly extended her arm. Her face twisted in agony at his touch and she let out a long, wailing scream. Oblivious, the man jammed the device against her skin and released another dose of the fast-acting narcotic. Gillian's scream was cut off and her features went slack as she passed out in the man's arms.

He lowered her until she lay on the ground, not gently but carefully. Then he came over to Grayson.

"Did he at least say why?" Grayson asked, standing motionless as the man reached out with the hypodermic and pressed it against the side of his neck.

"We don't take orders from the Illusive Man anymore," Pel replied.

There was the now familiar sound of the spring's recoil, and the world slipped away before Grayson had time to ask what he meant.

He had no idea how much time had passed before he finally woke up, but it felt like he'd been out for several hours at least. The familiar craving to dust up was there waiting for him, but it was more mental than physical. Red sand was a drug that tended to clear the body's system quickly; the physical symptoms of withdrawal usually faded within twelve to sixteen hours.

That was probably a good thing, considering that he now found himself lying on the floor in what appeared to be a makeshift holding cell. There was a door, presumably locked, on the far wall, and the only illumination came from a high-efficiency LED light overhead. The room was devoid of all furniture and decorations, though there was a small camera up in the corner to keep an eye on him.

Pushing himself into a sitting position, it took a moment for his still groggy mind to register the fact that he wasn't alone. Kahlee was sitting with her back against the wall in the opposite corner.

"Guess your friend is going to hand us over to Cerberus after all," she said.

He was confused for a moment, until he realized she hadn't heard his final conversation with Pel. She still thought he was a drug dealer, and she had no idea who Grayson was really working for.

"I don't think he's working with Cerberus," he admitted, figuring that small bit of information could do no harm. "Do you know what happened to Gillian?"

She shook her head. "I haven't seen her or Hendel."

Grayson chewed his lip, thinking hard. "Pel knows they're biotics," he muttered. "He must be taking extra precautions with them. Probably keep them both unconscious until . . ." he trailed off, realizing he had no idea what Pel had planned for them.

"You checked the door?" he asked her.

"They disconnected the access panel. It only opens from the outside." She shifted and crossed her legs, trying to find a more comfortable position on the hard floor. "Any idea how we can get out of this?"

The only answer he could give her was a shake of his head. There wasn't anything more to say, and so they sat like that for a good ten minutes before the door opened with a loud swoosh, startling them both.

Pel came into the room, accompanied by a pair of

armed guards, and set a small wooden chair down in the center of the floor. As he settled into his seat the guards took up positions on either side of the door, which remained open.

"Figured I owed you an explanation after all we've been through," he said.

"Where's my daughter?" Grayson demanded angrily, not caring to listen to Pel's attempts at justifying his betrayal.

"Don't worry, she's safe. We wouldn't want to hurt her. She's too valuable. Same with your friend," he added, turning to Kahlee.

"How much is Cerberus paying you?" she asked.

Pel laughed, and Grayson felt his stomach clench. "Cerberus pays pretty well," the big man admitted. "Isn't that right, Killer?"

Kahlee looked over at him, but Grayson couldn't meet her gaze.

"So Hendel was right," she said, her voice hopeless and defeated rather than angry as the truth dawned on her. "You and Jiro were working together. How could a father do that to his own child?"

Grayson never even considered defending himself by claiming that he wasn't Gillian's real father. There was no biological link between them, but he had raised her from infancy. For ten years he alone had cared for her, teaching and nurturing her until she'd been accepted into the Ascension Project. She had been, and still was, the center and totality of his world. There was no doubt in his mind she was truly his daughter; if she hadn't been, everything would have been so much easier.

"It was never meant to be like this," he said softly. "Gillian is special. All we were trying to do was help her tap into her biotic abilities. We just wanted her to reach her full potential."

"Kind of sounds like your Ascension Project, doesn't it?" Pel said to Kahlee, grinning.

"We would never do anything to endanger the life of a student!" she shot back at him, finally showing some anger. "Nothing is worth that risk!"

"What if it meant helping dozens—or even thousands—of other lives?" Grayson asked quietly. "What if your child had the potential to be a savior of the entire human race? What is that worth? Then what would you risk?"

"In other words," Pel chimed in, still grinning, "if you want to make an omelet, you have to break a few eggs."

"They're not eggs!" Kahlee shouted. "They're children!"

"Not everyone can be saved," Grayson said, repeating the words of the Illusive Man, though he stared down at the floor as he spoke. "If humanity is to survive, sacrifices must be made for the greater good. The Alliance doesn't understand this. Cerberus does."

"Is that what we are?" Kahlee demanded, her voice filled with contempt. "Martyrs to the cause?"

"Not really," Pel said, gleefully interrupting once more. "See, Cerberus pays well. But the Collectors pay better."

"I thought the Collectors were just myth," Kahlee muttered, as if she suspected Pel was toying with her.

"Oh, they're real. And they're paying good money for healthy human biotics. We'll make enough off that girl and your friend to live like kings for the rest of our lives."

"What do the Collectors want with them?" she asked.

Pel shrugged. "I figure it's probably better if I don't know all the grisly details. Might give me nightmares. You know what that's like, right, Killer?"

"You're a traitor to the cause. A traitor to the entire human race."

"Cerberus really sunk their hooks into you," Pel said with a laugh. "You know, if all their agents were this dedicated, the Man might actually accomplish something. But the fact is, it's human nature to look out for number one. Too bad you never figured that out."

"What's going to happen to the two of us?" Kahlee asked.

"I figure the Collectors will pay us a little bonus for you, sweet-cheeks, seeing as you're something of an expert on human biotics.

"As for my old friend over there, we'll throw him in for free. Should help buy us some time to disappear before Cerberus figures out what happened."

"The Illusive Man will hunt you down like dogs," Grayson snarled.

Pel stood up from his chair. "With the kind of rewards they're offering, that's a chance I'm willing to take."

He nodded toward Kahlee. "Throw her in with the other two. If we leave the two of them alone together she'll probably scratch his eyes out."

One of the guards stepped forward and hauled Kahlee to her feet, dragging her from the cell.

Pel, chair in hand, paused just before closing the door.

"Nothing personal, Killer," he said, getting the last word in as always.

SIXTEEN

Pel followed the guard and Kahlee down the hall to the room on the far end, then opened the door so they could toss her in. The woman gasped when she saw the two figures lying motionless on the floor.

"Relax, sugar," Pel said with a wink. "They're just unconscious."

The guard shoved her into the room and the door slid shut before she could reply.

"Keep a close eye on the cameras," Pel warned the two guards charged with watching the monitors that showed the inside of each cell. "If either one of those biotics even rolls over in their sleep, you hit them with another dose of the night-night juice. We're not taking any chances with them."

They nodded in acknowledgment, and Pel left them there, heading for his bed on the ground floor. It was already past midnight, and he was ready for some shut-eye.

Of course, he first had to traverse the maddening labyrinth of the building's interior. As if mirroring the streets in the district outside, the warehouse had been constructed as a confusing maze of corridors and stairwells. It was actually necessary to take one flight of stairs down to the ground floor, weave through several alternating left and right turns of branching hallways, then climb up another flight of stairs to a small landing that overlooked the garage, before finally taking a third set of stairs down to the large common room they had converted into a barracks.

"Message came in from Golo awhile ago," Shela, the woman who was his unofficial second in command, told him once he finally reached his destination.

She was sitting on the edge of her cot, removing her boots as she got ready to bed down for the night. Apart from the two guards stationed to keep an eye on the prisoners and the one patrolling the garage, everyone else was already sleeping.

"He have an update on when the Collectors are supposed to show?"

She shook her head. "When I asked he just said they'll come to us when they're ready. He told me we have to be patient."

Sitting down with a weary sigh, he asked, "So why'd he call?"

"He wanted to warn us. He says there's another quarian who's going to try to sneak into the building tomorrow night. He sent us all the details."

Pel raised an eyebrow in surprise. Golo might be a cowardly, backstabbing, double-dealing little quarian, but he was damned resourceful.

"Okay, we'll set something up to take care of him tomorrow."

"What about the other one down in the basement?" Shela wanted to know.

In all the excitement of Grayson's arrival, Pel had

almost forgotten about the quarian pilot they had captured from the *Cyniad*. They had finally managed to make him give up the info they wanted, but he doubted they'd get much more out of him. Between the torture and the fever from whatever diseases he had contracted when Golo had broken his mask, their quarian prisoner had been reduced to a barely coherent babbling madman. Of course, now that they were breaking off all ties with Cerberus it had all been a waste of time . . . though it had allowed Shela to show him some rather interesting new interrogation techniques.

"We've got no use for him now. Put him down in the morning," he said.

"He looked pretty bad last time I saw him," Shela remarked. "I don't think he'll make it until morning."

"Care to put your money where your mouth is?"

"Twenty credits says he doesn't see the sunrise."

"Done."

As Pel leaned over to shake on the wager the entire building was rocked by the sound of multiple shotgun blasts fired in quick succession. The noise came from the floor above them.

Lemm was young, but he wasn't stupid. He knew better than to trust Golo, so after the other quarian had fallen asleep Lemm had snuck out of his apartment and made his way back to the rooftops in the Talon district. He figured there was a fifty-fifty chance Golo was in deeper with the humans than he admitted, and he had no intention of walking into an ambush. The best way to avoid the possibility was to strike a day early. If Golo hadn't tipped off the humans, it made little difference. But if he had alerted them, Lemm would now have the upper hand, as they wouldn't be expecting him until tomorrow.

He moved quickly over the rooftops, blood pumping with adrenaline as he worked his way toward the small two-story building he'd been scouting earlier in the day. Space was precious on Omega, so traveling from one building to the next required little more than a leap of fifteen or twenty feet to cross the empty air between them. Even with his pack full of gear strapped to his back, the greatest danger wasn't that he would fall. Rather, it was the chance he would run into the inhabitants of one of the buildings out to enjoy the night air above the stink of street level. If that happened, the encounter would almost surely end with someone getting shot.

Fortunately, he made it there without running into anyone, rolling to absorb the impact and muffle the sound as he made the final jump from the three-story building beside the warehouse to the rooftop ten feet below.

He got to his feet and paused, listening for sounds that would indicate he'd been spotted. Hearing nothing unusual, he made his way to the edge of the roof, peering down at the large window beneath him.

It was impossible to see through the one-way glass. But he wasn't interested in what lay beyond the window—at least not yet. Instead, he pulled his omnitool from his belt and flipped on the flashlight. The thin beam of soft illumination allowed him to locate the tiny infrared emitters along the outside of the window frame. Adjusting a setting on the omnitool, he used it to tap into the wireless signal, overriding the alarm system.

There was no latch on the window, so Lemm would have to make his own opening. He slung his backpack from his shoulder and set it down on the roof, then rummaged around until he found the glass cutter. The tight-beamed laser sliced through the window with a barely audible, high-pitched whine. He carved off a tiny piece in the upper corner; just large enough for a small video camera on the end of a stiff wire to poke through and look around.

Images from the camera were transmitted back to the readout on his omnitool, allowing him to see what awaited him on the other side. The window was at one end of a corridor. Several doors that looked to be storage rooms lined either side. At the far end was a small table, where a pair of armed guards played cards and cast occasional glances at a bank of monitors resting on the table.

Using the camera magnification, he zoomed in to get a closer look at the images on the monitors. There were six in all: four showed only empty rooms, but one of the rooms had a lone figure huddled in a corner, and another showed three occupants, two lying on the floor and the third sitting between them.

Lemm withdrew the camera quickly; it was obvious the storage rooms had been converted to holding cells, and these guards were in charge of watching their prisoners. There were no police or law enforcement officials on Omega, so that left only one reasonable explanation.

Slavers. And he had a pretty good idea who the slaves were.

Enraged at seeing his fellow quarians caged like animals, Lemm stashed the camera, strapped his pack back over his shoulders, readied his shotgun, then lowered himself down from the rooftop until he was balanced precariously on the window's narrow bottom ledge. He didn't bother to use the glasscutter this time, but simply threw himself forward, relying on the tough fabric of his enviro-suit to protect him from the shards of glass.

His momentum carried him into the corridor, where he hit the floor, tucked into a forward role and came up firing. Neither guard was expecting the attack and he caught them completely unprepared. Most of the first two blasts from his shotgun were deflected by the kinetic shields in their combat suits, keeping them alive just long enough to jump to their feet. But the third and fourth blasts killed the men before they had a chance to draw their weapons, hurtling their bodies back with such force that they slammed into the table, sending the monitors crashing to the floor.

Knowing he had to work fast, Lemm turned his attention to the cells. Four of them stood empty, doors open. He slapped his hand against the access panel of the nearest closed door, hoping it wasn't protected by a security code. To his relief it slid open, revealing the room with the three figures inside. And that's when Lemm realized he'd made a horrible mistake.

They weren't quarians at all—the prisoners were human! A man and two women. *No,* his mind corrected: *a man, a woman, and a girl.* The woman sprang to her feet when she saw him, but the others didn't move. To his great surprise, Lemm thought he recognized her.

"Are you Kahlee Sanders?"

She nodded quickly. "Who are you?"

"Not now," he told her, his mind casting back to the achitectural plans he had memorized. "We only have a minute or so until reinforcements get here. Come on."

"I can't leave them," she said, nodding to the two on the ground.

The girl was small enough that she could be carried, but the other one was far bigger than either Lemm or Kahlee. He rushed over to the man's side and dropped to one knee, scanning him quickly with his omnitool.

"I think I can wake him up," he said. "Grab the guns from the guards outside and let your friend out of the other cell."

"Leave him behind," she said, her voice dripping with venom. "He's one of them."

Lemm pulled a booster shot from his pack and administered it to the unconscious man as Kahlee disappeared into the hall. By the time she returned with the guards' assault rifles, the man was moaning and trying to sit up.

"Help me get him to his feet."

Kahlee set the weapons down and came over. Together they managed to lift the big man off the ground. To Lemm's relief, he was actually able to stand on his own.

"What's his name?"

"Hendel."

"Hendel!" he shouted, hoping to penetrate the narcotics that were still clouding his mind. "My name is Lemm! We're going to get you out of here! Do you understand?"

The big man nodded, though the action caused him to sway on his feet. Lemm realized that even if he woke the girl, she probably wouldn't be strong enough to walk for a good twenty minutes.

"We'll move quicker if I just carry the little one," Lemm said.

Kahlee nodded, and the quarian adjusted his back-pack, bent down, and scooped the girl up with his left arm, carrying her over his shoulder like a sack of flour. She was heavier than she looked, and even with his right hand free and the weight of his pack offsetting the load, he knew it was going to be tough for him to carry her and still shoot effectively.

"Did the Alliance teach you how to handle one of those?" he asked Kahlee, tilting his head toward the assault rifles on the ground.

She nodded and bent to pick them up. "How did you know I was in the Alliance?"

"Later," he answered. "We need to move."

Kahlee handed one of the weapons to Hendel, but it slipped through his hands and clattered to the floor.

"Forget it," Lemm said. *He couldn't hit the broadside of a building right now anyway.* "Follow me!" he added, shouting in the hopes the drugged man would respond to his voice.

He led them through the twisting hallways, knowing their best chance was to get to one of the vehicles in the garage. Unfortunately, the enemy probably knew that, too.

When he reached the stairs leading down to the

ground floor, he cast a quick peek behind him. Hendel was keeping up, thanks in part to Kahlee half pulling, half carrying him along. With the girl still draped over his shoulder, the four of them stumbled awkwardly down the stairs, across a small landing and into the garage. Various containers and shipping crates of all sizes were piled haphazardly about the room; perfect cover for any guards waiting to ambush them.

"Over there," Kahlee said, pointing to a pile of metal boxes stacked in the corner of the far wall. "You three make a run for it. I'll lay down some covering fire."

Lemm nodded and took off, moving as quickly as possible while carrying his awkward load. For a brief moment he was aware of Hendel lumbering after him, and then movement on the other side of the room drew his attention.

A woman popped up from behind one of the crates, taking a bead on him. He realized with horror that while his kinetic shields gave him some protection, the girl and Hendel were completely vulnerable. Before the woman managed to get off a shot, however, Kahlee let loose with a spray of bullets that forced her to duck back down again.

From the corner of his eye, Lemm saw a man halfhidden in the boxes off to the right. The human fired his pistol as they ran by less than a dozen feet away, concentrating his fire on Lemm rather than taking aim at Hendel or the girl. The quarian retaliated with a pair of wildly aimed shots that echoed like thunder in the cavernous warehouse.

At this close range accuracy barely mattered; the

autotargeting systems of both weapons ensured direct hits. Lemm's kinetic barriers deflected all the rounds from the pistol except for one that embedded itself harmlessly in the padded shoulder of his combat suit and another that ripped through the corner of his backpack. His opponent wasn't so lucky. The concentrated scatter of the shotgun blasts overwhelmed his shields, and a handful of pellets penetrated the kinetic barriers. The impact tore great holes in the exposed flesh of his face and hands, and the man dropped lifeless to the floor.

And then they were sliding into the safety of the cover behind the containers. Lemm quickly shook the pack loose from his shoulder and lowered the girl to the floor, then popped up to provide cover for Kahlee. Seeing what he was doing, she sprinted across the warehouse toward them, keeping her head low.

A shotgun wasn't the best weapon for laying down a field of cover fire. Unlike an assault rifle, it didn't spray a nearly endless stream of bullets. But Lemm remembered where the woman who had popped up before was hiding. If she was foolish enough to peek out again without changing position, he'd have her right in his sights.

The woman did exactly that, and Lemm pulled the trigger the instant her head came into view. The echo of the shotgun rang out once more, and the crate she was using for cover actually shifted from the impact of his shot. Her kinetic barriers saved her life, absorbing the tightly packed cloud of incoming projectiles, and she ducked behind cover once again. Lemm doubted she'd make the mistake of showing herself in exactly the same place a third time.

Kahlee skidded to a stop beside him, breathing hard. At almost the same instant two more guards, a man and a woman, burst into the warehouse through the same entrance they had come through only a few seconds before. A coordinated barrage of shotgun and assault-rifle fire sent them scurrying back around the corner.

"They'll go around to the other side," Lemm warned, recalling that there were two entrances to the warehouse, along with the landing up above and the big vehicle doors on the far wall. "Try to flank us."

"You think you can get to those rovers?" Kahlee asked him, pointing at the two vehicles parked out in the open near the center of the garage.

"There's not much cover. I'll have to work my way around to the far side. Can you hold position here?"

"For a little while. Any idea how many we're up against?"

"They started with nine, as far as I know. Two dead upstairs, one more down here."

"Six against two," she muttered. "Without one of those rovers we don't stand much of a chance."

Hendel mumbled something neither of them understood. He seemed to be more alert, but his words were still incomprehensible as the booster fought against the drugs still coursing through his system.

"You stay here with me and Gillian," Kahlee told him, patting him on the thigh. "And keep your head down."

Peering through a small gap between the wall of boxes shielding them from enemy fire, Lemm tried to plan a route from cover point to cover point that would eventually lead him to the vehicle. It was there, but he'd have to keep moving. And Kahlee would need to stay sharp.

Even as he was wondering if she was up to the task, another slaver appeared in the door they had used to enter the garage. Kahlee popped up from behind her cover and took him down with a short, well-aimed burst from her assault rifle.

Two against five now.

"Okay, I'm ready," he said, taking a deep breath.

"Good luck," she replied. She didn't turn to look at him, but kept her attention on the battlefield.

As he broke from the boxes, she started firing.

Grayson heard the shotgun blasts in the hall outside, but wasn't sure what to make of them. A few minutes later he heard gunfire coming from a distance, though he guessed it was still inside the building.

Somebody's assaulting the base. Now's your chance to get out of here.

He was trapped in a storage room, not a real jail cell, and the walls imprisoning him were nothing but the turian equivalent of drywall. Standing up, he went over to one of the side walls and began to slam the bottom of his foot hard against the surface.

If the guards were still out there they'd see what he was up to on the cameras. But Grayson was banking on them being otherwise distracted.

After a few hard kicks his foot broke through to the other side. He put his eye to the hole to see what lay beyond. It appeared to be another makeshift cell, much like his own. But this one was empty, and the steel door leading out to the hall was open.

He continued his assault on the wall, and five minutes later he had broken away enough of the material to crawl through. No one had come to check on him during his slow-developing escape, so he assumed none of the guards were around. Based on the continuing sound of gunfire from somewhere else in the building, he guessed they had gone to help fight off the attackers. As he stepped out into the hall and saw the two bodies, he realized he was wrong.

A quick look around told him just about everything he needed to know. All the other cells were empty; Gillian and the others were gone. Someone had obviously busted them out . . . though he couldn't even begin to guess who it might have been.

Whoever it was, they were kind enough to leave me an assault rifle, he thought, picking up the discarded weapon from the floor of one of the cells.

Grayson didn't know where he was, but he knew where he wanted to go—he needed to find Gillian. The most logical way to do that seemed to be to follow the sound of the gunfire.

It didn't take him long to realize that this task was harder than it seemed, and he quickly became hopelessly lost in the building's nonsensical floor plan.

Lemm darted back and forth between the containers, constantly changing direction, stopping and starting without warning, and never staying in one place too long. His hands clutched his shotgun tightly, but he wasn't looking to fire at anyone—he was simply trying to make it to the vehicles.

Kahlee was doing her best to cover him, but she was badly overmatched. The one time he'd dared to stop long enough to look back, he saw two slavers firing at her from cover positions behind a pile of containers on the floor, and another two, newly arrived, shooting down at her from the small landing overlooking the garage from above.

The two teams coordinated their attacks, never giving her a clear opening to retaliate. But that didn't stop her from occasionally popping her head out and firing back.

Brave thing to do, considering she doesn't even have any shields.

With Kahlee occupying four of the remaining five slavers, that left only one more for him to deal with. Unfortunately, he had no idea where his enemy was. Every time he ran out into the open he could be stepping into a spray of lethal assault-rifle fire.

Don't think about it. Just stay focused on the vehicle. You're almost there.

Only a short stretch of bare floor still separated him from the rovers; a quick sprint and it was all over, one way or the other.

He broke from cover and dashed for the vehicle. The fifth slaver was waiting for him, popping up from behind a crate not twenty feet away as he ran past. She opened fire from close range on his flank; clouds of concrete flew up from the floor as she fired low, where his barrier shields were most vulnerable, trying to take his legs out from under him.

Head down, Lemm knew his best shot at survival was just to keep running. He was half a step away from safety when a hollow-point round entered his left calf. It mushroomed then split apart on impact, sending a spray of metal fragments through his lower leg, shredding the muscles and tendons. Screaming in agony, he pitched forward, his shotgun falling from his hand. His momentum allowed him to manage two more stumbling, off-balance steps that carried him far enough to put the metal-plated rover between him and his attacker before he collapsed to the ground.

He rolled over onto his back, clutching at the bloody pulp below his knee that used to be his leg. He heard footsteps coming toward him, and he realized his shotgun had been left behind, skittering across the floor when he'd dropped it after being hit.

A second later the woman materialized from around the front of the vehicle. She smiled and aimed the weapon at him.

Then suddenly she was flying across the room.

Lemm followed the path of her body as it arced high through the air before slamming into one of the walls and crashing down to the floor. She lay there motionless, her neck twisted at a gruesome angle. It was only when he heard Hendel screaming at him that he realized what had happened: the man was biotic!

"The rover! Hurry!"

The quarian knew it would take thirty or forty seconds before Hendel recovered enough to use his biotics again . . . time they didn't have. Gritting his teeth and hoping he wouldn't pass out from the pain, he used the rover's front bumper to haul himself up. Standing on his one good leg, he pulled the driver's side door open and crawled inside. Blocking out the pain as best he could, it took him half a minute to override the operator codes and get the engine fired up.

There was no windscreen on the vehicle; it was

more like an armored transport carrier, with a navigation screen on the inside to give him the layout of his surroundings. Organic creatures picked up by the vehicle's infrared and ultraviolet sensors showed as small dots on the nav screen, revealing the locations of everyone in the warehouse, both friend and foe.

The rover wasn't equipped with weapons, but it was four tons of bulletproof metal. He threw the vehicle into gear, the tires leaving patches of smoking black rubber on the garage floor as he peeled out and spun in a crazy circle, fighting with the steering in his haste.

He careened into a pile of crates, sending the heavy metal boxes flying. He spun the wheel and stomped on the accelerator. Ignoring the agonizing jolt of pain as his wounded left leg bumped against the side door, he headed straight for Kahlee and the others.

Along the way he plowed through the containers providing cover for the remaining two slavers on the ground, mowing them down under his wheels before bringing the rover to a skidding halt, only inches short of running over Hendel.

Lemm threw open the door and the biotic clambered up into the backseat of the vehicle, the still unconscious girl gripped tightly in his arms while Kahlee lay down another stream of cover fire at the last two surviving slavers atop the landing. They returned fire, the sound of their bullets ricocheting off the armored roof and hull in a metallic, staccato symphony.

"They're loading up a rocket launcher!" Kahlee shouted, tossing Lemm's bag into the back with Hendel as she leaped into the front of the vehicle. "Get us the hell out of here!"

"You better drive," Lemm panted through clenched teeth as he tried to slide awkwardly over to the passenger seat.

She glanced down at his mangled leg, then shoved him out of the way as she slid behind the wheel, causing him to scream in pain.

"Sorry!" she shouted, slamming the door shut and throwing the rover into reverse.

She pinned the accelerator and they took off backward. A fast-moving projectile appeared on the nav screen: an incoming missile fired from the rocket launcher. Lemm thought they were all dead, but Kahlee wrenched the wheel to the right at the last possible second. Instead of blowing the rover apart, the missile struck the ground beside them. There was a deep boom as it detonated, and the vehicle bucked hard from the explosion, the wheels on the near side lifting high into the air before crashing back down to the ground.

Somehow Kahlee kept control, using the nav screen to steer as they raced in reverse across the length of the garage, quickly building up speed. Lemm was horrified to see she was about to send them full tilt into the garage's heavy metal loading door.

"Everyone hold on!" she warned them. "This is going to hurt!"

They hit the door with enough force to wrench one side partially off its rails, the metal twisting in its frame. The back end of the rover crumpled, absorbing the brunt of the impact. Everyone inside was thrown against the rear of their seat as the sudden de-

celeration of the crash brought them to an immediate
stop.

Lemm's leg slammed against the dashboard as he
was bounced around, and he screamed again, struggling not to lose consciousness. He glanced over at
Kahlee, who was lolling to the side in her seat, momentarily dazed from the crash.

"Kahlee!" he shouted. "You have to drive!"

His voice seemed to snap her back to full awareness. Sitting up with a shake of her head, she
slammed her foot down on the accelerator once
more. The vehicle lurched, still traveling in reverse,
and slammed into the door again. Kahlee kept the engine revving as they tried to force their way through
the twisted metal sheet blocking their escape.

"Come on, you son-of-a-bitch!" she swore. "Give
me all you've got!"

The door bent and buckled under the relentless
push of the rover's six churning tires, but it refused to
give way completely, leaving them sitting ducks for
the next inevitable assault from the rocket launcher.

This is NOT happening!

Pel had been thinking this one thought over and
over, ever since he'd heard the first of the shotgun
blasts down in the barracks.

Screaming at his team to get out of their bunks and
over to the warehouse to cut off that avenue of escape, he and Shela, the only other member of his crew
not already in bed, had grabbed their weapons and
raced upstairs. They'd arrived to find the guards dead
and their biotic prisoners gone.

Racing back down to the landing that overlooked

the warehouse, they'd taken a high point above the battlefield, firing down at where the woman, Kahlee, had taken up a defensive position. There was a half-assembled rocket launcher on the landing; a new addition to the warehouse's defenses. He briefly debated slapping it together, then decided against it; he still wanted to try and recapture one of the biotics alive so they could sell them to the Collectors.

It wasn't long before he regretted that decision. From his vantage point above the action, Pel had a perfect view as the rest of his team was slaughtered by a mix of Kahlee's gunfire, Hendel's biotics, and one of their own rampaging rovers.

This is NOT happening, he thought once again. Out loud, he shouted to Shela, "Get that rocket launcher operational! Take out the vehicle!"

She scrambled to put it together even as he fired in vain at the prisoners piling into the rover, the position of the vehicle preventing him from getting a clear shot. There was only one way to stop them now, and it didn't involve taking any of them alive.

"Armed and ready!" Shela cried out as the rover began to speed away from them in reverse.

"Fire, damn it!"

The rocket shot toward the vehicle, but the target swerved at the last second and the missile exploded harmlessly into the floor of the garage. The rover continued to accelerate, then crashed into the reinforced-steel loading door with a deafening crash. The door buckled, but held.

"Finish them!" Pel shouted, and Shela took aim with the rocket launcher for a second, and final, shot.

* * *

Grayson wound his way through the unfamiliar halls and stairwells for nearly ten minutes, hopelessly lost.

Maybe all that red sand over the years messed up your sense of direction.

The only thing that kept him going was the fact that the sound of gunfire was getting steadily closer, and the knowledge that whoever had broken the others out had taken Gillian as well.

He was on the verge of slamming his fist through another wall in frustration when he heard an incredibly loud explosion, like a grenade or rocket launcher, followed by a tremendous crash coming from beyond the corner just up ahead. Moving quickly but quietly, he rounded the bend to find himself standing on a small landing overlooking a large, two-story garage.

Crates and containers were strewn about on the floor beneath the landing, along with several bodies. At the far end a vehicle had obviously just slammed into the garage's door. And on the landing not ten feet away, their backs to him, stood Pel and a woman he didn't know. The woman had a rocket launcher braced on her shoulder.

The vehicle's engines began to rev as it tried to force its way through the door. Given the situation, Grayson was almost certain that Gillian and the others were inside.

"Finish them!" Pel shouted, and the woman aimed her weapon.

Grayson opened fire with the assault rifle; he had no hesitations about shooting a woman in the back. The stream of bullets ripped through her shields, shredded her body armor, and turned everything between her shoulder blades and belt into hamburger. The rocket launcher fell from her nerveless hands and she staggered forward against the landing's waist-high railing. Another burst from Grayson sent her flipping over the edge to the floor below.

Pel was already spinning around, trying to bring his own assault rifle to bear, when Grayson fired again. He concentrated on Pel's right arm, the spray of gunfire nearly severing it from his shoulder as it blew the rifle from his grasp and sent it hurtling over the railing.

His former partner fell to his knees, his eyes glazing over in shock as sprays of arterial blood spurted from his maimed limb. He opened his mouth to speak, but another burst from Grayson silenced him forever. It was the first time in almost twenty years Pel hadn't been able to get the last word in.

The horrible shriek of wrenching metal from the far side of the garage drew his attention. Glancing over, he saw the rover had managed to push itself against a corner of the loading door so that it bent up and out. Grayson watched, motionless, as the vehicle squeezed through the opening, the rover bursting forth to the other side as if the garage were somehow giving birth to it.

For the next sixty seconds he didn't move, listening carefully for sounds of other survivors. All he heard was the rover's engines growing ever fainter as it raced off into the night.

SEVENTEEN

Inside the rover, Kahlee heard the metal door screeching across the armored roof as the vehicle forced its way past and out into the dark streets of Omega. Still driving in reverse, she went half a block before locking the brakes and turning the wheel, sending them into a 540-degree spin. It ended with them heading in the same direction, but they were no longer traveling backward.

They had escaped the warehouse, but their getaway wouldn't be complete until they'd left Omega well behind them.

"Do you have a ship?" she asked, directing her question to the quarian in the passenger seat.

"Head to the spaceports," he answered. "Right at the end of the block. Take the third left, then the next right." His voice sounded strained and thin from behind his mask.

Kahlee pulled her attention away from the nav screen to sneak a quick glance at his injured leg. The wound looked bad, but not life threatening.

"Hendel," she called out to the backseat. "See if you can find a med-kit back there."

"There's medigel . . . in . . . my backpack," the

quarian managed to pant out, struggling against the pain.

Kahlee didn't dare stop while they treated the injury. Fortunately, Hendel had basic medical field training; fixing up a bad leg while bouncing along in the rover would be easy enough.

Following the quarian's directions, they quickly cleared the close-packed buildings and emerged on the outskirts of the district's docking bays. Racing along the open ground, the nav screen picked up three small starships clustered together at the far end of the spaceport.

"Lemm, which shuttle is yours?" Kahlee asked.

"Whichever one you want." His voice sounded stronger now. She noticed Hendel had splinted his leg and wrapped it in sterile bandages to minimize germ exposure, and the medigel would have dulled the pain even as it began to heal and disinfect his wounds.

She brought the rover to a halt a few dozen feet away from the closest vessel's airlock and hopped out, then turned back to help the injured quarian. He slid gingerly across the seat to the door, then leaned on Kahlee for support as he stepped out of the vehicle with his good leg. Hendel emerged a few seconds later, carrying the still unconscious Gillian in the crook of one arm and clutching Lemm's bag in his other hand.

"I'll be damned," he muttered, staring through the station's viewport at the shuttle docked just outside. Kahlee couldn't help but smile when she realized what he was looking at: they were about to steal Grayson's ship.

The quarian set to work on overriding the vessel's

security system. It took just over a minute before the airlock opened with a faint click and the landing ramp descended with a soft whoosh of hydraulics.

Inside the ship, Hendel set Gillian down in one of the passenger seats. He reclined the seat and buckled her in as Kahlee helped Lemm hobble his way up to the cockpit.

"Can you fly this thing?" she asked him.

He studied the controls for a few seconds, then nodded. "I think so. Everything looks pretty standard."

The quarian settled into the pilot's seat and reached out toward the console with a gloved, three-fingered hand. Kahlee was suddenly reminded that, though quarians might look vaguely human, under their enviro-suits and filtration masks they were definitely aliens. And this alien had risked his life to save them.

"Thank you," she said. "We owe you our lives."

Lemm didn't acknowledge her gratitude, but instead asked, "Why were they holding you prisoner?"

"They were going to sell us to the Collectors."

He shuddered, but didn't say anything else. A second later the display screens came online.

"No sign of any immediate pursuit," he muttered.

"Cerberus won't give up on us that easy," Hendel warned him as he entered the cockpit.

"They aren't working for Cerberus," Kahlee explained, remembering that Hendel hadn't been part of the conversation in Grayson's cell. "Not anymore. I guess they figured they could make more by going freelance."

It was only then she realized Hendel hadn't yet bothered to ask why Grayson had been left behind.

He must have hated him even more than I thought. Given how things turned out, she couldn't really blame him.

"You were right about Grayson," she told him. "He was a Cerberus agent. He must have been working with Jiro the whole time."

The ship trembled slightly and there was a low rumble as Lemm fired up the engines.

The news of Grayson's true identity didn't seem to surprise Hendel at all. To his credit, the security chief didn't take the opportunity to say "I told you so." Instead, he only asked, "Did you kill him?"

"He's still alive, as far as I know," Kahlee admitted. "They were holding him prisoner, just like us. I left him in his cell."

"If they turn him over to the Collectors, he'll wish you had killed him," Lemm chimed in.

Kahlee hadn't thought about that, but the idea brought the hint of a grim smile to Hendel's lips.

The quarian made a few final adjustments and the thrusters engaged, lifting the shuttle slowly into the air.

"What course should I set?" he asked.

Good question, Kahlee thought.

"Nothing's changed," Hendel said, giving voice to her own concerns. "Cerberus will still want to get their hands on Gillian, and we still can't risk going to the Alliance. Grayson and his former friends may be out of the picture, but Cerberus has plenty of other agents.

"No matter where we go, they're going to find us sooner or later."

"Then we have to keep moving," Kahlee said. "Stay one step ahead of them."

"It'll be hard on Gillian," Hendel warned her.

"We don't have much choice. For all we know, they could have someone stationed on every human accessible world, colony, and space station in the galaxy."

"I know one place you can hide where Cerberus is guaranteed not to find you," Lemm said, turning in his seat to join the conversation. "The Migrant Fleet."

In the aftermath of the battle Grayson made a thorough exploration of the warehouse from top to bottom. For a moment he had debated racing down to the second rover on the garage floor and trying to chase after Gillian, but he knew the other vehicle would be long gone by the time he got there. If he wanted to find Gillian, he had to be patient and smart.

An examination of the warehouse floor revealed several bodies, including the woman he'd shot in the back. Two more had been shot, two had been run over by the missing vehicle, and one woman lay crumpled against a wall, her neck broken. Grayson recognized the corpse as a telltale sign of biotics, and he suspected it was Hendel, not Gillian, who had inflicted the damage.

He also found a shotgun sitting in the middle of the floor. It appeared to be of turian manufacture, but the mods on it were of an improvised yet effectively cunning design that was the hallmark of the quarian species.

Recognizing the value of the weapon, he picked it

up and carried it with him as he left the garage and went to explore the remainder of the base. He became lost several times in the confusing halls, but eventually he found himself back on the main floor, in a room that had been converted into a barracks.

There were twelve bunks, but only nine showed signs of use. Grayson had found seven bodies in the warehouse; adding these to the two guards in the hall near his cell explained why he hadn't run across anyone else during his search. With all the occupants of the warehouse accounted for, he was able to relax his guard.

On any other station or world he would have been worried about law enforcement responding to the sounds of the battle. But Omega had no police, and gunfire and exploding rockets generally encouraged the neighbors to mind their own business. Someone would come to investigate the premises eventually—probably whoever had been renting the location to Pel and his team. However, Grayson didn't expect anyone for at least a few days.

The barracks led down a short hall to several offices Pel had set up as intel and command posts. Looking through the computers and OSDs, Grayson found the reports from their original assignment. They were coded, of course, but only with a basic Cerberus cipher, and Grayson had no problem making sense of them.

Pel had been sent to Omega to try and find a way to infiltrate the quarian fleet. Unfortunately, the reports were incomplete. They mentioned a ship they had captured called the *Cyniad,* and a single prisoner that had been taken for interrogation, but the results of the interrogation weren't recorded. Pel had obviously given up keeping the logs once he threw his lot in with the mysterious Collectors, and he wasn't stupid enough to keep any records, electronic or written, of his plan to betray the Illusive Man.

The mention of the quarian ship and prisoner, combined with the discovery of the quarian modified shotgun, left little doubt in Grayson's mind as to who had busted the others out. A quarian rescue team must have come for their compatriot, and for some reason they had decided to take Gillian, Kahlee, and Hendel with them as they shot their way to freedom.

Satisfied he had learned as much as he could from the files, he resumed his slow, careful search of the premises. In another office, this one located near what he guessed to be the center of the building, he discovered a small door built into the floor. It was primitive in design; rather than sliding on rails it simply swung upward on a pair of metal hinges. It was closed and locked with a simple deadbolt latch.

Grayson took aim at the door with his newly acquired shotgun and used the toe of his boot to slide the deadbolt aside. He waited for several seconds, and when nothing happened he leaned forward cautiously and threw open the door, ready to fire if a target presented itself.

The cellar beneath was completely dark. A rickety wooden staircase descended into the blackness. Grayson flicked on the flashlight built into the shotgun's barrel, using its powerful beam to pierce the gloom as he made his way slowly down the stairs.

When he reached the bottom he cast about in a quick circle, sending the illumination into every corner. The room was square, maybe twenty feet on each side. The walls were finished with brick and mortar, the floor was bare cement. It was completely empty except for a motionless figure lying on its back near one of the walls.

Training the beam of his flashlight—and the muzzle of the shotgun—on the body, Grayson approached. He was within a few feet before his mind finally recognized what he was seeing; he had found the quarian captive.

Running the flashlight slowly from head to toe, he saw that the prisoner was bound hand and foot, and had been stripped completely naked. Grayson had never seen a quarian without its enviro-suit and helmet before, though he doubted this individual could still be called anything close to a representative example of his species. His face was a deformed mess of lumps, bruises, cuts, and burn marks—clear evidence of the torture he had endured. Someone had knocked out all his teeth and caved in one cheekbone. The other cheek gaped wide, as if someone had slit it lengthwise from lip to what passed for the quarian version of an ear.

One eye was swollen completely shut. The other had both upper and lower eyelids missing, the ragged edges of the flesh left behind attesting to the fact that they had been savagely torn off with a pair of pliers. Grayson recalled with distaste how much Pel had enjoyed that particular method of torture: in addition to the excruciating pain of the brutal removal, the victim would go slowly and agonizingly blind as the exposed eyeball became dehydrated.

The rest of the body showed similar signs of abuse.

The fingers and toes were all broken, and several had been yanked from their sockets. Every inch of exposed skin showed signs of being beaten, cut, burned or dissolved by acid. However, there was something even more unusual about the body that caused Grayson to crouch down for a closer look.

There appeared to be some kind of loamy, gray growth spreading out from the quarian's wounds to crawl slowly across the skin. It took Grayson a moment to realize it was some kind of bacterial fungus; in addition to the sadistic torture, the quarian must have contracted a strange alien disease.

He gave a grunt of disgust and stepped back from the body. To his surprise, the quarian reacted with a short yelp of fear.

Jesus Christ, the poor bastard's still alive!

He was actually trying to talk, saying the same phrase over and over in a shaky, raspy voice. The words were distorted from his missing teeth and misshapen face, and it took Grayson's automated translator several repetitions before it could decipher what he was trying to say.

"Frequency 43223. . . . My body travels to distant stars, but my soul never leaves the Fleet. . . . Frequency 43223. . . . My body travels to distant stars, but my soul never leaves the Fleet. . . . "

He kept repeating the same phrase over and over, his voice rising and falling in a trembling, terrified warble. Grayson crouched down close to him, though he was careful not to touch the infected flesh.

"It's okay," he said softly, knowing his translator would repeat the words in the quarian's own language. "Nobody's going to hurt you now. It's okay."

The quarian didn't seem to hear him, but continued babbling, his words coming more and more quickly as his broken mind spewed out the information in a desperate attempt to avoid continued torture.

"It's over now," Grayson shushed, hoping to calm the frantic captive down. "It's over."

His words seemed to have the opposite effect, as the quarian began to thrash against the bonds holding his wrists and ankles. He let out a cry of frustration, then began to sputter and cough. A fine mist of black, foul-smelling ichor spewed from his lips and the gash in his cheek, causing Grayson to jump back to avoid the spray.

The fit ended with the quarian letting out a series of hitching, gurgling sighs, and then he finally went still and silent. Steeling himself against the fecund stench that was now emanating from the body, Grayson got close enough to verify that the quarian had stopped breathing.

He left the body in the blackness of the cellar and climbed the stairs back to the ground floor. Closing and bolting the door behind him, he then scrounged up everything of value he could carry. Fifteen minutes later he was behind the wheel of Pel's second rover, making his way down the unfamiliar streets of Omega with a pack full of supplies and the shotgun resting on the seat beside him.

Staying focused on his true purpose allowed him to ignore the little voice in the back of his skull telling him to track down a dust dealer for a quick hit. Instead, he set off to locate a transmit station so he could link into the comm network and send a message off to the Illusive Man, telling him everything that had happened.

Pel had turned his back on Cerberus, but Grayson was still loyal to the cause . . . and he knew they could help him find Gillian again.

EIGHTEEN

Six hours had passed since Kahlee and the others had escaped the warehouse on Omega.

Lemm had managed to find the current location of the quarian flotilla by linking into the comm network and scanning the news updates. The Migrant Fleet was passing through a remote volus-controlled system near the edges of Council Space. According to the news reports, several volus diplomats were petitioning the Citadel to do everything in its power to hasten the quarians' departure.

Kahlee doubted their political appeals would have any noticeable impact. The Citadel was still coming to grips with the changes wrought by Saren and his geth army. Their primary focus was on eliminating the few remaining pockets of geth resistance scattered across the galaxy; an objective being pursued by an emergency coalition force headed up by humanity and the Alliance. Once the geth were pushed back beyond the Perseus Veil, she suspected the next order of business would be to address the restructuring of the Council, along with the massive political fallout that would entail. The last thing anyone on the Citadel wanted to deal with was the Migrant Fleet.

Kahlee knew that even during the long period of interstellar peace that had preceded humanity's arrival, the various species of the galaxy tended to view the activities of the Fleet as little more than a minor inconvenience or nuisance . . . until they passed through one of their systems. Then the most effective course of action was to offer unwanted resources in the form of decommissioned ships, raw materials, and spare parts to the quarian Admiralty.

The quarians allowed themselves to be bought off with such gifts, with the understanding the flotilla would quickly move on to become a thorn in someone else's side. Kahlee hated to pass judgment, but she couldn't help but see it as the interstellar equivalent of panhandling.

And in another forty hours we'll be hoping to join up with them, she thought, shaking her head in disbelief at the course of events over the last few days.

Lemm had plotted their course into the navigation, then gone to lay down in the sleeper cabin in the back once they'd made the jump to FTL flight. Kahlee still had plenty of questions for him—like how he knew who she was—but in light of all he had done for them, she could afford to be patient. She'd give him a few hours to rest and start recovering from his injury before she began peppering him with questions. Besides, she was anxious to check on Gillian now that the girl had woken up.

The first words out of her mouth upon gaining consciousness had been, "I'm hungry." Hendel had easily solved that problem by preparing a double-portioned serving for her from the ship's rations.

With the ship's navigation following the preprogrammed course, there was no need for anyone to keep an eye on the helm. So the three of them—Kahlee, Gillian, and Hendel—had gathered in the passenger cabin, the two adults seated side by side facing her, while the girl ate from the hard plastic tray of food on her lap.

She was just now finishing the last of her meal. As she had done back at the Academy, she chewed with focused determination, never pausing or breaking rhythm as she steadily consumed her food one methodical bite at a time. Kahlee, however, noticed she didn't stick to her normal pattern of taking only one single mouthful from a dish before moving on to the next item on her plate. In fact, she didn't even touch the apple crumble dessert until everything else was gone.

Once she was done she carefully set the tray on the seat beside her and spoke for the second time since regaining consciousness.

"Where's my dad?" There was no emotion in her voice; it was flat and monotone, like the primitive speech synthesizers from the twentieth century.

There was no simple answer to this question. Fortunately, she and Hendel had discussed what to say while Gillian was still sleeping off the drugs their captors had given her.

"He had some business to take care of," Kahlee lied, figuring the truth would be too much for the girl to handle right now. "He's going to catch up with us later, but for now it's just you, me, and Hendel, okay?"

"How will he find us if we took his ship?"

"He'll find another ship," she assured the girl.

Gillian stared at her and squinted her eyes slightly, as if she suspected deception and was trying to peer through her to the truth. After a few seconds of this she nodded, accepting the situation.

"Are we going back to the school?"

"Not yet," Hendel told her. "We're going to meet up with some other ships. Quarian. Do you remember when you studied the quarians last year in history class?"

"They made the geth," she said simply.

"Yes," Kahlee admitted, hoping this wasn't the sole fact she associated with the species of their rescuer. "Do you remember anything else about them?"

"Driven from their home system by the geth nearly three centuries ago, most quarians now live aboard the Migrant Fleet, a flotilla of fifty thousand vessels ranging in size from passenger shuttles to mobile space stations," she answered, and Kahlee realized she was reciting the entry verbatim from her history e-book.

"Home to seventeen million quarians, the flotilla understandably has scarce resources," the girl continued. "Because of this, each quarian must go on a rite of passage known as the Pilgrimage when they come of age. They leave the Fleet and only return once they have found something of value—"

"That's okay, Gillian," Hendel said gently, cutting her off before she gave them the entire chapter.

"Why are we meeting a quarian ship?"

Kahlee wasn't sure how much Gillian remembered about the violent greeting they had received upon landing at Omega, so she was intentionally vague in her answer. "We met a quarian named Lemm while you were sleeping. He's going to help us hide from some people who are trying to find us."

"Cerberus," she said, and the adults cast a nervous glance at each other, uncertain where she had picked up the name.

"That's right," Hendel said after a moment. "They want to hurt you, and we won't let that happen."

Gillian frowned and bit her lip. She was silent for several long seconds before she asked the same question that had been bothering Kahlee. "Why is Lemm helping us?"

Neither of them had a ready answer for that one.

"I guess we'll have to ask him when he wakes up," Kahlee finally admitted.

Fortunately, they didn't have long to wait. Less than an hour later she heard the uneven, clumping steps of Lemm coming down the hall. His leg was covered by a hermetically sealed, hard-shelled boot that protected and supported everything from the tips of his toes up to the joint of his knee. He was still wearing his mask and enviro-suit, of course; Kahlee suspected he wouldn't take them off again until they reached the flotilla.

"Lemm," she said as he entered the passenger cabin and stopped. "This is Gillian. Gillian, this is Lemm."

The quarian stepped forward and bowed slightly, extending his gloved hand in a gesture of greeting common to both species. To Kahlee's amazement Gillian reached out and shook it.

"Nice to meet you," she said.

"Nice to meet you, too. I'm glad to see you up and about," he replied, releasing her hand and sitting gingerly down in the seat beside her, facing Kahlee and Hendel.

"Why are you helping us?" Gillian asked him.

Kahlee winced. They hadn't been able to warn the quarian about Gillian's condition, and she hoped Lemm wouldn't take offense at the girl's lack of tact.

Fortunately, he took her question in stride. "You get right to the point, don't you?" he said with a laugh from behind his mask.

"I'm autistic," Gillian replied, again with absolutely no hint of emotion.

It wasn't clear if Lemm fully understood the meaning of the word, but Kahlee figured he was smart enough to grasp the basic concept. Before he could formulate a response, Gillian repeated her earlier question.

"Why are you helping us?"

"I'm a little curious about that myself," Hendel added, leaning back in his chair and bringing his right leg up so he could rest it on his left knee.

"I'm on my Pilgrimage," the quarian began. "I was on the world of Kenuk when I met two crew members from the *Bavea,* a scout ship for the cruiser *Idenna.* They told me another scout ship, the *Cyniad,* had gone to Omega to broker a deal and not returned.

"I came to Omega in search of the *Cyniad* crew. I hoped I could rescue them, or at least discover their fate. On Omega another quarian, a man named Golo, told me the *Cyniad* had arranged a deal with a small group of humans.

"I broke into their warehouse hoping to find the crew. Instead, I found you."

"But why risk your life to save us?" Hendel asked.

"I suspected your captors were slavers. No species deserves to be bought and sold. It was my moral obligation to free you."

Kahlee had no doubt he was being sincere, but she also knew there was more to the story.

"You recognized me," she said. "You knew my name."

"The name Kahlee Sanders has become very well known among my people in the past few months," he admitted. "And I recognized your appearance from an old image we picked up off the Extranet. You have hardly changed in eighteen years."

The pieces began to click together in Kahlee's mind. Eighteen years ago she had been involved in an illegal Alliance AI project headed by a man named Dr. Shu Qian. But Qian had betrayed the project, forcing Kahlee into a desperate flight for her life. It was how she had met Captain Anderson . . . and a turian Spectre named Saren Arterius.

"It's because of my connection to Saren," she said, looking for confirmation.

"Your connection to him, and his connection to the geth," Lemm clarified. "The geth revolt was the single most significant event in the history of my people. They drove us into exile; an army of synthetic machines—ruthless, relentless, and unstoppable.

"But Saren led an army of geth against the Citadel. He found some way to make them follow him. He found a way to control them and bend them to his will. Is it any wonder we are so interested in him, and anyone who has ever had anything to do with him?"

"Kahlee?" Hendel asked, uncrossing his legs and sitting up straight, his muscles tensing. "What's he talking about?"

"Back when I was with the Alliance, Saren was the Spectre sent to investigate a research project I worked on." She had never really talked about what had happened on that mission with anyone other than Anderson, and she didn't want to start now.

"How did the quarians find out about all this?" she demanded. Her voice was rising; she was beginning to get a little bit scared, and that in turn made her angry. "Those Alliance files were classified."

"Any information can be acquired for the right price," the quarian reminded her. It was hard to read his expression behind his mask, but his tone seemed calm. "And as I said, we have an understandable obsession with the geth.

"Once we knew Saren was leading their armies we began to gather all the information we could on him: personal history, past missions. When it was discovered he had close dealings with a human scientist working on an illegal AI research project, it was only natural we would delve into the scientist's background as well."

"Illegal AI?" Hendel muttered, shaking his head in disbelief at what he was hearing.

"That was a long time ago," Kahlee told the quarian.

"The Captain of the *Idenna* will want to speak with you."

"I can't help you," she insisted. "I don't know anything about Saren or the geth."

"You might know more than you think," Lemm replied.

"You make it sound like we don't have any choice in the matter," Hendel noted, his voice dark.

"You are not prisoners," the quarian assured them. "If I take you to the Fleet it will be as honored guests. If you do not wish to go, we can change course right now. I can take you to any world you choose.

"However, if we do join up with the Fleet, it is possible they won't allow you to leave right away," he admitted. "My people can be overly cautious when it comes to protecting our ships."

The security chief glanced over at Kahlee. "It's your call. You're the celebrity."

"This will end your Pilgrimage, won't it?" she wanted to know. "Meeting me is your gift to the captain."

He nodded, but didn't speak.

"If I don't do this, you can't go back to the Fleet yet, can you?"

"I will be forced to continue my journey until I find something of value to bring back to my people. But I will not force you to do this. The gift we bring must not be won through causing harm or suffering to another—quarian or nonquarian."

"It's okay," she said after thinking on it. "I'll talk to them. We owe you our lives, and this is the least I can do. Besides," she added, "it's not like we'll be safer anywhere else."

* * *

Forty hours later they dropped from FTL travel less then 500,000 kilometers from the Migrant Fleet. Lemm was once again occupying the pilot's chair, with Kahlee seated beside him. Hendel was in his now typical spot, standing just inside the door heading back to the passenger cabin, and even Gillian had come up to join them in the close confines, standing directly behind the quarian's chair.

The girl seemed to have taken to Lemm. She had started following him around, or just sitting and staring at him whenever he sat down or caught a few hours of sleep. Gillian didn't initiate conversations with him, but she answered promptly whenever he spoke to her. It was unusual, but encouraging, to see her responding so well to someone, so neither Kahlee nor Hendel had tried to stop her when she'd come up to the cockpit to join them.

The Migrant Fleet, with its thousands upon thousands of ships flying in tight formation, showed up on the nav screens as a single, large red blob as they approached. Lemm punched up their thrusters, and they began to move steadily toward the flotilla.

When they reached a range of just under 150,000 kilometers the nav screen showed several smaller ships detaching themselves from the main armada, arcing around on an intercept trajectory with their own course.

"Navy patrols challenge every ship approaching the Fleet," Lemm had informed them earlier. "Heavily armed. They'll open fire on any vessel that doesn't identify itself or refuses to turn back."

From what Kahlee knew of quarian society, their reaction was completely understandable. Deep in the heart of the Migrant Fleet floated the three enormous Liveships: gigantic agricultural vessels that supplied and stored the majority of the food for the seventeen million individuals living on the flotilla. If an enemy ever damaged or destroyed even one of the Liveships the inevitable result would be a catastrophic famine, and the grim prospect of slow starvation for millions of quarians.

Lemm responded to the quickly approaching patrol by thumbing open a comm channel. A few minutes later it crackled with a voice speaking in quarian, though of course the tiny translator Kahlee wore as a pendant on her necklace automatically converted it into English.

"You are entering a restricted area. Identify."

"This is Lemm'Shal nar Tesleya, seeking permission to rejoin the Fleet."

"Verify authorization."

Lemm had previously explained to them that most quarians who left on their Pilgrimage tended to return to the flotilla in newly acquired ships. With no records of the registration or call signs for the vessel, the only way to confirm the identity of those on board was through a unique code phrase system. Before leaving on his right of passage, the captain of the *Tesleya*, Lemm's birth ship, had made him memorize two specific phrases. One, the alert phrase, was a warning that something was wrong, such as hostiles on the ship forcing the pilot to try and infiltrate the Fleet. The alert phrase would cause the heavily armed patrols to open fire on their vessel immediately. The second phrase, the all clear, would get them safely past the patrols, where they would join the densely packed mass of other ships, shuttles, and cruisers.

"The quest for knowledge sent me away from my people; now the discovery of wisdom has brought me back."

There was a long pause as the patrol relayed the exchange back to the *Tesleya*, somewhere deep inside the flotilla, for confirmation. Kahlee's palms were sweating, and her mouth felt dry. She swallowed hard in the silence and held her breath. Grayson's shuttle was built for speed and long-distance travel; it had no weapons, no GARDIAN defense systems, and virtually no armor on its hull. If Lemm had mixed up the alert and all-clear codes, or if something else went wrong, the patrol would tear them apart in seconds.

"The *Tesleya* welcomes you home, Lemm" came the reply, and Kahlee let her breath out in a long, low sigh of relief.

"Tell them it's good to be back," he responded, then added, "I need to contact the *Idenna*."

Again there was a long pause, but this time Kahlee didn't feel the same unbearable tension as she waited.

"Sending coordinates and hailing frequencies for the *Idenna*," they finally replied.

Lemm verified receipt of the message, then disconnected the comm channel. They continued their approach to the Fleet, and the single giant red blob on the nav screens became countless tiny red pixels jammed so close together Kahlee wondered how the vessels they represented avoided crashing into each other.

Moving with a steady, expert hand their quarian pilot maneuvered them into the mass of ships, working his way slowly toward where the *Idenna* floated along with the rest of quarian society. Twenty minutes later he flicked the comm channels open again and sent out a hailing call.

"This is Lemm'Shal nar Tesleya requesting permission to dock with the *Idenna*."

"This is the *Idenna*. Your request is granted. Proceed to docking bay three."

Lemm's trifingered hands flew over the controls, making the necessary adjustments to bring them in. Two minutes later they felt the slight bump as docking clamps fastened onto their ship to hold it in place, followed by a sharp clang as a universal airlock connected to the airlock of their own ship.

"I'm requesting a security and quarantine team," Lemm said into the comm channel. "Make sure they wear their enviro-suits. The ship is not clean."

"Request confirmed. The teams are on the way."

The quarian had warned them about this, too. The quarantine team was a necessary step whenever a new vessel was first brought into the flotilla. The quarians couldn't risk bacteria, viruses, or other impurities from former nonquarian owners accidentally being released into the flotilla.

Similarly, requesting a security team to inspect your ship upon first arrival was considered a common courtesy among the quarian people—it showed you had nothing to hide. Typically, the team would come aboard, introductions would be exchanged, and no search would ever actually be conducted.

However, this situation was as far from typical as it could get. In the three hundred years of their exile, no nonquarian had ever set foot on a flotilla ship. As much as Lemm wanted to bring Kahlee before the captain of the *Idenna*, it simply wasn't in his power. And the unexpected sight of humans on a ship that had slipped past the Fleet's patrols was likely to cause shock and alarm.

There was no protocol for this unprecedented event, but Lemm had explained that there were procedures that could be followed to minimize the risk to both the crew of the *Idenna* and the humans on board the shuttle.

"Let's go meet our guests," Lemm said, standing up awkwardly on his injured leg. "Remember, just stay calm and everything will be fine. We just need to take it slow."

The four of them made their way into the passenger cabin, and the three humans sat down in the seats. Lemm made his way to the airlock to greet the security and quarantine teams coming on board.

Again, Kahlee felt the stress of being forced to sit and wait. What if Lemm was wrong about how the other quarians would react to their presence? What if somebody saw the humans and panicked? They were putting a lot of faith in someone who was, technically, not even an adult yet in the eyes of his own people.

I think he's earned a bit of trust after everything he's done for us.

Kahlee couldn't argue with the infallible logic of her own mind, but it did little to quell her fears. She could hear voices coming from the airlock, though they were too far away to pick up what was being said. One of the voices was rising, either in anger or fear. Someone—it sounded like Lemm, though she couldn't be sure—was trying to calm the upset speaker down. And then there were footsteps coming through the airlock and into the ship.

A few seconds later four masked quarians, one female and three males, entered the passenger cabin, armed with assault rifles. The one in front, the female, actually did a double take on seeing the humans, then turned back over her shoulder to speak to Lemm, who was standing just behind them.

"I thought you were joking," she said. "I really thought you were joking."

"This is unbelievable," one of the others muttered.

"What were you thinking?" the female, clearly the one in charge, wanted to know. "They could be spies!"

"They're not spies," Lemm insisted. "Don't you recognize the woman? Look closely."

The three humans sat silently as the female quarian stepped up to get a better look. "No . . . it can't be. What's your name, human?"

"Kahlee Sanders."

There was an involuntary gasp from the other quarians, and Kahlee thought she heard Lemm chuckle.

"My name is Isli'Feyy vas Idenna," the female quarian said, bowing her head in what seemed to be a gesture of respect. "It's an honor to meet you. These are my ship mates, Ugho'Qaar vas Idenna, Erdra'Zando vas Idenna, and Seeto'Hodda nar Idenna."

Kahlee bowed her head in return. "These are my friends, Hendel Mitra and Gillian Grayson. We are honored to be here."

"I brought Kahlee here so she could speak to the

captain," Lemm interjected. "This meeting is my gift to the *Idenna.*"

Isli glanced over at Lemm, then turned her mask back to Kahlee.

"Forgive me, Kahlee Sanders, but I cannot permit you to board the *Idenna.* That decision must come from the captain, and he will want to consult with the ship's civilian council before deciding."

"So what are you saying?" Hendel asked, judging the mood to be calm enough for others to join into the conversation. "We have to leave?"

"We cannot allow you to leave yet, either," Isli told him after a moment's consideration. "Not without the captain's approval. Your shuttle must stay here in the dock, and you must stay aboard your own vessel until a ruling is reached on this matter."

"How long will that take?" Kahlee asked.

"A few days, I would guess," Isli answered.

"We're going to need some supplies," Hendel said. "Food, primarily. Human food."

"And they will need suitable enviro-suits when the captain finally decides to let them onto the ship," Lemm added, taking the optimistic view.

"We will make every effort to accommodate your needs," Isli told them. "We don't have any stores of nonquarian food aboard the *Idenna,* but we will contact the other ships to see what we can find."

She turned once more to Lemm. "You will have to come with me. The captain will want to speak to you in person." Then she turned back to the humans. "Remember, you are not to leave the confines of this vessel. Either Ugho or Seeto will be posted outside your airlock at all times. If you need anything, they can help you."

And with that, the quarians, including Lemm, left them alone. A minute later they heard a loud clang as the door to the *Idenna*'s external airlock slammed shut, sealing them inside the shuttle.

"Hmph," Hendel grunted, "that's a hell of a way to treat a celebrity."

NINETEEN

Even with all he had done for Cerberus, even after hundreds of missions and almost sixteen years of service, Grayson could count on one hand the number of times he had met the Illusive Man face-to-face.

As charismatic and impressive as he appeared over a vid screen, he was far more imposing in person. There was a seriousness about him, an air of authority. He possessed a cool confidence that made it seem as if he was completely in control of everything that unfolded around him. There was unmistakable intelligence in his steely eyes; coupled with his silver-gray hair and his daunting presence, it gave the sense that he had wisdom far beyond that of ordinary men.

This impression was further enhanced by the surroundings of the office the Illusive Man used for his personal meetings. The room was decorated with a classic dark-wood finish, giving it a serious and subdued, almost somber, feel. The lights were soft and a little dim, leaving the corners obscured by shadows. Six black meeting chairs surrounded a frosted glass table on the far side of the room, allowing him to accommodate larger groups.

This meeting, however, was a private session. Grayson was seated in one of the two oversized leather chairs in the center of the office, directly across from the Man himself. He'd noticed a pair of guards posted just outside the door as he entered the room, but inside the office it appeared to be just the two of them.

"We haven't found any hard evidence to back up your story yet," the Illusive Man said, leaning forward in his own chair with his elbows resting on his knees and his hands clasped before him.

His features were sympathetic and his voice understanding, but there was a hard edge just below the surface. Grayson once again found him to be compelling yet intimidating at the same time. He made it so that you *wanted* to confide in him. Yet if you chose to lie, his eyes seemed to say, he would know . . . and there would be grave consequences.

Fortunately for Grayson, the truth was on his side. "I stand by my report. I pulled Gillian from the Ascension Project as ordered. During the mission, I was forced to alter the plan because of interference from Kahlee Sanders and Hendel Mitra, who insisted on coming with Gillian. I made arrangements with Pel to deal with them, but when I arrived on Omega he imprisoned us all so he could sell us to the Collectors."

The Illusive Man nodded as if agreeing with every word. "Yes, of course. But I'm still not clear on what happened next."

The question was innocent enough, but Grayson recognized it as a potential trap. Within two days of receiving his message, Cerberus had sent an extraction team to bring him from Omega back to Earth to meet with the organization's leader. Considering Pel and his entire team were dead—some of them by his hand—it was an invitation he wasn't given the option of refusing.

Upon landing they had hustled him into a waiting car and taken him directly to the nondescript office tower that served as the corporate headquarters of Cord-Hislop Aerospace, the legitimate business front for Cerberus. Virtually the entire building was staffed with everyday men and women engaged in the business of manufacturing and selling ships and shuttles. None of them had any idea they were really working for an anonymous individual who inhabited the secure penthouse at the very top of the building, above the privately accessed suites of the more well known corporate executives.

Grayson had been itching for a sand hit during the seemingly endless elevator ride to the top of Cord-Hislop. But it would have been sheer idiocy to dust up before a meeting as important—and dangerous—as this one. He had one chance to convince the Illusive Man that Pel was a traitor. If he failed, he likely wouldn't leave the building alive, meaning he'd never see Gillian again.

"I've told you everything I know about Pel's death. An unknown person or persons, probably quarian, broke into the warehouse. I presume they helped the others escape. Most of Pel's team were killed during the escape. During the battle I broke out of my cell. I killed Pel and one surviving member of his team myself. Then I contacted you."

The Illusive Man nodded again, then stood up slowly. At just over six feet tall, he towered above Grayson, still seated in his chair.

"Paul," he said softly, gazing down on him from on high, "are you addicted to red sand?"

Don't lie. He wouldn't be asking if he didn't already know.

"I wasn't high on this mission. I wasn't hallucinating when I shot Pel, and I didn't kill him and his team to cover up some mistake I made while stoned. I just did what was necessary."

The Illusive Man turned his back to him and took a step away, pondering his words. Without turning back to face Grayson, he asked, "Do you care for Gillian?"

"Yes," he admitted. "I care for her as much as any father cares for his child. You told me to raise her as my own, so I did. It was the only way to get her to trust me." *And you already knew the answer to that question, too.*

The Illusive Man turned back to face him again, but remained standing. "Do you ever have doubts about what we do here at Cerberus, Paul? Do you ever feel conflicted over what's been done to Gillian?"

Grayson didn't speak for several moments, trying to carefully formulate his response. In the end, he couldn't find the words to answer while evading the question, so he replied as honestly as he could.

"It tears me apart whenever I think about it." Then he added with conviction, "But I understand why it must be done. I see how it serves the greater good. I believe in our cause."

The Illusive Man raised one eyebrow in surprise, tilting his head to fix his gaze on the man sitting before—and beneath—him.

"Your former partner would never have given me

an answer as honest as yours." Grayson wasn't sure if the words were meant as a compliment or an insult.

"I'm not like Pel. He made a deal with the Collectors. He betrayed humanity. He betrayed Cerberus. He betrayed you."

Grayson felt a small hint of relief when the Illusive Man sat down again.

"We've had no reports on your shuttle's location since it left Omega. Not a single sighting at any space station or colony in either Council Space or the Terminus Systems."

"I think I know why," Grayson announced, exhaling a breath he didn't even know he was holding as he played his trump card. "I think they're hiding amid the quarian flotilla."

Again, the Illusive Man raised an eyebrow in surprise. "I'm curious as to what led you to this rather unlikely conclusion."

He didn't have a good answer. His theory was based on a few pieces of highly circumstantial evidence: the shotgun he'd found at the warehouse, the prisoner in the basement, and the unshakable certainty that he just *knew* where Gillian was.

"Instinct," he finally replied. "I feel it in my gut. The quarians took my daughter."

"If they did," his boss replied, "then she is beyond our reach."

Grayson shook his head, silently refuting the other man's statement. "I found Pel's mission reports in the warehouse. I know he was gathering information to infiltrate the Migrant Fleet, and I think that's what drew the quarian rescue team to the warehouse. But they left one of their own behind; a prisoner Pel had tortured to the brink of insanity. He gave me a transmission frequency and what I believe to be some kind of pass code before he died.

"Pel's reports also mentioned a quarian scout ship he'd acquired, the *Cyniad*. I think we can load a team onto the ship and use the frequency and code to get inside the flotilla and get Gillian back."

The Illusive Man didn't try to deny the purpose of Pel's mission. Instead, he considered Grayson's plan, most likely weighing the risks against the potential rewards. "It could work . . . assuming you're right about the quarians taking Gillian."

He stood up again, but this time the action seemed to signal an end to their meeting, as if he'd gotten what he wanted out of Grayson.

"I will have some of our operatives in the Terminus Systems see if they can find any information to support your theory. If they do, we'll send an extraction team to get her out.

"We have a quarian contact on Omega who could help us," he added. "I will give him the code to see if he can verify the authenticity."

Grayson had achieved half of what he wanted from this meeting: Cerberus was sending troops to bring Gillian back. But that wasn't enough for him this time; he was done letting others control his daughter's life while he sat idly by.

"I want to be part of the extraction team."

The Illusive Man simply shook his head. "The mission will require exacting precision and flawless execution. The smallest mistake could put the entire team at risk. And I'm concerned your feelings for Gillian have compromised your judgment."

"I need to be part of this," Grayson insisted. "I need to get my daughter back."

"I give you my word no harm will come to her," the Illusive Man assured him, his voice slipping into a low, soothing register. "We'll do everything to keep her safe. You know how important she is to us."

That's what I'm counting on.

Gillian represented over a decade of intense Cerberus research. Tens of thousands of hours and billions of credits had been invested in his little girl in the hope she would one day become the key to unlocking new frontiers in the field of human biotics. The Illusive Man wanted Gillian back just as much as Grayson, though for different reasons. And that gave the father something few people ever had when dealing with the Illusive Man: leverage.

"You don't have any other choice," Grayson warned him, delivering his ultimatum in a sure, steady tone. "I won't give up the pass code. Not until I'm on a ship heading right into the heart of the Migrant Fleet. If you want to get Gillian back, then I'm your only shot."

It was a dangerous gamble. They could always torture him for the information, and their techniques would make the methods Pel had used on his quarian prisoner seem merciful by comparison. But Grayson could still be useful, especially when it came to Gillian. Cerberus knew of his daughter's condition; they knew she could be unresponsive to strangers. Her father was worth keeping around . . . or so he hoped.

"You are very dedicated to her," the Illusive Man said with a smile that didn't quite hide the rage beneath it. "I hope that does not become a problem later on."

"So I can go?"

The Illusive Man nodded. "I will set up a meeting with Golo, our quarian contact on Omega."

He motioned with one hand and Grayson stood up, fighting to keep his elation well hidden. It was quite likely there would be repercussions for his defiance somewhere down the road—the Illusive Man had a long, long memory. But he didn't care about that now. He was willing to pay any price if it meant he could get his daughter back.

TWENTY

"Remember what I told you, Gillian," Hendel said. "Get the image in your mind, then clench your fist and concentrate."

Gillian followed Hendel's instruction, scrunching up her face as she focused all her attention on the pillow at the foot of the bed they were sitting cross-legged on. Kahlee watched them with interest from the other side of the bedroom, leaning against the frame of the open door.

Though Kahlee wasn't biotic, she was familiar with the techniques Hendel was teaching. The Ascension Project used simple biomechanical feedback, such as clenching a fist or thrusting a hand high into the air, as a tool for unleashing biotic power. Associating basic muscle movements with the necessary complex thought patterns created a triggering mechanism for specific biotic feats. Through practice and training, the corresponding physical action became a catalyst for the required mental processes, increasing both the speed and strength of the desired biotic effect.

"You can do it, Gillian," Hendel urged. "Just like we practiced."

The girl began to grind her teeth, her fist clenched so tight it began to tremble.

"Good girl," Hendel encouraged. "Now throw your arm forward and imagine the pillow flying across the room."

Kahlee thought she saw a faint shimmering in the air, like the rippling heat rising off a sun-scorched blacktop. Then the pillow launched itself from the bed, hurtling toward Kahlee and smacking her square in the face. It didn't hurt, but it did catch her off-guard.

Gillian laughed—a nervous bark of excitement and surprise. Even Hendel cracked a small smile. Kahlee scowled at them both in mock exasperation.

"Your reaction time's a little slower than it used to be," Hendel commented.

"I think I better leave you two alone before I catch a lamp in the teeth," she replied before exiting the room and making her way aft toward the seats in the passenger cabin.

Three days had passed since their shuttle had docked with the *Idenna,* and they were still waiting for the captain to give them clearance to come aboard his ship. During that time they had been well looked after, but Kahlee was starting to develop a serious case of cabin fever.

Gillian and Hendel had fought against the boredom by focusing on developing her biotic talents. She had made astounding progress in an incredibly short time. Whether that was from all the one-on-one training Hendel was giving her, or if it was because her outburst in the cafeteria back at the Academy had broken through some kind of internal mental barrier,

Kahlee couldn't say. And though she was glad to see Gillian making progress, there was little she could do to help.

It was clear, however, that Gillian was coping surprisingly well with their situation. She had always had good and bad days; the severity of her condition had an irregular ebb and flow. Over the past several days there were still times when Gillian seemed to simply zone out or disconnect from what was happening around her, but overall she seemed more consistently aware and engaged. Again, Kahlee wasn't sure of the exact reason. It could be the fact that she was receiving far more personal attention than she ever had at the Academy. It might have had something to do with their inability to leave the tight confines of the shuttle; Gillian was intimately familiar with every square inch of the ship. She likely felt safe and protected while on board, as opposed to being exposed and vulnerable while wandering the classrooms and halls of the Grissom Academy. Or it simply could have been the fact that she had to interact with fewer people—apart from Hendel and Kahlee, the only visitor to the shuttle had been Lemm.

He stopped by once or twice a day to give them updates on what was happening aboard the *Idenna,* and share any important news coming in from the rest of the vessels in the Fleet. With almost fifty thousand ships—many of them frigates, shuttles, and small personal craft—there was a constant stream of information and traffic within the flotilla.

Fortunately, in the quarians' endless efforts to seek out resources for their society, there were also dozens of vessels arriving and departing from nearby worlds on a daily basis. As promised, the *Idenna* had requested from the other vessels food stores that were suitable for humans, as well as human enviro-suits. One day after their arrival supplies began to come in, and the shuttle's hold was now stocked to overflowing.

Not surprisingly, the request had set off suspicions and rumors among the rest of the Fleet. As Lemm explained it, that was one of the reasons the decision was taking so long. The captain of each ship was given absolute authority over his or her vessel, provided that authority wasn't abused and didn't endanger the rest of the flotilla. Apparently the harboring of nonquarians definitely fell beyond the scope of what was permitted.

In the wake of the *Idenna*'s strange request for human-centric supplies, the Conclave and the Admiralty—the respective civilian and military leaders of the quarian government—had become involved in the discussions of what was to be done. Ultimately, Lemm had explained to Kahlee, the final decision would be given to the *Idenna*'s captain, but not before everyone else had weighed in with their opinions and recommendations.

To pass the time between Lemm's visits, Kahlee had begun speaking with the quarians posted at the airlock as their guards. Ugho, the older of the two, was polite, but somewhat cold. He responded to her questions with short, almost clipped, answers, and she soon gave up bothering to speak with him while he was on duty.

Seeto, however, was the exact opposite. Kahlee guessed he was about Lemm's age, though hidden behind his mask and enviro-suit her only clue was the "nar" identifier in his name. But for some reason Seeto seemed more naïve and youthful than their rescuer. Lemm spending several months away from the flotilla on his Pilgrimage no doubt had something to do with that, but Seeto also struck her as having a childlike exuberance about him that she simply chalked up to an excitable, outgoing personality.

She learned very quickly that he was a talker. One or two questions from her were all it would take to get the words flowing, and then they came out in a gushing river. Kahlee didn't mind, however. It helped pass the time, and she had learned a lot about the quarians in general, and the *Idenna* in particular, from Seeto.

At only thirty years old, he had explained, the *Idenna* was still considered a new ship. Understandable, considering some of the ships in the flotilla were manufactured over three centuries ago, before the quarians' defeat and exile at the hands of the geth. Over time they had been upgraded, repaired, and retrofitted to the point they hardly resembled the original vessel anymore, but they were still seen as less reliable than newer ships.

Seeto also told her that the *Idenna* was a medium-sized cruiser, large enough to have a seat on the Conclave, the civilian board that advised the Admiralty on setting Fleet policy and passed rulings on specific disputes and decisions within the flotilla. She learned that there were 693 men, women, and children who called *Idenna* home—694 if Lemm's proposed gift from his Pilgrimage was ultimately accepted by the captain and he joined their crew. Kahlee was astonished by that number; in the Alliance, a medium-sized cruiser would have a crew of 70 or 80 at the most. In her mind's eye she envisioned the inhabitants of the *Idenna* living in squalid, overcrowded misery.

The more she had talked with Seeto, the more comfortable he'd become. He'd told her about Ysin'Mal vas Idenna, the ship's captain. Ship captains tended to be men and women bound by tradition; Mal, however, was generally regarded as an aggressive proponent of change and progress. He'd even, Seeto had confided in a low whisper, put forth a proposal for the flotilla to start sending out cruisers on long-term exploratory missions to uncharted regions of space, in the hopes of discovering uninhabited, life-bearing worlds the quarians could settle as their own.

This particular view had often brought him into conflict with the other ship captains and the Conclave, who believed the quarians needed to remain united in the Migrant Fleet if they were to ensure their survival. However, from the way the young quarian spoke, it was clear to Kahlee that Seeto supported his captain's position, rather than common convention.

As she passed through the passenger cabin on her way to the airlock, she hoped it would be the more interesting Seeto, and not the stoic Ugho, who was standing on duty outside. Still forbidden to leave the ship, she was about to use the airlock's intercom to contact the guard outside and ask him to come aboard when the seals on the door suddenly released on their own.

Surprised, she stumbled back from the door as it opened and a group of seven quarians entered.

Kahlee felt a brief moment of alarm as they marched onto the shuttle, but when she realized none of them had their weapons drawn she relaxed.

She recognized both Seeto and Ugho among them. And she thought the one standing at the head of the group was Isli, the leader of the security patrol that had first greeted them. The other four she didn't know.

"The captain has agreed to meet with you," Isli said by way of greeting, confirming her identity.

About damn time, Kahlee thought. Out loud she only asked, "When?"

"Now," Isli told her. "We will escort you to the bridge to see him. You will need to wear your enviro-suit, of course."

"Okay. Let me tell Hendel and Gillian where I'm going."

"They need to come, too," Isli insisted. "The captain wants to meet with all of you. Lemm is already there waiting."

Kahlee didn't like the idea of forcing Gillian to leave the shuttle and dragging her through the crowded decks of the *Idenna,* but given the circumstances she didn't see how she could refuse.

Hendel shared her concern when she told him, but Gillian didn't seem bothered by the idea. Five minutes later, once they had all donned their enviro-suits, they were off. Isli, Ugho, and Seeto went with them as their escorts, while the other four quarians stayed behind.

"They need to sterilize your shuttle," Isli told them. "It's better if you aren't on the vessel while they're working."

Kahlee wondered if they were really decontaminating the vessel, or if this was just an opportunity for the quarians to thoroughly search the shuttle from top to bottom without offending them. Not that it made a difference; they had nothing to hide.

Isli led them through the ship while Ugho marched silently along beside her. Seeto fell back with the humans so he could provide the occasional comment or explanation on what they were seeing during the journey.

"This is the *Idenna*'s trading deck," he said as they passed from the docking bays into what would have served as the cargo hold on an Alliance vessel.

The room was packed with quarians, all in their enviro-suits, milling about. Each one carried a bag or backpack. Storage lockers lined the walls. Most of them were open, revealing the contents to be a mishmash of mundane items, from clothes to cooking utensils. Similar piles of goods were loaded into large, open-topped steel crates and oversized metal storage containers scattered haphazardly about the floor, filling the room except for the narrow aisles that ran back and forth between them.

The quarians were moving from container to container and locker to locker. They would rummage through them, occasionally picking up an item and examining it before either keeping their find or putting the item back and resuming their search.

"Anyone who has unneeded goods and items stores them here," Seeto explained, "so others can come and take what they need."

"You mean you just let anyone take anything from anyone else?" Hendel asked in surprise.

"Not if someone else is using it," Seeto said, his voice making it clear that, to him, the answer was blatantly obvious.

"But if you're not using it, you're just supposed to bring it here and give it away for free to someone else?"

"What else would you do with it?" the young quarian asked, the question making it clear that the concept of selling surplus merchandise to your neighbor was completely foreign to him.

"What if somebody hoards their possessions?" Hendel asked. "You know, keeping everything for himself?"

Seeto laughed. "Who would do such a thing? Your living space would become so crowded you'd have to sleep standing up, just for the sake of having items you don't even use." He shook his head and chuckled softly at Hendel's foolishness.

As they passed through the trading deck, Kahlee cast a quick glance over at Gillian. It was hard to read her emotional state behind her mask, but she seemed to be okay.

Satisfied, Kahlee turned her attention back to the quarians hunting through the merchandise. At first glance the scene resembled the crowded market square of any colony world. A closer look, however, showed it was very, very different. It lacked the aggressive, bustling energy of a typical bazaar. Despite the crowd—forty or fifty people by her guess—nobody was pushing, shoving, or fighting over items. Often, two or three people would stop and talk, though they were always careful to move aside so they didn't block the aisles when they did so.

It took her a moment to realize what else was missing: the noise. There were no merchants loudly hawking their wares, and no angry shouting of customers and proprietors haggling over prices. Only the soft sounds of people searching through the lockers and bins, and the low, good-natured conversation of neighbors and friends.

They were nearing the large freight elevator that would take them up to the next level of the ship when Kahlee noticed something else. A small desk fashioned from an unidentifiable alien hardwood had been set up in front of a door leading to a supply room off to the side of the cargo hold. A female quarian sat at the desk behind a computer, where a line of five or six others stood waiting. Two male quarians stood behind her.

The man at the front of the line said something to the woman, who punched some information into the computer. He handed her an empty pack, which she passed to one of the men behind her. He disappeared into the room, then emerged again a few seconds later and handed the pack, now filled, back to the man in line.

"What's going on over there?" she asked.

"Essential items, such as food or medicine, are stored separately," Seeto explained. "We need to keep track of our reserves to make sure we always have enough for everyone in the colony."

"What happens when the reserves run low?" Hendel asked.

"If we manage them carefully, they never will," Seeto replied. "Weekly shipments arrive from the Liveships to provide for our basic needs. And specific

or luxury items are acquired by the scout ships we
send out to explore the worlds of the systems we pass
through, or through trading with other vessels in the
Fleet."

They boarded the elevator and began to ascend,
leaving the trading deck behind them. When they
reached the next level the elevator door opened, and
Kahlee's jaw dropped at the sight before her.

They were on what would have been the crew deck
of an Alliance cruiser. But instead of the expected
mess hall, sleeper pods, medical bay, or rec room, she
got her first good look at how the vast majority of
quarians lived.

Most of the interior walls of the deck had been torn
out to maximize the use of space. Replacing them was
a massive grid of cubicles, arranged in groups of six:
three running fore and aft along the ship's deck by
two running port to starboard. Each individual cubicle was maybe a dozen feet on a side, with three walls
fashioned from steel plates that ran three quarters of
the way up to the ceiling. The fourth side, the one facing out toward the aisles that crisscrossed fore to aft
and port to starboard between each group of cubicles, was open, though most had heavy sheets of
bright, multicolored cloth hanging down from the
ceiling like curtains to cover the opening. The noise
that had been absent from the markets seemed to
have migrated here, a general din of sound and voices
that rose up from each cubicle.

"This is the deck where I live," Seeto told them
proudly as Isli led them down one of the aisles running through the center of the cubicle grid. As on the
trading deck, the lanes running in both directions

were crowded with people. These individuals moved with more purpose than the idly browsing shoppers, though they were still unfailingly courteous in making way for others.

As they passed cubicle after cubicle, Kahlee wondered if the colors and intricate designs sewn onto the cloth curtains that served as the doors had any significance, such as identifying individuals from a specific clan or family. She tried to look for signs of common or repeating patterns in the artwork that might hint at meaning, but if it was there it eluded her.

Many of the cloth curtains were only partially drawn, and Kahlee couldn't resist the urge to glance from side to side at each cubicle as they passed, catching occasional glimpses of ordinary quarians living their everyday lives. Some were cooking on small electric stoves, others were tidying up their cubicles. Others were playing cards or other games, or watching personal vid screens. Some were gathered in small groups, sitting on the floor while they visited a friend's or relative's space. A few were even sleeping. All of them were wearing their enviro-suits.

"Are they wearing their suits because of us?" Hendel wondered.

Seeto shook his head. "We rarely take off our enviro-suits, except in the most private settings or intimate encounters."

"We work hard to maintain our ships," Isli added from up ahead, "but the chance of a hull breach or engine leak, remote though it may be, is something we must be constantly and acutely aware of."

On the surface her explanation made sense, but Kahlee suspected there was more to it. Hull breaches and engine leaks would indeed be extremely rare, even in older, run-down vessels. And simple air-quality monitors, combined with element zero detectors, could alert people on board to don their suits in the event of an emergency long before any serious harm was done to them.

It was quite likely wearing the enviro-suits had become a deeply ingrained tradition, a custom born from the inescapable lack of privacy on the overpopulated ships. The masks and layers of material could very well be a physical, emotional, and psychological buffer in a society where solitude was virtually impossible to find.

"How do you go to the bathroom?" Gillian asked, much to Kahlee's surprise. She had expected the girl to withdraw into herself in an effort to escape the crowds and overabundance of noise in the unfamiliar surroundings.

Maybe she's getting some kind of psychological privacy from her mask and enviro-suit, too.

"We have bathrooms and showers in the lower decks," Seeto explained, in answer to Gillian's query. "The room is sealed and sterile. It is one of the few places we feel comfortable removing our enviro-suits."

"What about when you're not on a quarian ship?" Gillian wanted to know.

"Our suits are equipped to store several days worth of waste in sealed compartments between the inner and outer layer. The suit can then be flushed, discharging the waste into any common sanitation facility—like the toilet on your shuttle—without exposing the wearer to outside contaminants."

Seeto suddenly darted up ahead and pulled back the curtain on one of the cubicles. "This is my living quarter," he said excitedly, ushering them over.

Peering inside Kahlee saw a cluttered but tidy little room. A sleeping mat was rolled up in one corner. A small cooking stove, a personal vid screen, and a computer rested against one of the side walls. Several swatches of bright orange cloth hung on the walls, the color matching the curtain that was used to block the open entrance.

"You live here alone?" Kahlee asked, and Seeto laughed again at the foolishness of humans.

"I share this space with my mother and father. My sister lived here for many years, too, until she left on her Pilgrimage. Now she is with the crew of the *Rayya*."

"Where are your parents now?" Gillian asked, and Kahlee thought she heard a hint of longing in her voice.

"My father works on the upper decks as a navigator. My mother is usually part of the civilian Council that advises Captain Mal, but this week she is volunteering on the Liveships. She will be back in two more days."

"What about all the orange cloth hanging from the walls," Kahlee asked, changing the topic away from missing parents. "Does it mean anything?"

"It means my mother likes the color orange," Seeto chuckled, letting the curtain fall back into place as they continued on their way.

They made their way through the remaining cubicles until they reached another elevator.

"I will escort the humans alone from here," Isli informed Seeto and Ugho. "You two go report back for normal work detail."

"I'm afraid this is where we part company," Seeto said with a courteous nod. "I hope we shall see each other again soon."

Ugho nodded, too, but didn't bother to speak.

The elevator opened and they followed Isli aboard. The doors closed and it whisked them up to the bridge. As they stepped off, Kahlee was surprised to see several more cubicles built along one side of the hall running from the elevator. Apparently space was so valuable that even here, only a few dozen feet from the bridge itself, every available inch was used.

"Those are the captain's quarters," Isli pointed out as they walked past one of the cubicles toward the bridge, filling the role of tour guide now that Seeto was no longer with them. The blue and green curtain was completely drawn, blocking any view inside. But based on the width of the corridor and the two steel plates that formed the side walls, Kahlee estimated the captain's room was the same size as every other.

When they arrived on the actual bridge Kahlee noted with some surprise that this was the one place the ship didn't seem unusually crowded. There were still a lot of bodies crammed into a small area—a helmsman, two navigators, a comm operator, and various other crew—but the same could be said of any Alliance vessel. The captain was seated in a chair in the center of the bridge and Lemm, his injured leg still encased in the protective boot, stood just behind him. The captain rose and approached as they entered, while Lemm clumped along behind him.

"Captain Ysin'Mal vas Idenna," Lemm said, making the introductions, "allow me to present Kahlee Sanders, and her companions Hendel Mitra and Gillian Grayson."

"You and your friends are welcome aboard the *Idenna*," the captain said, extending his hand to each of them in turn. Once again, Gillian didn't flinch or shy away from the contact, though she didn't find the courage to speak this time.

It has to be the enviro-suits, Kahlee thought.

Captain Mal looked, to Kahlee's eye, exactly like every other male quarian she had met. She knew her observation was more than just interspecies bias. Even accounting for the fact that many of the physical differences were obscured by their environmental suits, it was a safe generalization to say that quarians all tended to look pretty much the same. They were of an almost uniformly similar size and build, with far less variety than what was found in humans.

Apart from Lemm, who was easy to identify because of his boot, she had learned to rely on specific subtle differences in their clothing to tell the quarians apart. For example, Seeto had a small but noticeable discoloration on the left shoulder of his enviro-suit, as if it had been rubbed or worn at constantly over many months. However, if Hendel and Grayson were both wearing enviro-suits, it would have been easy to tell them apart without relying on similar tricks— Hendel was half a foot taller and seventy pounds heavier than Gillian's father. That same degree of variance simply didn't exist in the quarian population.

It's like that with all the other races, Kahlee thought to herself. *For some reason, humans just have more genetic diversity than the rest of the galaxy.* She hadn't really noticed it before, not consciously, but here on the bridge of the *Idenna* it seemed to strike home.

It's happening to us, too, she realized as Hendel shook the captain's hand. The big man's mix of Nordic and Indian ancestry was the norm on Earth now, and the inevitable genetic by-product was a more physically homogeneous population. In the twenty-second century, blond hair like hers was a rarity, and naturally blue eyes were nonexistent. *But with hair dye, skin toning, and colored contact lenses, who really cares?*

"I extend to each of you the warm welcome of my ship and her crew," the captain was saying, causing Kahlee to snap her mind back to the present. "It is an honor to meet you."

"The honor is ours, Captain Mal," Kahlee replied. "You have taken us in when we had nowhere else to go."

"We are wanderers ourselves," the captain replied. "We have found safety and community here in the Migrant Fleet, and I offer that safety to you now, as well."

"Thank you, sir," Kahlee replied.

The captain bowed his head in acknowledgment of her gratitude, then reached out and placed a hand on her shoulder, drawing in close so he could speak to her in a tone so soft she could barely hear it through the voice modulator of his mask.

"Unfortunately, the safety of the Migrant Fleet is a false one," he whispered.

Kahlee was caught off-guard by the cryptic warning, too surprised to give a reply. Fortunately, he didn't seem to expect one. He took his hand from her shoulder and stepped back, resuming the conversation in his normal voice.

"Representatives from the Conclave and the Admiralty are coming to the *Idenna* to speak with you," he told her. "This is a great honor for my ship and my crew."

From the tone of his voice, Kahlee suspected he felt the honor was more of an inconvenience.

"Sir," one of the crew members informed the captain, "the *Lestiak* is requesting permission to dock."

"Send them to bay five," Mal replied. "We'll meet them there.

"Come," he said to Kahlee and her companions, "we shouldn't keep such important visitors waiting."

TWENTY-ONE

Once again Kahlee and her companions were led through the ship by three quarians. This time, however, their escort consisted of Isli, Lemm, and the captain.

They took them back down to the lower levels and over to the docking bays. Instead of going back to Grayson's shuttle, however, they made their way to one of the other occupied bays, where the *Lestiak,* along with its crew of VIPs, was already waiting for them.

Considering the political status of those on board, Kahlee was surprised to see the captain didn't request permission before opening the airlock and entering the vessel.

"I guess the captain gets to go wherever he wants on his own ship," Hendel whispered to her, making note of the strange behavior as well.

Inside the shuttle they were brought into a large conference room that appeared to be set up for what looked to be some type of official inquiry. *Or a court-martial,* Kahlee thought. There was a long, semicircular table with six chairs behind it. Five of the chairs were occupied by quarians, though one on the end was empty. Several armed guards stood at the back of the room, behind the seated dignitaries.

Mal led them to the center of the room, where they stood while he made a full round of introductions. Kahlee didn't bother trying to remember all the names as they were tossed out. She did, however, make a point of noting which three of the quarians in attendance were elected representatives from the civilian Conclave, and which two were members of the military's Admiralty board.

She also noticed that when Mal introduced Lemm, he referred to him as "Lemm'Shal vas Idenna"; apparently the young quarian's Pilgrimage was officially over, and he had been accepted into Mal's crew.

When the introductions were finished, Mal went over and sat down in the lone unoccupied seat at the table. Isli went and stood behind him, joining the other honor guards watching over the scene from the back wall. Lemm didn't move, but stayed with the humans who remained standing in front of the table.

"Kahlee Sanders," one of the Admiralty representatives asked, beginning the proceedings, "do you understand why we have brought you here?"

"You think I might know something about Saren Arterius and how he was able to control the geth," she replied.

"Could you describe your relationship with Saren?" another representative asked, this one from the civilian Conclave.

"There was no relationship," Kahlee insisted. "I only met him briefly two or three times. As far as I knew, he was just the Spectre assigned to investigate the activities of my mentor, Dr. Shu Qian."

"And what were those activities, exactly?"

"Qian had discovered some kind of alien artifact," she said, choosing her words carefully. "It might have been Prothean. Maybe it even predated them. None of us really knew.

"He thought it was the key to creating a new kind of artificial intelligence. But he kept the rest of us in the dark; we were just lab monkeys for him, running data he gathered from his tests and experiments. Qian was the only one who knew any of the details about the artifact: where it was, what it was, what it did.

"But Qian went missing, and he was never found. Neither were his files."

"Is it possible Saren found his files?" one of the Conclave asked. "Is it possible he found this artifact, and used it to gain control of the geth?"

"It's possible," Kahlee answered, somewhat reluctantly. The idea had occurred to her before, but she didn't like speculating that she had played some role, however small, in the devastation wrought by the geth.

"Have you ever heard of a species called the Reapers?" the first quarian wanted to know.

Kahlee shook her head.

"There is word coming from the Citadel that Saren's flagship, *Sovereign*, was actually an advanced AI. It was alive; just one of an entire race of enormous, sentient ships called the Reapers."

"Those are just rumors," Hendel interjected. "There's no proof to support those theories."

"But it could explain why the geth followed Saren," the quarian countered. "An advanced AI might have been able to override the geth's rudimentary intelligence systems."

"I can't really say," Kahlee answered. "I don't know anything about the geth, other than what I've seen on the vids. And I have no idea why they followed Saren."

"But if *Sovereign* was a Reaper," one of the Admiralty members pressed, "then there could be more of its kind. They could be lying dormant in unexplored regions of space, just waiting for someone to accidentally discover and awaken them."

"Maybe," Kahlee said with an indecisive shrug.

"It seems obvious to me that this is something we would want to avoid at all possible costs," one of the Conclave representatives chimed in. "One Reaper nearly destroyed the Citadel. Another could finish the job. The galaxy already blames us for the geth. We don't need to give them another reason to hate us."

"Or maybe if we found one of these Reapers," Mal countered, joining the conversation for the first time, "we could use it as Saren did—to take control of the geth! We could return to our homeworlds and reclaim what is rightfully ours!"

There was a long silence, then one of the Admiralty asked Kahlee, "Is Captain Mal correct? Do you believe it might be possible to discover a dormant Reaper and use it to gain control of the geth?"

Kahlee shook her head, bewildered. "I can't say. There are too many unknown variables."

"Please," the quarian urged, though his request seemed more like a command, "speculate. You are one of the galaxy's foremost experts in synthetic intelligence. We are eager to hear what you think."

Kahlee took a deep breath and considered the problem carefully before answering. "Given what I knew of Dr. Qian's research, if Saren's flagship was the alien artifact we were studying, it might have been possible to use it to control the geth. And *if* there are more ships out there like *Sovereign,* then yes, it is logical to assume they could also be used to control or influence the geth . . . assuming that's what Saren did."

It was difficult to read the body language of the quarians at the table while their expressions were obscured by their masks. But Kahlee thought she detected anger or frustration in several of their postures. Mal, however, seemed to be sitting taller than before.

"Is there anything else you can tell us, Kahlee Sanders?" one of the Admiralty asked. "Anything about Saren, or the geth, or Dr. Qian's research?"

"There's really nothing to tell," Kahlee said apologetically. "I wish I could be more helpful."

"I believe we have everything we need," Mal said, standing up. "Thank you, Kahlee."

Realizing they weren't going to get anything more out of their guest, the rest of the participants deferred to his decision and similarly rose from their seats.

"We thank you for your time," one of them said. "Captain Mal, we would like to continue this discussion with the rest of the Conclave. We hope you will accompany us."

Mal nodded. "I am eager to speak with them."

"We should leave as soon as possible," one of the other quarians noted. "Perhaps you could have your security chief escort the humans back to their shuttle?"

"Kahlee and the others are honored guests of the *Idenna*," Mal said pointedly. "They do not need a security escort. They are free to come and go as they please."

There was an awkward silence that was finally broken by one of the Admiralty. "Understood, Captain."

Having won his point, Mal turned to Kahlee and the others. "As long as you are careful not to interfere in the operations of the ship, I am granting you free run of my vessel. Should you wish to have a guide, Lemm would be honored to show you around."

"Thank you, Captain," Kahlee said, eager to get off the *Lestiak* and leave the increasingly tense situation behind.

"Perhaps when I return from the Conclave, we can speak again," he said.

"Of course," she replied. "You are always welcome on our shuttle."

Unsure if there was some kind of formal protocol still required before they were dismissed, Kahlee simply stood there until Lemm gave her elbow a gentle tug.

"Come on," he whispered, "let's go."

Mal and Isli stayed behind as he led them away. Once they were beyond the airlock and back on the *Idenna*, Hendel turned to Lemm.

"What the hell was that all about?"

"Politics" was the short, and uninformative, answer.

"You can't be a little more detailed?" Kahlee pressed.

"I'm sure the captain will make everything clear when he returns from the Conclave," Lemm assured her. "Please, just be patient for a few more days."

"It's not like we have any other choice," Hendel said with a grunt. "But my patience is growing awful thin lately."

Grayson didn't like Golo.

The Illusive Man had arranged a meeting between Grayson and the quarian on Omega to plan their assault on the Migrant Fleet. The meeting was taking place in a small rented apartment in the Talon district, not two blocks away from the warehouse where he had killed Pel. The room was empty except for two chairs, one table, and the two of them.

"You might as well give up," Golo declared to start off the conversation. "Infiltrating the quarian fleet is impossible."

"They have my daughter," Grayson replied, keeping his voice neutral despite the bile in his throat. "I want her back. I was told you could help us."

Golo may have been an ally of Cerberus, but he was a traitor to his own people. Grayson couldn't respect anyone who would turn on his own kind simply to make a profit. It went against everything he believed in.

"There are fifty thousand ships in the Migrant Fleet," Golo reminded him. "Even if they do have her, how are you going to figure out which vessel she's on?"

"The pilot of the scout ship, the one Pel tortured for information, said his name was Hilo'Jaa vas Idenna. I think the *Cyniad* was a scout ship for the *Idenna*. Whoever came looking for him was part of the same crew. They're the ones who took Gillian."

"That makes sense," Golo admitted. Something about the way he said it made Grayson feel as if he were being played, as if Golo already knew all this. "But it hardly matters. You won't get anywhere near the *Idenna*. Even if you're in the *Cyniad*, the patrols will shoot the vessel down if you don't use the proper codes and hailing frequencies."

"I have the frequency and the code," Grayson assured him. "The pilot gave them to me before he died."

Golo laughed. "How do you know they're real? What if he gave you a false code?"

Grayson thought back to the quarian he had discovered in the cellar. Pel had possessed a sixth sense for knowing when his victims were lying under torture; interrogation had always been one of his strong suits.

"The information's good," he said. "It'll get us past the patrols."

"Your confidence is inspiring," the quarian replied, and Grayson could hear the smirk in his voice. He knew Golo had been Pel's contact on Omega. He'd been instrumental in acquiring the *Cyniad*, and Grayson couldn't help but wonder what else the quarian and Pel had been involved in together.

"We're offering ten times what you were paid for the last mission," Grayson said, struggling to keep his rising anger in check.

He needed Golo. Having the codes wasn't enough; if the mission had any hope of succeeding they had to have someone familiar with the protocols of the Migrant Fleet on the ship to keep them from making a mistake that would expose them. And they needed someone fluent in the quarian tongue on the radio to relay the codes back and forth with the patrols; an automated translator wasn't going to cut it.

"Ten times?" Golo said, considering the offer. "Generous. But is it worth risking my life for?"

"This is also a chance for revenge," Grayson reminded him, sweetening the pot. He'd read Golo's profile in Pel's mission reports. He knew the quarian harbored a deep hatred for the society that had exiled him, and he wasn't above exploiting that hatred. Not if it helped him get Gillian back.

"The Fleet banished you. They cast you out. This is your chance to strike back at them in a way they will never forget. Help us and you can make them pay."

"A man after my own heart," Golo said with a cruel laugh, and Grayson felt his stomach turn.

"Does this mean you're in?" Grayson demanded.

"We still have several problems to consider," Golo said by way of confirmation. "The *Cyniad* and the codes will get us past the patrols. But we'll need some way to disrupt the *Idenna*'s communications after we dock so they don't alert the rest of the flotilla once the assault begins."

"We can take care of that," Grayson said, knowing Cerberus had that technology readily available. "What else?"

"We'll need blueprints of the ship's interior layout."

"It was originally a decommissioned batarian Hensa class cruiser," Grayson replied, relaying information the Illusive Man's agents had already gath-

ered in preparation for the mission. "We have the layout."

"Impressive," Golo replied. "There is a chance this
could work, after all. Provided you and your team do
exactly as I say."

"Of course," Grayson said through gritted teeth,
offering his hand to symbolically seal the deal. "I
wouldn't have it any other way."

TWENTY-TWO

Three more days passed before Mal returned to the *Idenna*. Kahlee had spent much of that time exploring the quarian ship, becoming more familiar with its inhabitants and their culture.

She had come to realize that most of her previous beliefs about the quarians were either outright wrong or gross distortions of the truth. She had always considered them to be scavengers, beggars, and thieves: a culture of petty criminals not to be trusted. Now she saw them simply as resourceful and determined. They were a people struggling to survive with limited space and resources, yet they refused to allow their society to degenerate into selfishness and anarchy. To accomplish this, they clung fiercely to their powerful sense of community.

There was something noble in this unity, enforced though it might be by their circumstances. Every quarian truly believed they needed to work together to survive. The strong family bonds among shipmates, and the willingness of individuals to sacrifice for the greater good, were values Kahlee thought other species could aspire to . . . should they ever learn to see past their own prejudices and preconceived notions about the quarians.

While Kahlee was exploring the ship, Hendel and Gillian spent most of their time on Grayson's shuttle practicing biotics. Even while wearing her envirosuit, Gillian still wasn't entirely comfortable around strangers, and she preferred to stay isolated in the more familiar surroundings.

Occasionally Lemm or Seeto would come to visit, though both were closed lipped when Kahlee or Hendel tried to pry information from them about the quarian political situation. It was frustrating, being a pawn in a game she didn't fully understand, but Kahlee was confident they would get some answers soon: Captain Mal was finally coming to speak with them.

Kahlee, Hendel, and Gillian were all wearing their enviro-suits in preparation for his visit to their shuttle. Lemm had suggested the idea yesterday as a way for them to show respect for quarian customs and traditions in honor of the captain's arrival. Until they knew more about the purpose of this meeting, Hendel had noted, it was probably best to do whatever they could to stay on his good side.

With some reluctance, Kahlee had agreed. She didn't like wearing the suit if she didn't have to, although she couldn't quite say exactly what she disliked about it. The suits were fully climate controlled, so she never felt hot or sweaty while wearing it, and the thin, pliant material barely restricted her movement. And with the vis-glass of the faceplate and the audio enhancements in the helmet, she could actually see and hear better while wearing the suit than without it.

· Still, she never felt comfortable in it. The suit completely cut her off from normal tactile sensations, like the feel of the warm leather under her palm when she placed her hand on the arm of her seat, or the cool, hard metal of the tabletop as she drummed her fingers against it. It even made it impossible to run her fingers through her hair.

In contrast, Gillian seemed to love wearing the suit, only taking it off once since their meeting with the captain on the bridge. She even wore it during her biotic training with Hendel. Kahlee knew the security chief found her behavior odd, but he put up with it for her sake. He did, however, insist that she remove the helmet and mask during their sessions. Gillian had complied, though not without some grumbling and complaining.

The mere fact that she grumbled and complained, rather than mutely obeying, was further evidence of how much she had changed. Kahlee had commented to Hendel on how much improvement Gillian had shown, and she'd even shared her theory that the suit might make the girl feel psychologically safe and more confident. Hendel, however, had offered a different theory.

"I think she's just getting better because Cerberus isn't drugging her anymore."

The thought was disturbing, but Kahlee was surprised she hadn't come up with it on her own. It was doubtful Gillian's condition could be blamed solely on whatever chemical concoctions Jiro had been feeding her, but it was very possible they had made her symptoms worse. Somehow that knowledge made what Grayson had allowed them to do to his daughter seem even more monstrous.

The sound of the airlock opening startled her out of her recollections.

"Not big on knocking, are they?" Hendel muttered, rising from his seat to greet their visitors. Kahlee and Gillian did the same.

Kahlee had been expecting some kind of honor guard or security detail to accompany the captain, but if they came they must have stayed outside the ship. Apart from Lemm, Mal was alone.

"Thank you for this invitation," he said, once handshakes had been exchanged all around.

"We're honored to have you here," Kahlee replied. "Please, sit down and make yourself comfortable."

There were only four chairs in the passenger cabin, so once all the adults took their seats, Gillian hopped up into Hendel's lap. Yet again, Kahlee was amazed at how far she had come in a little less than two weeks.

Before any of them could speak, they were interrupted by a short, muffled beep coming from behind Mal's mask—the sound of an incoming message transferred to his in-helmet radio. He held up one hand, asking the others to be silent as he listened to the message. Kahlee couldn't hear what was being said in his ear, but she saw him nod.

"Send them to docking bay seven," he instructed. "And tell them it's good to have them back."

"Forgive me," he said a moment later to Kahlee and the others. "I have to approve all arriving vessels before they can dock."

"Do you have to go?" she asked.

He shook his head. "Isli and her team will greet them. We can continue our business."

"And what exactly is that business?" Hendel said, casting tact and decorum aside. Kahlee couldn't blame him; she was about ready to do the same thing. Fortunately, Mal seemed willing to be completely candid.

"The Migrant Fleet is dying," he said flatly. "It is a long, slow, almost invisible death, but the facts are undeniable. We are nearing a time of crisis for our species. In another eighty or ninety years, our population will be too large for our ships to support."

"I thought you had zero population growth," Kahlee said, remembering Seeto describing the universally enforced policies of birth control during one of her tours of the lower decks.

"Our population is stable, but the Fleet is not," the captain explained. "Our ships continue to age and break down faster than we can replace or repair them. Little by little we are running out of livable space, yet neither the Conclave nor the Admiralty are willing to take action. I fear that by the time they finally realize something drastic must be done, it will be too late to stem the tide."

"What does that have to do with me?" Kahlee wanted to know. "Why were they asking me all those questions about the geth and Reapers?"

"There is a small but growing coalition of ship captains who believe we must take immediate action if the quarian nation is to survive," Mal explained. "We have proposed that several of the Fleet's largest vessels be equipped for long-distance voyages. We want to send them on two- to five-year journeys into uncharted regions of space or through unexplored mass relays."

"Sounds dangerous," Hendel noted.

"It is," Mal admitted, "but this could be our only hope to secure the long-term survival of the quarian species. We need to find life-bearing, uninhabited worlds we can call our own. Or, failing that, we need to find some way to return to the Perseus Veil and reclaim our home from the geth."

"Do you really believe you'll find one of these so-called Reaper ships somewhere on the fringes of unexplored space?" Hendel asked.

"I believe it is better than doing nothing, and waiting for our numbers to begin an irreversible decline."

"Seems logical," Kahlee admitted. "So why is there so much opposition to sending out these ships?"

"Our society is extremely fragile," Mal explained. "The smallest change can have huge repercussions. Sending away several of our larger vessels will weaken the Fleet as a whole, at least until they return. Most of the representatives in the Conclave are not willing to take that risk.

"Their caution is understandable," the captain admitted. "For nearly three hundred years the Admiralty and the Conclave have fought to protect what little we have from crumbling away. They had no choice but to adopt careful and conservative policies.

"Those policies served us for a time," he continued, "but now we need to adapt. We need new policies if we are to survive. Unfortunately, the weight of tradition hangs heavily over the Fleet, and there is a widespread fear of change.

"That is why your testimony before the representatives was so important, Kahlee," he added. "We need to win others over to our cause, to make them see that taking a risk is our best chance to survive. Even if we don't find the Reapers or discover a way to drive the remaining geth from the Perseus Veil, we still might find new worlds we can settle."

"But my testimony was meaningless," Kahlee objected. "It was all speculation and maybes. I don't know anything useful about the geth or the Reapers. And I never said sending ships into the uncharted void would help you find them."

"That's beside the point," Mal explained. "People believe you have knowledge that can defeat the geth; it doesn't matter if you really do. You have become a symbol of hope for the future among our society. If other captains see you allied with me, it will win support to our cause. That is why those who oppose us want to see you leave the *Idenna*."

"Leave?" Hendel said worriedly. "You mean they're kicking us out of the Fleet?"

"They won't do that," Mal assured him. "It would turn you into martyrs for my cause, drumming up even more support for those of us who advocate change.

"But there are many captains who oppose us," he continued. "Several have offered to give you sanctuary on their vessels, should you choose to leave the *Idenna*. They believe if you travel with them, it will gain support for their side."

"I don't like being a political pawn," Kahlee muttered darkly.

"I understand," Mal said sympathetically, "and I

am sorry I have put you in this position. If you really don't want to be involved, you are free to leave the Fleet."

Kahlee frowned. Leaving the Fleet wasn't an option; not while Cerberus was still looking for them.

"Please, Kahlee," Lemm added. "Sending out the exploration ships is the best hope for my people to survive."

Lemm probably could have gotten her to agree simply by saying she still owed him for saving them on Omega. But Kahlee had learned enough about quarian culture to realize he would never try to force her like that. Still, she did owe him. And Mal's arguments made sense to her.

Before she could answer, however, they heard the distant but unmistakable sound of the *Idenna*'s shipboard alarms.

"We're about to find out if your information is reliable," Golo whispered as the *Cyniad*'s nav screens showed several patrol frigates breaking off from the main body of the Migrant Fleet.

The quarian shuttle was packed with ten highly trained Cerberus commandos, along with Golo, Grayson, and a pilot trained to fly the quarian modified vessel. Everyone on board was wearing a full combat hard-suit equipped with kinetic dampeners, and they each carried a heavy assault rifle.

"Open the hailing channel," Golo instructed, and the Cerberus pilot did as he was told. Grayson was technically in charge of the mission, but for much of it he would be deferring to Golo and his greater understanding of the quarians.

A few seconds later the radio crackled with the challenge of the quarian patrols. "You are entering a restricted area. Identify."

"This is the scout ship *Cyniad*, of the *Idenna*," Golo responded, "seeking permission to rejoin the Fleet."

"Verify authorization."

Grayson held his breath as Golo recited the code phrase. "My body travels to distant stars, but my soul never leaves the Fleet."

Several seconds passed before they got their response. "*Idenna* confirms your identity. Welcome back, *Cyniad*."

Golo flipped off the comm channel. "Bring us in nice and slow," he instructed the pilot. "We don't want to spook anyone."

Locating the *Idenna* amid the armada of ships was surprisingly simple. Every vessel in the Fleet transmitted a short-range homing signal on a unique frequency. As a scout ship, the *Cyniad* was preprogrammed with the *Idenna*'s frequency, so that the vessel showed up as a green pixel on the nav screen, in contrast to the red of the other ships.

As they drew close, Golo opened the comm channel again. "This is the *Cyniad*, requesting permission to dock with the *Idenna*."

There was a delay of several seconds before the radio crackled with, "This is the *Idenna*. Your request is granted. Head to docking bay seven. And the captain says it's good to have you back."

"It's good to be back," Golo replied. "Better send a security and quarantine team," he added, before clicking the comm channel closed.

"A security team?" Grayson asked, suspicious.

"Standard protocol," Golo replied. "If I didn't request one, they'd get suspicious."

"Will they be armed?"

"Probably, but they won't be expecting any trouble. Your squad should be able to take them down without too much difficulty."

Grayson felt his stomach clenching as they drifted into the docking bay. For the first time in several days he felt the sudden craving to dust up, but he pushed it aside by focusing on the mission.

The three men in the cockpit were silent until they heard the docking clamps secure the ship in place.

"Lock onto your target," Grayson instructed, and the pilot nodded. "But hold fire until my order."

Cerberus had made some additions to the *Cyniad,* including the addition of a small but powerful short-range laser. One well-placed shot could knock out the *Idenna*'s tight-beam transmitter, killing the ship's external communications and preventing them from alerting the rest of the Fleet.

The timing had to be perfect, though. The *Idenna* would still have internal communications, and as soon as the transmitter was knocked out the bridge would alert everyone on board. Grayson wanted to wait until the security team coming to meet them had been dealt with before that happened.

"Alpha team," Grayson said into his combat helmet's transmitter, "you're going to have company when the airlock opens. Report in as soon as you take them out."

A few seconds later they heard several sharp bursts of gunfire coming from just outside the ship.

"Enemy is down," the Alpha team leader replied. "No casualties on our end."

"Take out the transmitter," Grayson said, and the pilot fired the laser, shearing off the dish in a quick, clean cut. The shipboard alarms kicked in almost immediately.

"Now the fun begins," Golo said, and behind his mask Grayson knew he was grinning.

TWENTY-THREE

"What's happening?" Kahlee demanded, shouting over the distant alarms.

The captain listened intently to an incoming message, then relayed the news to the rest of them. "The *Cyniad*, one of our scout ships, just docked with us. They knocked out our tight-beam transmitter."

"I was searching for the crew of the *Cyniad* when I found you in that warehouse," Lemm told them, speaking quickly. "I thought your captors had some connection to the scout ship."

"Cerberus," Hendel said. "They're coming for Gillian."

"What about the security team you sent to meet them?" Kahlee asked, remembering the captain's earlier instructions. "Isli and the others?"

"No response," Mal said, his voice grim. They all knew what that likely meant.

"If it's Cerberus, they'll be coming straight for this shuttle," Hendel warned them. "They'll want to grab Gillian and get out quick, before you can organize any resistance."

"Do you have any weapons on board?" Lemm asked.

Kahlee shook her head. "The rifle we took from the warehouse is nearly out of ammo. Hendel's biotic, but that's all we've got."

"Call for a security detail," the big man said.

"They won't get here in time," Mal replied. "The *Cyniad*'s only two bays over."

We can't even seal the shuttle and make a run for it, Kahlee realized. *We'd never disconnect the docking clamps in time.*

"Come on," she said, jumping to her feet. "We can't hold them off in here."

The five of them—two quarians and three humans—raced from the shuttle through the airlock out into the landing bay of the *Idenna*. Hendel had to half-drag and half-carry Gillian to keep up; the alarms were disorienting her, and she was moving with slow, distracted steps.

"Trading deck!" Mal shouted. "We have weapons in the storeroom."

As they ran through the crowded halls and corridors of the ship, Kahlee couldn't help imagining what would happen when the Cerberus troops arrived to find Grayson's shuttle empty. The quarians had no reason to ever expect an attack inside the confines of their Fleet vessels, and ready access to firearms in such crowded living conditions was normally a recipe for disaster. As a result, no one except a handful of security details carried weapons. If armed Cerberus agents started searching for Gillian through the populated decks, it would turn into a massacre.

Mal was shouting instructions into his radio, trying to organize reinforcements to drive back the enemy.

"We need to make a stand!" Kahlee shouted. "Hold

them on the trading deck. If we don't, hundreds will die."

He nodded, and relayed the instructions to the bridge.

How did they find us here? Kahlee wondered as she ran, followed quickly by, *Is there nowhere in the galaxy Gillian can escape them?*

The Cerberus team arrived at Grayson's old shuttle to find it abandoned.

"They must have gone into the ship to hide," Golo guessed.

"How many quarians on board?" Grayson demanded.

"Between six and seven hundred," Golo estimated. "But only a couple dozen will be armed. You stay here with a small team to secure the shuttle, and I'll take the rest with me. We'll find Gillian and bring her back here."

Grayson shook his head. "She's my daughter. I'm coming with you."

"Forget it," Golo replied. "We don't need you in there."

"I'm in charge of this mission," Grayson reminded him.

"And I'm the only one who knows his way around a quarian ship," Golo countered. "You can't do this without me, and I'm not going in there with you as part of my team.

"You're too emotionally involved," he continued, almost apologetic. "You're not thinking straight, and you're not ready for this."

Grayson didn't argue the point. He'd barely slept

since escaping Pel's warehouse; he was just a duster running on adrenaline and desperation. Exhaustion and withdrawal would slow his reaction time and impair his judgment, putting the entire team in jeopardy.

"If you really want your daughter back," the quarian added in a sensitive whisper, "the best thing you can do is wait here and get the shuttle ready for our escape."

Golo was playing him; pushing his emotional buttons. The quarian didn't care what happened to Gillian. He was just a lying, manipulative, son-of-a-bitch who was only looking out for his own self-interest. But that didn't mean he was wrong.

They're better off without you. For the sake of the mission—for Gillian's sake—you have to sit this one out.

"You, you, and you," Grayson said, pointing to the pilot and two others. "Stay here with me. The rest of you go with Golo. Remember, we only have thirty minutes to get off this vessel."

"If the humans went into the ship they're probably wearing enviro-suits," Golo noted almost casually.

Grayson swore silently at the extra complication. "The Illusive Man wants Gillian alive and unharmed," he reminded the eight soldiers going with Golo, stressing the point to make sure they understood. "Don't shoot at anything smaller than a full-grown quarian."

"Not unless you're close enough to count the fingers," Golo added with a laugh.

"The bridge is sealing off sections of the ship," Mal told them as he passed out the guns stored in the stockroom with the food, medicine, and other care-fully tracked supplies. "It won't stop them, but it might slow them down. The civilians are being evac-uated to the upper decks, and I've ordered all security teams to meet us down here."

Kahlee took the assault rifle he handed her, hefting it to test the weight. It was a cheap volus knock-off of a turian design—a substandard weapon, but it was better than nothing.

Glancing around the room, she considered their chances. There was only one entrance onto the trad-ing deck from the loading bays: Cerberus would have to come straight down a long, narrow hall right to them. But if they got past that first door, they would find plenty of cover among the oversized crates and bins used to store merchandise that were scattered all about the room. A well-organized strike team would have no problem spreading out and trying to flank Mal's people. And if they had to fall back there was only one place to go—up to the heavily populated liv-ing quarters of the deck above.

Two quarian security teams were already on the trading deck. By the time Mal had finished passing out weapons to Kahlee, Lemm, and Hendel, four more security teams had arrived from the decks above.

"Everyone spread out and find cover," the captain ordered. "Hold the doors to the landing bay for as long as you can. If I give the order, fall back to the level above."

The quarians scrambled to find their positions, and Kahlee turned to Gillian. She wasn't moving or looking around; she simply stared straight ahead at nothing, her arms hanging limp by her sides.

"Do you remember where Seeto's room is?" Kahlee asked, trying not to think about the fact that the young quarian, along with Isli and Ugho, was probably already dead.

Gillian didn't answer her at first, but simply stood still and quiet, gazing off into the distance from behind her mask.

"Gillian!" Kahlee shouted. "This is important!" The girl turned her head slowly toward her.

"Do you remember when Seeto showed us his room?" Kahlee repeated. The girl nodded once. "Do you know where it is?"

"The deck above us," she answered, in a flat monotone that indicated she was slipping farther and farther away from her surroundings. "The first cubicle in the group along the fourth column and the sixth row."

"I need you to go there and wait for me or Hendel to come get you!" Kahlee shouted. "Do you understand? Go to Seeto's room and hide!"

Gillian gave the familiar single nod, then turned and walked slowly over toward the freight elevator.

"The stairs, Gillian," Kahlee shouted after her, knowing the elevator wouldn't be operational with the ship in emergency lockdown. "You have to take the stairs!"

The girl didn't look back at her, she simply altered her course and headed for the stairs.

"You sure about sending her off alone?" Hendel asked, checking the sights and autotargeting system on his own weapon.

Kahlee wasn't sure. In fact, she hated it. But she didn't see any other option.

"She can't stay here," she said. "And we can't send anyone with her. Mal's going to need every possible body if we have any hope of holding this position."

Hendel nodded, agreeing with her assessment of the grim situation, then ran off to find a cover spot behind one of the overflowing metal bins that gave him a clear shot at anyone coming in from the landing bay. Kahlee did the same, hunkering down behind a large steel crate filled with pots and pans.

Cerberus didn't keep them waiting long.

The assault began with a handful of grenades lobbed through the door and into the trading deck. None of Mal's team were positioned close enough to the entrance to be caught in the blast range, but when the grenades detonated they sent several of the crates, and their contents, flying through the air. No one was injured, but it served as a distraction as the first wave of two Cerberus soldiers pushed forward to the edge of the door.

Kahlee and the others opened fire, trying to drive them back. Trusting in their armor's kinetic barriers, the enemy returned fire as they sprinted forward through the entrance toward one of the nearby crates that promised them cover.

The plan would have worked if not for Hendel. While Kahlee and the quarians were unloading round after ineffective round into the enemy shields, the biotic had been gathering his strength. Just as the Cerberus soldiers ducked behind the crate they assumed would give them shelter, Hendel lifted it high into the air, exposing them to another barrage of concentrated assault-rifle fire.

Their shields, still depleted from their initial charge through the door, couldn't save them from a second hail of bullets. Both men were torn to shreds, and Kahlee felt a burst of triumphant exultation.

Her euphoria was short lived. The second wave of Cerberus soldiers—this time a group of three—followed only a few seconds after the first, using the same techniques. Hendel needed more time to recharge before he could unleash his powers again, so this time the trio made it safely to the cover of one of the bins. Protected from enemy fire, they were able to regroup and recharge their shields, then quickly strike out again.

They burst from their cover at the same time, all three moving in different directions as they scattered to and fro among the maze of crates and containers. Kahlee focused on the nearest enemy, losing track of the other two. She tried to take him down with well-aimed bursts as he moved from cover point to cover point, but he knew the limits of his shields, and he always managed to duck out of the line of fire just before they were completely drained.

She saw he was trying to work around to the far side of the room, attempting to get to a position where he could sneak up on the defenders from behind. From the corner of her eye Kahlee saw one of the quarians step out from the crate he was hiding behind to try and cut him off, only to get mowed down by the weapons of the third wave of four Cerberus troops charging through the door.

It was then that Kahlee realized how hopeless the

situation was. Despite having a two- or three-to-one edge in numbers, the tactical and technological advantages of the Cerberus agents were too much to overcome. They had better weapons, better armor, and better training. Half of Mal's team—including Lemm, the captain, Hendel, and Kahlee herself—weren't even wearing body armor.

And Cerberus had grenades.

As if on cue, she heard a loud boom over on the far side of the deck. Whipping her head around she saw the smoke from the explosion clearing to reveal the burned and lifeless bodies of two quarians who had been caught in the deadly blast.

At least they had Hendel on their side. The big man poked his head out from behind his crate and unleashed another biotic attack, this one hurling two Cerberus soldiers backward from their hiding places, sending them both crashing against a nearby wall. One landed hard, quickly scrambling to her feet and making it safely back behind cover. Kahlee squeezed the trigger of her weapon and made sure the other one didn't.

An instant later, however, Hendel was the one flying backward through the air—Cerberus apparently had a biotic on their team, too. He shouted out in surprise, then slammed hard against the wall behind the desk outside the stockroom where they had grabbed their guns. He crumpled to the ground and didn't rise.

"Hendel!" she cried out, fighting against the suicidal urge to leap up and rush over to check on him.

Instead she turned her attention back on the enemy, drawing on her years of Alliance training to stay focused. Soldiers went down in combat, even friends.

Usually there wasn't anything you could do to help them until the enemy was neutralized.

She held her position, picking her targets carefully. She saw one more Cerberus soldier go down—by her count that left five, including the biotic. But all around her she could hear the screams of Mal's people. When the Cerberus biotic launched another attack, batting aside the bin shielding a quarian armed with a sniper rifle so she could be gunned down, the captain finally gave the order Kahlee had known was coming.

"Fall back!" he shouted. "Fall back!"

She didn't want to leave Hendel behind, but attempting to reach him now would almost guarantee her getting shot. Blinking away the harsh tears in her eyes, she lay down a line of cover fire as she began to make her retreat.

Gillian wandered back and forth along the grid of cubicles, silently counting until she reached the one blocked by the bright orange curtain. Far away she could hear the sharp retorts and ricochets of sounds she couldn't—or didn't want to—consciously identify.

She knew something was wrong, and she knew it was somehow her fault. But though she fought to piece together what was going on, the truth eluded her. Shocked into a trancelike state by the stress of the situation, all her fractured mind could latch on to were disconnected bits and pieces.

For example, she realized that there should have been more people around. She had hazy, incomplete memories of crowds moving in and among the cubicles. She could recall the buzz of chatter; it had circled around her head like a swarm of angry bees. Now, however, the cubicles were empty. Everything was still and silent.

Again, she knew this was wrong. She just couldn't quite figure out why.

Kahlee said hide in Seeto's room, she thought, as she reached out and pulled the curtain aside. The room didn't look as she remembered it. The sleeping mat had been moved half a foot to the side of where it had originally been placed, and someone had turned the cooking stove ninety degrees since the last time she was here.

Gillian knew that people moved things around sometimes. But she didn't like it. Things should always be put back in the same place.

I don't like it here. I want to go back to the shuttle.

She let the curtain fall from her hand and turned away from the cubicle. Walking with slow, uncertain steps she began to make her way back through the crisscrossing aisles toward the stairs leading to the deck below, taking a long, meandering route far different from the one that had brought her here originally.

Kahlee fell back up the stairs, knowing all hell would break loose when Cerberus followed them and the fight spilled over into the cubicle grids. Even with all the civilians cleared out, the battle would become a run-and-gun skirmish up and down the crisscrossing aisles, giving Cerberus and their superior weaponry an even greater advantage.

While several of Mal's people took up positions

around the corners of cubicles near the staircase, aiming their weapons at the door Cerberus would have to come through, Kahlee made her way straight to Seeto's room to grab Gillian.

By the time she got there, she could already hear steady bursts of gunfire being thrown back and forth. She knew she didn't have long; as easy as it had been for Cerberus to break through the quarian defenses on the lower deck, it would be even harder to hold position up here. There were simply too many options; the quarians would have no hope of pinning an enemy down when they could simply double back to one of the other aisles and come at them from the opposite side.

She pulled the orange curtain back, only to discover an empty room staring back at her.

Gillian was still wandering up and down the halls when the loud noises her mind had refused to identify earlier began to ring out even louder. She saw a quarian run across the far end of the aisle she was standing in, and the gun in his hand forced her to recognize the sounds as gunfire.

I don't want to be here, her mind screamed at her. *Go back to the ship.*

Gillian intended to do just that. She could hear the gunfire all around her now, sporadic bursts coming from in front, behind, and off to either side. But her overwrought mind simply blocked it out and she continued to make her way toward the stairs.

She took a left turn and came face-to-face with a man and a woman. She could tell right away they weren't quarian—they had no environmental suits.

They were wearing helmets, but the visors only covered the first three quarters of their faces, and they had big, bulky vests that hid their chests, shoulders, and arms. Each was carrying a gun, and when they saw her they raised their weapons up and pointed them in her direction.

Gillian simply continued to walk toward them, as if oblivious of their presence.

"Hold fire!" the woman shouted, lowering her gun as the girl approached. "It's her! Grayson's daughter!"

The man lowered his weapon and rushed forward, reaching out to grab her. Without even thinking about it, Gillian made a fist and snapped her hand out, just like Hendel had taught her. The man hurtled away from her, slamming his back against the edge of one of the cubicle walls. There was a sharp crack and he bent in a funny way.

"Holy mother—" the woman gasped, but Gillian cut her words off. Moving on pure instinct, she reached out with an open hand, palm upward, and flicked her wrist. The woman launched up to the ceiling, smashing against it so hard her helmet cracked. She dropped down at Gillian's feet, her eyes rolling back into her head and blood trickling from her nose, mouth, and ears. Her leg twitched once, her boot kicking against the side of a nearby cubicle, then went still.

The girl simply stepped over her and continued on her way. She reached the staircase without running into anyone else, then went down to the lower deck.

She could still hear the gunfire from up above, but it was quieter down here. Feeling a little better, she began to hum a tuneless song as she headed toward the shuttle.

Kahlee was in a near panic as she raced up and down the aisles, desperately searching for Gillian. Fortunately, her training allowed her to keep her wits together just enough not to do anything stupid, and instead of dashing blindly around corners, she would poke her head out at each intersection, taking a quick peek for enemy combatants.

All around her she could hear the sounds of fighting, but she didn't encounter any Cerberus troops until she came across two dead soldiers lying in the middle of one of the aisles. For an instant she thought she'd found proof that Hendel had survived being thrown twenty feet through the air: it was obvious the soldiers had been killed by a biotic attack. Then another thought occurred to her.

Gillian.

Since coming to the *Idenna* Hendel had worked closely with the girl, teaching her to develop and control her biotic abilities. But despite the remarkable improvement in her condition over the past few weeks, she was still an emotionally fragile, easily disturbed little girl. Something had set her off in the cafeteria back at the Academy, unleashing a storm of biotic powers. Now Kahlee had clear evidence that the storm had been unleashed yet again.

She's scared, Kahlee thought to herself. *Confused. She's going to want to go somewhere she feels safe.* An instant later she had it.

She's heading back to the shuttle.

Leaving the two dead soldiers where they lay,

Kahlee continued to work her way carefully through the aisles back toward the stairs.

Golo was thoroughly enjoying the battle against his former people. While he hadn't been a crew member of the *Idenna,* he had no trouble imagining the quarians he gunned down as being the ones who had banished him from the *Usela,* his old ship.

Heavily armed and armored, he had already notched six kills during the battle—two on the trading deck and four more hunting through the cubicles up above. Given the superior weaponry Cerberus had provided him, it wasn't even a fair fight . . . which was exactly how Golo liked it. In fact, he was enjoying himself so much that he nearly lost track of the time.

It was only when the timer in his helmet began beeping softly that he realized they had only ten minutes left. They hadn't found the girl yet, but that didn't really matter to him. It was time to head back to Grayson's shuttle and get off the *Idenna.*

He knew the rest of the team would keep fighting and searching for Gillian for another five minutes before pulling back, but he didn't like cutting it that close.

With a sigh of regret he abandoned his hunt among the cubicle maze, and made his way quickly and cautiously back toward the stairs leading to the deck below.

Inside the passenger cabin of the nameless shuttle that had been stolen from him on Omega, Grayson paced anxiously. Checking his watch, he realized they were down to just under ten minutes.

"You and you," he said, pointing at two of the three soldiers left behind to help him secure the shuttle. "Get out there and find the controls to release the docking clamps."

He intended to wait to the last possible second before leaving, but that didn't mean he couldn't have everything ready beforehand.

The two soldiers rushed out to the airlock, while Grayson and the other man—the pilot who had flown the quarian vessel in—waited in silence.

He heard a loud, heavy thump coming from outside the ship. Curious, he made his way cautiously toward the airlock and saw a small, female figure covered head to toe in an enviro-suit standing in the center of the landing bay.

"Daddy?" the figure said. Though the voice was partially obscured by the mask and breathing apparatus, he recognized it instantly.

"Gigi," he said, dropping to one knee and holding out his hand to her.

She approached him in her familiar, stiff-legged walk until she was close enough for him to touch. Knowing her condition well, he dropped his hand without making contact. And then, to his great surprise, she lurched forward another step and hugged him.

Only when he was clasping his daughter to his chest did he notice the two soldiers he'd sent out only moments before—they were pinned beneath an overturned forklift the quarians would have used to load and unload cargo vessels. It looked as if the six-ton vehicle had somehow been picked up and dropped on them, crushing them like ants and killing them instantly.

Their private reunion was broken an instant later when he heard the copilot speaking behind him.

"S-s-sir," he said in a stuttering, trembling voice, staring at the mangled bodies of the two dead soldiers peeking out from beneath the forklift. "What happened to them?"

"Never mind," Grayson said sharply, releasing his hold on his daughter and standing up. "Just get on board and fire up the engines. It's time to go."

"We can't go yet," Gillian said. Grayson was surprised to hear real emotion in her voice, rather than the flat monotone he was used to. "We have to wait for my friends."

"Your friends?" he asked, humoring her.

"Hendel and Kahlee and Lemm," she answered. "Lemm's a quarian."

"We can't wait for them, honey," he told her gently.

She crossed her arms and stepped away from him—a gesture he'd never seen her use before.

"I'm not going without them," she said defiantly.

Grayson blinked in surprise, then nodded. "Okay, honey, we'll go find them."

As she turned away to head back toward the *Idenna*'s interior, he stepped up behind her and drew a small stunner from his belt. One quick shot between the shoulder blades and she slouched over into her father's waiting arms.

Feeling guilty over using the weapon on her, but knowing they had precious little time to spare, he scooped her up and carried her aboard the shuttle.

Once inside, he took her to the bedroom, setting her gently down on the bed. He removed the enviro-suit helmet, and for a long moment he just stared at her face, only glancing up when he heard the pilot addressing him again.

"Sir?" he said, standing at the door. "The docking clamps are still attached."

"Go release them," Grayson ordered. "I'm not leaving my daughter's side."

The man nodded, then turned and left them alone.

"Don't worry, Gigi," he whispered. "I'll make sure they take good care of you from now on."

TWENTY-FOUR

Kahlee ran through the deserted trading deck, heading for the shuttle Gillian now thought of as her home. She was so focused on finding the girl before something happened to her that she didn't even think to check on Hendel behind the desk.

She slowed down as she moved through the hall separating the trading deck and the landing bays, moving quietly in case any of the Cerberus troops were waiting for her. Her caution proved well founded; there was a single guard just outside the shuttle. He was standing with his back to her, one hand punching at a control panel to disengage the docking clamps on the vessel while his other hung at his side, casually gripping his assault rifle.

Gunfire might alert anyone else nearby, but that didn't mean she couldn't use her assault rifle as a weapon. She knew his armor was equipped with kinetic barriers, but they were programmed to respond specifically to speed. If you sat down or slapped someone on the back they didn't activate; it took a high-velocity round to trigger them. A sharp incoming blow to the head wouldn't be fast enough to set them off.

Moving quickly, Kahlee crept up behind him, wrapping her arms around the end of the barrel and holding the gun like a baseball bat. As soon as she got within range she took three quick running steps to build up momentum, then swung her makeshift club as hard as she could.

The sound of her feet clanging against the metal floor of the landing bay during her quick charge gave the soldier just enough warning to react. He half-turned toward her, bringing one arm up and ducking his head so that the blow landed on his shoulder rather than the side of his helmet. The force of the impact knocked his assault rifle from his grasp, and it clattered to the floor as he was knocked sideways, staggering to keep his balance.

Kahlee swung again, but she was in too close to get the leverage she needed. The blow struck him on the side of his helmet, but not hard enough to knock him out. Dazed, the soldier stumbled away from her, his hands fumbling for the pistol on his hip.

Spinning the assault rifle in her hands, Kahlee repositioned her grip so that she could jab forward with the heavy butt of the gun. She came in low, just beneath the edge of the three-quarter visor, smashing in the front teeth of his lower jaw. His head snapped back and he fell over. Kahlee leaped on top of him, driving the butt of the rifle down on his head with both hands.

Even his helmet couldn't protect him from the savage force of repeated impacts. After six consecutive blows Kahlee was certain he would never get up again. She gave him two more shots just to make sure.

Rising to her feet, she saw the assault rifle had been bent out of alignment by the attack.

Useless piece of volus crap, she thought as she grabbed the pistol from the dead soldier's belt.

With her enemy down, she took a quick glance around the rest of the landing bay. When she saw the bodies of the two Cerberus troopers beneath the fork-lift, she knew the girl had been by.

She crept into the shuttle, moving as quietly as possible. The passenger cabin was empty so she headed up to the cockpit, only to discover it was deserted as well. When she made her way to the sleeping quarters in the back, she was only mildly surprised to find Gillian lying on the bed, her father protectively sitting over her.

Raising the soldier's pistol, she pointed it at Grayson. "Get away from her, you son-of-a-bitch."

He glanced up at the sound of her voice, and his eyes widened in shock. It took him a moment to recognize her behind the enviro-suit and mask.

"Kahlee?" he muttered.

She nodded and gestured with the pistol, and Grayson slowly stood up and backed away from the bed.

Kahlee glanced down at Gillian and realized she was unconscious. "What did you do? Drug her again?" she demanded.

"Stunner," Grayson whispered, and Kahlee thought he actually sounded ashamed of himself. She realized that, despite everything he had done, he truly cared for his daughter. Somehow it made his devotion to Cereberus seem both more terrifying and more pathetic.

Then she felt the hard jab of a pistol digging into the side of her ribs.

"Drop the gun," a voice from behind her said.

For a split second Kahlee considered shooting Grayson. But killing her father wouldn't save Gillian, and it would almost certainly get Kahlee killed. Instead, she let the pistol fall from her hands.

"Lay facedown on the ground, hands behind your head," the voice ordered, jabbing her again with the pistol.

She did as ordered, and then she heard the sound of her unknown assailant walking past her over toward the bed.

"Don't touch her, Golo," Grayson warned, the cold anger in his voice causing the footsteps to stop.

Flat on her belly, Kahlee dared to tilt her head to look up. She was stunned to see he was speaking with a quarian.

The world came back to Hendel in a wave of pain. Every bone and muscle in his body ached from being slammed into the wall, and as consciousness slowly returned, he just lay there, trying to get his bearings. After a few seconds, it all started to come back to him. He was on the trading deck, where the quarians had been battling Cerberus.

He could still hear gunfire, but it was coming from far away.

The fight moved to the deck above.

Ignoring his protesting muscles, he forced himself to stand up. There were a few seconds of vertigo before he steadied himself. Looking around, he located his assault rifle where it had fallen on the floor and picked it up.

Gotta go help Kahlee and the others.

Before he could clamber out from behind the desk, however, he heard heavy footsteps running down the stairs. Two Cerberus guards burst into view from the deck above, their attention not focused on Hendel, but rather on the quarians pursuing them.

They're retreating! Hendel realized. *We've won!*

Biotics were out of the question. His head was still spinning slightly from being thrown, and he suspected he had a mild concussion. But he was feeling well enough to use his assault rifle.

Relying on the weapon's autotargeting systems to overcome any lingering unsteadiness he might be feeling, he lined up the nearest Cerberus soldier and opened fire.

From this range, the bullets made short work of his shields. They lasted just long enough for him to turn toward Hendel, but not long enough for him to bring his weapon up and return fire.

The second soldier wheeled on him as the first fell to the ground, and Hendel had to duck behind the heavy desk for cover. The first burst from his enemy chewed away huge chunks of hardwood, but the cover held together in time for Hendel to dart into the safety of the stockroom.

He poked his head through the door to return fire, only to see that the Cerberus soldier was about to be caught in a crossfire. Hendel opened fire, as did several quarians coming down the stairs from the deck above. With enemies both in front and behind, the soldier didn't last more than three seconds.

"It's me, Hendel!" he shouted out from the stock-room, not wanting to suddenly pop into view and get accidentally shot.

"Hendel!" he heard Lemm shout. "You're alive!"

He walked out from the storeroom and climbed gingerly over the desk. Lemm, Mal, and four other quarians were gathered at the foot of the stairs.

"Is that the last of them?" Hendel asked, nodding toward the dead Cerberus troopers on the ground. He figured the fight was over, as he didn't hear any-more gunfire.

"There might be one or two left," the captain an-swered, "falling back to the *Cyniad*."

"They had us on the run, when all of a sudden they broke into a full retreat," Lemm added.

"Why would they—" Hendel began, then stopped short. "Where's Kahlee? Where's Gillian?"

Nobody answered.

"Cerberus has her!" Hendel shouted. "That's why they're pulling out!"

As a group, they broke into a run, heading for the landing bays.

"Should I shoot her?" Golo asked.

Grayson looked at Kahlee, still lying facedown on the ground in her enviro-suit. The quarian had his pistol pointed at the back of her head.

"No," Grayson said. "Keep her alive. She's an ex-pert in biotic amp configurations. Cerberus might want her to help with Gillian's new training."

"I'll never help you with your sick experiments," Kahlee spat out from the floor.

"Quiet," Golo warned, kicking her hard in the ribs. Grayson winced.

Kahlee grunted and rolled over onto her back, her hands clutching at her side. "Gillian will hate you for this," she gasped, trying to catch her breath. "She'll never forgive you."

The quarian hauled off and kicked her again, causing her to pull her knees up into a fetal position to try and protect herself.

"Enough!" Grayson snapped.

"How can you let them do this to your own daughter?" Kahlee asked through gritted teeth, still balled up from the pain.

"Did you see the forklift out there?" Grayson demanded. "Do you see what Gillian is capable of? That's because of what Cerberus did!"

"They want to make her into a weapon," Kahlee countered, panting behind her mask. Grayson guessed several of her ribs were broken. "They're turning her into some kind of monster."

"They're transforming her into a savior of the human race," he countered.

"We don't have time for this," Golo warned.

"They're destroying her," Kahlee snarled, her words filled with pain and anger. "Those drugs made her condition worse. Without them, she has a chance to be almost normal!"

Unbidden, the memory of Gillian actually hugging him outside the airlock filled Grayson's mind. He remembered her words, and her surprising defiance.

We have to wait for my friends. I'm not leaving without them.

"Gillian was happy here," Kahlee continued. "Have you ever seen that before? She was actually happy!"

"Shut up!" Golo shouted, kicking her again.

This time he didn't stop, but continued to beat on her until Grayson snapped, "No more! That's enough. It's over."

Golo looked over at him, panting slightly from the exertion, and shrugged. On the ground Kahlee was rolling feebly from side to side, moaning and whimpering from behind her mask.

Grayson's eyes flicked away from her and over to Gillian on the bed. She looked so small, vulnerable and helpless.

Salvation comes with a cost, he seemed to hear the Illusive Man saying in his head. His mind flashed back to the mutilated quarian in the cellar of Pel's warehouse.

Judge us not by our methods, but by what we seek to accomplish.

"We're almost out of time," Golo reminded him. "We have to leave now. We can't wait for the others."

Grayson was suddenly struck by the similarities between the quarian and his former partner. Both were sadistic and cruel. Both had no compunction about torturing or killing others for personal gain.

And both were traitors to their own people. It sickened him to think about the kind of individuals he had allied himself with.

We take terrible burdens on ourselves for the greater good. This is the price we must pay for the cause.

"Get the engines fired up and get us out of here," Grayson ordered.

As the quarian turned to leave, Grayson calmly bent over and picked up the pistol Kahlee had let fall to the floor. He stepped up behind the quarian and jammed the barrel against the back of his helmet, too close for the kinetic barriers to save him. And then he shot Golo once through the head, the bullet exiting through the front of his mask and lodging itself in the shuttle's bulkhead.

As the quarian toppled forward, Grayson let the pistol fall from his hand. He turned and looked down at Kahlee, but he couldn't tell what she was thinking behind her mask.

"The ship we arrived on is filled with explosives," he told her. "We have about two minutes before they detonate and rip a hole in the side of the *Idenna*. I'll need your help if we want to stop it.

"Can you walk?" he asked, reaching down and offering a hand to help her to her feet.

She hesitated for a split second before grabbing it and hauling herself up with a groan.

"I can damn well try," she answered.

Hendel and the quarians were running at a full sprint as they burst into the loading docks. The *Cyniad* was in bay seven, on the far end past all the other ships. The former security chief's long strides had pulled him slightly ahead of the others, but they caught up when he stopped to stare in amazement at the two figures coming out of the airlock in bay three.

Kahlee, still in her enviro-suit, and Grayson, wearing Cerberus armor, were exiting the shuttle. She had one arm wrapped around Grayson's neck, and he appeared to be holding her up, as if she couldn't stand on her own. Neither one of them was armed.

"Hendel!" Kahlee shouted, but her voice was cut off in a gasp of pain and her free hand clutched at her side.

"The *Cyniad*," Grayson called out to them. "The ship in bay seven. It's filled with explosives!"

Hendel, bewildered by the scene before him, could only shake his head. "What's going on? Where's Gillian?"

"She's safe," Grayson answered, speaking quickly. "But you have to get to the *Cyniad*. Disarm the bomb before it detonates!"

"What the hell are you talking about?"

"Cerberus. We never intended to escape on the *Cyniad*. We were going to take my shuttle. The *Cyniad* is filled with explosives and set to go off on a timer to provide a distraction as we escaped."

"How many explosives, and how much time?" Hendel demanded.

"Two minutes, and enough to rip a hole in the *Idenna*'s hull."

"Watch him!" Hendel said, pointing at Grayson as he turned to go.

"Wait!" Grayson shouted, freezing him in his tracks. "It's a dual sync arming system. You need two people to enter the code simultaneously or it'll detonate."

"What's the code?" Mal demanded.

"Six two three two one two."

"Everyone else evacuate the loading bays," the captain ordered, then turned to Hendel. "Let's go."

It took them less than thirty seconds to reach the

Cyniad's airlock. The bodies of Isli, Seeto, and Ugho lay just beyond it. The airlock itself had been sealed.

"Wait," Mal said, grabbing Hendel by the arm. "What if it's a trap?"

The security chief had been thinking the same thing. "That's a chance we have to take."

They opened the airlock and raced up into the quarian shuttle. The cargo hold was filled with enough explosives to blow apart a small asteroid. At least fifty drums of liquid rocket fuel, each as high as Hendel's shoulder, were clustered in the center of the floor, held together by a mess of wires. From somewhere in the middle of the canisters, completely inaccessible, he heard the rhythmic *beep-beep-beep* of a timer counting down.

"Find the overrides!" Hendel shouted, and the two of them split up, one going clockwise around the ring of explosives, the other counterclockwise.

Hendel tried to sync the high-pitched beeps with the imaginary clock ticking down in his head. He figured they had maybe thirty seconds to spare when he finally found what he was looking for: a small keypad attached to the side of one of the drums. Two wires ran from the base into the cords woven around the explosives. Hendel had no doubt that detaching either of the wires would set the whole mess off.

"I've got mine!" Mal shouted from the far side of the canisters.

"Me too," Hendel called back. "Enter the code on three? Ready? One . . . two . . . three!"

He punched in the numbers, knowing there was a lag of only a couple seconds for Mal to do the same. If they weren't in sync, if either one of them hesitated or made a mistake, they'd both be instantly vaporized.

The steady beep of the timer suddenly changed to a single long, shrill whistle. Hendel instinctively closed his eyes as he braced himself for the boom . . .

And nothing happened.

The shrill whistle slowly faded away, and Hendel reached up to wipe the sweat from his brow, only to have his gloved hand bump against the mask of his enviro-suit.

"Hell of an all-clear signal," he muttered to himself. And then he began to laugh.

TWENTY-FIVE

In the aftermath of the battle, the quarians had taken Grayson into custody. For nearly a week his fate hung in the balance as the Admiralty, the Conclave, and the civilian Council of the *Idenna* weighed in on what was to be done.

He had saved dozens, possibly even hundreds, of lives by warning them about the explosives. But Kahlee, along with everyone else, knew that the only reason their lives were ever in danger was because of what he had done. And there was still plenty of blood on his hands to be accounted for. Over twenty of the *Idenna*'s crew had been killed in the attack, along with eleven Cerberus soldiers and Golo, the quarian traitor. The cost was high, but it was far less than it could have been.

Mal understood all this, and he took it into account while passing the final judgment on Grayson, as was his right as captain. Kahlee had feared there could be consequences for her and Hendel, as well; none of this would have happened had the quarians not taken them in when they first arrived. However, she had underestimated the value quarian culture placed on community and crew. They had been accepted as guests on his ship, Mal had explained to her. They were part of the *Idenna* family. He wasn't about to cast them out now, and he wasn't going to hold them accountable for the actions of Cerberus.

In the end, the captain even agreed to allow Kahlee to take Grayson back to the Alliance as her prisoner, giving them Grayson's own shuttle for transportation. Lemm agreed to accompany her as the pilot, and to help her keep an eye on their captive.

Hendel and Gillian, however, would not be going with them.

"Are you sure you know what you're doing?" she asked Hendel as they stood in the landing bay, saying their good-byes.

"Gillian needs this," he said. "You saw how far she's come since we've been here. I don't know if it's the ship, the enviro-suits, the lack of drugs . . . all I know is that she's happy here on the *Idenna*.

"And soon she'll be beyond the reach of even Cerberus," he added after a moment.

Kahlee nodded, accepting the fact that she couldn't change his mind.

The news of an enemy force infiltrating the Migrant Fleet had shaken the quarian society to its very core. Faced with the shocking realization that they were vulnerable even within the flotilla, many of the ship captains had changed their views on the idea of sending exploratory vessels out into the depths of space on extended missions.

The Conclave had fiercely debated the matter, but in the end those who favored the exploratory missions, like Mal, were the majority. The Admiralty could have overturned the Conclave's ruling, but they, too, seemed to have had a change of heart. They acquiesced to the decision, though they did impose strict rules and restrictions on how many vessels could go, and when they could leave.

Not surprisingly, the *Idenna* was chosen to be the first of those vessels. In three weeks it would set off through a recently activated mass relay in an uninhabited system, heading into parts unknown. Even now it was being refitted with new technology to allow it to survive on its own for up to five years without any outside contact or resources. To make such a journey feasible, however, the crew would have to drop from its current population of nearly seven hundred to just over fifty, all handpicked by Mal himself.

The captain had already given Hendel and Gillian permission to go.

"Do you really think Cerberus will stop looking for her after five years?" Kahlee asked.

Hendel shrugged. "I don't know. But at least it'll give her a chance to grow up some before she has to deal with them again."

He glanced over at the shuttle, where Gillian was inside saying a last, private good-bye to her father. Hendel had opposed the idea initially, but Kahlee had worn him down. Grayson deserved that much, at least.

"What do you think he's telling her in there?" the security chief wondered.

"I don't know."

She couldn't even imagine what Grayson was going through. Everything he had done in his adult life—every action, every decision he had made—had been in the service of Cerberus and their so-called great and glorious cause. But in the end he had finally chosen his daughter over these nebulous ideals. Unfortunately, that choice meant it was impossible for her to stay with him.

"What are you going to tell Gillian if she ever asks about him?" she asked Hendel.

"I'm going to tell her the truth," he said. "Her father is a complicated man. He made some mistakes. But he loves her very much, and he only wants what's best for her. And in the end he did the right thing."

Kahlee nodded again, and pulled Hendel close for a hug. "You two be careful out there," she whispered.

"We will."

They broke the embrace when they heard the familiar clump of Lemm's boots coming toward them.

"Are we ready to go?" he asked her.

Kahlee knew the young quarian was eager to take her and Grayson to the nearest Alliance colony so he could drop them off and get back in time to rejoin the *Idenna*. Like Hendel and Gillian, he had also been selected by Mal to be part of the long and dangerous journey.

She'd already said her good-byes to Gillian, and as much as she hated to take Grayson away from his daughter it was time for them to go.

"I'm ready," she said.

They were only a few hours away from decelerating from light speed in the vicinity of Cuervo, the nearest Alliance colony. Lemm had already programmed their destination into the nav systems, and Kahlee had sent off a comm message: there would be a security patrol waiting when they landed to take Grayson into immediate custody.

Now the quarian was taking a quick nap in the bedroom, while Kahlee and Grayson sat in the passenger cabin, facing each other. Grayson's hands were cuffed in front of him, resting in his lap. As a further precaution, Kahlee was armed with both a stunner and a pistol just in case he had a change of heart.

She could tell he was getting scared. His eyes kept darting around the cabin as if he was looking for an escape, and his fingers fidgeted nervously in his lap.

"You realize this is a death sentence for me," Grayson told her.

"The Alliance will protect you," Kahlee assured him. "You have valuable information on Cerberus. They'll want to keep you around."

"They can't protect me," Grayson answered, shaking his head. "It might take a month, or maybe even a year, but sooner or later one of their agents inside the Alliance will get to me."

"What do you expect me to do?" Kahlee asked him. "I can't let you go."

"No," he said softly. "No, I suppose you can't."

"You had to know this was going to happen," she told him. "But you helped us anyway. I think you wanted to atone for your past."

"I'd like to think I can atone without dying," he said with a grim smirk.

"Remember why you're doing this," Kahlee said, hoping to improve his mood. "It's for Gillian."

The mention of his daughter brought a forlorn smile to the thin man's lips.

"You were right," he said. "What you told me before I killed Golo. Gillian's happy now. I guess that's all I can really hope for."

Kahlee nodded. "You did the right—"

Her words were cut off as Grayson suddenly threw himself at her. He moved quick as a snake, throwing his head forward to strike at her unprotected nose. Kahlee ducked to the side at the last possible instant and he butted her in the shoulder.

His weight was bearing down on her, pinning her in her seat. His cuffed hands were trying to grab at her, until she jabbed her fingers, held flat and stiff, sharply into his windpipe.

Gasping and choking he fell away from the seat, then curled up in a ball on the floor. Kahlee leaped out of her chair and stood over him, her muscles coiled in case he lunged at her a second time.

"Try that again and I'll shoot you," she warned, but there was no real venom in her threat.

Her heart was pounding and her blood was racing with adrenaline, but he hadn't actually hurt her. She'd been expecting something like this for some time now; he was getting desperate. If anyone was to blame it was her for not recognizing he was still dangerous.

"Come on," she said in a softer voice, taking a step back from him. "I didn't hurt you that bad. Get up."

He rolled onto his side, and Kahlee realized he had something clenched between the fingers of his still-cuffed hands. It took her a second to realize it was a stunner—he must have torn it from her hip during the scuffle!

She tried to shout out a warning to Lemm, but Grayson fired and everything went black.

When she woke Lemm was standing over her, looking concerned. She realized she was in the shuttle's bed, but the effects of the stunner had left her feeling disoriented and confused.

"Where are we?" she asked, struggling to sit up.

"Daleon," Lemm answered. "A small volus colony."

"I thought we were supposed to land on Cuervo," she said, her foggy mind still putting the pieces together.

Lemm shrugged. "All I know is that somebody knocked me out with a stunner. When I came to we were sitting here at the Daleon spaceport."

"Where's Grayson? What happened to Grayson?"

"Gone," Lemm replied. "We could search for him, if you want. It's possible he might still be here on Daleon."

Kahlee shook her head, realizing what had happened. "He's long gone by now. We'll never find him."

"So what now?" the quarian asked.

"Take the shuttle and head back to the *Idenna*," she told him. "You've got a lot of preparations to make for your journey."

"What about you?"

"Just drop me off at the Grissom Academy," she said. "There are a lot of kids in the Ascension Program who still need my help."

With a smile, she added, "I'm pretty sure I can convince the board to take me back."

EPILOGUE

The vid screen beeped to indicate an incoming message. The Illusive Man looked up from the report he was studying at his desk and noted the call was coming over a secure line.

"Answer," he said, and an image of Paul Grayson flickered into view.

The Illusive Man blinked in mild surprise. He had assumed the mission to infiltrate the quarian flotilla was a failure, simply because two weeks had passed and he hadn't heard anything. With most Cerberus assignments he could get general updates by watching the news vids, but with no media coverage of what went on in the confines of the Migrant Fleet, it had rendered him as clueless and ignorant as any ordinary, average citizen.

"Paul," he said with a slight tilt of his head. "Has the asset been recovered?"

"Her name is Gillian," the man answered. The hostility in his tone was unmistakable.

"Gillian, then," the Illusive Man conceded, his voice cold. "What happened on the mission?"

"The team's dead. All of them. Golo. Everyone."

"Except you."

"I'm as good as dead," Grayson replied. "I'm a ghost now. You'll never find me."

"What about your daughter?" the Illusive Man asked. "How long will she be able to survive as a fugitive? A life on the run is no life for her. Bring her in, Paul, and we can talk about what's best for Gillian."

Grayson laughed. "She's not even with me. She's on a quarian deep-space exploration vessel out in the middle of some uncharted system beyond the edge of the galaxy. You'll never find her."

The Illusive Man's jaw clenched ever so slightly as he realized the girl was beyond his reach. The fact that Grayson was willing to taunt him with the information was clear evidence of how impossible it would be to track her down. He relied on a network of Cerberus informants throughout Council Space and the Terminus Systems to supply him with a constant flow of information. Out beyond that network he was literally blind.

"I thought you were loyal to the cause, Paul."

"I was," Grayson answered. "Then I saw the kind of people who share your vision, and I had a change of heart."

The Illusive Man sneered at the screen. "I'm in the business of saving lives, Paul. Human lives. You used to understand that. Now it seems you're suddenly trying to save your soul."

"I think my soul is too far gone to save."

"Then why are you calling?" the Illusive Man demanded, the smallest hint of frustration creeping into his voice.

"I'm giving you a warning," the man on the other end of the vid screen answered. "Stay away from

Kahlee Sanders. If you come after her, I go to the Alliance with everything I know."

The Illusive Man studied the image on the vid screen carefully. He noticed the familiar signs of Grayson's red sand use—the bloodshot pupils, the faintly luminous sheen on his teeth—were missing. And he realized the man wasn't bluffing.

"Why is she worth so much to you?"

"Does it matter?" Grayson countered. "She's hardly worth anything to you. Not compared to all the dirty little secrets I have. I figure my silence in exchange for her safety is a bargain."

"We will find you, Paul," the Illusive Man promised in a menacing whisper.

"Maybe," Grayson admitted. "But that's not why I called. Kahlee Sanders—do we have a deal?"

After taking a moment to weigh the offer, the Illusive Man nodded his acceptance. Gillian's loss would set their biotic research back a full decade, but Cerberus had too many other projects on the go to risk them all for this. On the screen Grayson smiled. An instant later the image went blank as the call was disconnected.

He didn't bother trying to trace the call—Grayson was too smart to slip up on something that simple. Instead, the Illusive Man just stared at the blank screen for a long, long time, slowly clenching and unclenching his jaw.